SIXKILLER, U.S. MARSHAL

This Large Print Book carries the
Seal of Approval of N.A.V.H.

Sixkiller, U.S. Marshal

William W. Johnstone
with J.A. Johnstone

THORNDIKE PRESS
A part of Gale, Cengage Learning

GALE
CENGAGE Learning·

Farmington Hills, Mich • San Francisco • New York • Waterville, Maine
Meriden, Conn • Mason, Ohio • Chicago

GALE
CENGAGE Learning®

LIBRARY OF CONGRESS CATALOGING-IN-PUBLICATION DATA

Johnstone, William W.
  Sixkiller, U.S. Marshal / by William W. Johnstone with J.A. Johnstone. — Large Print edition.
      pages cm. — (Thorndike Press Large Print Western)
    ISBN-13: 978-1-4104-6705-8 (hardcover)
    ISBN-10: 1-4104-6705-8 (hardcover)
    1. Large type books. I. Johnstone, J. A. II. Title.
  PS3560.O415S59 2014
  813'.54—dc23   2013046149

Published in 2014 by arrangement with Pinnacle Books, an imprint of Kensington Publishing Corp.

Printed in Mexico
2 3 4 5 6 7 18 17 16 15 14

Sixkiller, U.S. Marshal

CHAPTER ONE

Northeast Alabama, 1838

James Sixkiller was clearing a field with his father, Redbird, and three of the men who worked for them, when he saw smoke coming from the direction of his house.

"Edodah! Look! There is smoke!" James said, speaking to his father.

"What is that, Redbird?" one of the other men asked, pointing toward the smoke.

"I think it is our house," Redbird answered in alarm.

Throwing down their tools, James, his father, and the three others, ran toward the smoke. When they got there, James's mother, Wilma, and his two young sisters were standing under a live oak tree as the house was being consumed by flames. There were at least twenty other men present as well, all wearing military uniforms. The soldiers were standing around, watching the house burn.

"Why are you standing here?" Redbird demanded angrily. "Why aren't you fighting the fire?"

"Fighting the fire? Why you fool, we *started* the fire," a captain, who was in charge of the soldiers, said.

"What?"

"Can you read? And by that, I mean can you read white man's words?" the soldier asked.

"My son, James, can read."

"Then read this," the captain said, showing James a piece of paper.

Indian Removal Act
WHEREAS no state can achieve proper culture, civilization, and progress as long as Indians remain in its boundaries, and whereas true philanthropy reconciles the mind to the extinction of one race for another, therefore the INDIAN REMOVAL ACT has been proposed and acted upon by the Senate and House of Representatives of the United States of America in congress assembled.

Hereinafter it shall and may be lawful for the President of the United States to cause so much of any territory belonging to the United States west of the River Mississippi, not included in any state or orga-

8

nized territory, and to which Indian title has been extinguished, as he may judge necessary, to be divided in suitable numbers of districts for the reception of such tribes or nations of Indians to exchange the lands where they now live, and remove them there.

"What is this? Other than two long and incredibly convoluted sentences?" James asked.

"It is the Indian Removal Act, signed into law by President Andy Buck Jackson," the captain said.

"But surely that law does not apply to those of us who own our own private property?" James replied. "We have lived in peace with the white man for many years. We are neighbors, we sell our crops to the white man, we buy his goods."

"The law applies to all five tribes in North Carolina, Georgia, Alabama, and Mississippi. You are to be forcibly removed from these states and relocated into an area of land that has been set aside as Indian Territory."

"It doesn't say anything here about burning our house," James said, angrily.

"Why does it matter to you whether this house is burned or not?" the captain asked.

"From the moment the president signed this bill into law, it was no longer your house. We can do anything with it that we want."

"Do you expect us to just go peaceably?" James demanded.

"Port arms!" the captain shouted, and at his command, all the soldiers raised their rifles.

"Redbird!" Wilma shouted in fear.

"We expect you to go, whether it is peaceful or not," the army captain said.

As a result of the Indian Removal Act, 20,000 Creek, 17,000 Choctaw, and 16,000 Cherokee were forcibly relocated. It was approaching winter when the Cherokee left, and though Chief John Ross applied to let them remain until spring so that travel would be easier, his request was denied.

James's group of approximately one thousand, under Chief John Bushyhead, trekked through Tennessee where a hospital gave them blankets to be used against the cold. At first, the Cherokee were thankful; then they started dying in great numbers. A white doctor in one of the towns diagnosed the illness as smallpox, caught from the infected blankets.

The hospital blankets were burned, but

the word went ahead that the traveling band of Indians were spreading smallpox, so that they had to avoid every community they passed by in Kentucky, and then in Southern Illinois. The towns of Golconda, Vienna, Anna, and Ware refused even to sell them provisions.

Finally, their number reduced by over two hundred, they reached the Mississippi River on the Illinois side just opposite Cape Girardeau, Missouri.

"*Ayii*, I've never seen a river so large," Redbird said. "How are we going to cross it?"

Redbird's question was repeated by nearly all of the 800 men, women, and children who were still alive from the original 1,000 of their particular traveling party.

"Maybe we can buy boats from the whites who live here," Bushyhead suggested.

"Better to hire boats than to buy them," James said. "For if we buy them, what will we do with them once we are on the other side?"

James's suggestion was accepted, but they ran into immediate difficulty, because so many ice floes were coming downriver that none of the boat owners would risk a crossing. There was nothing left to do but wait until the river was clear of the ice. In the meantime, with only their few remaining blankets for shelter, the Cherokee made an encampment on the east bank of the Mississippi River.

For weeks they camped alongside the frozen river. Literally hundreds got sick, dying of exposure and pneumonia, including James's mother and father.

Of the one thousand who started the journey, a little less than seven hundred were left to cross the river into Missouri. There, weakened by their ordeal, and with several still sick, they decided to camp while their sick recovered enough to go on.

The citizens of Cape Girardeau were divided as to whether to allow the Indians to stay while they were recovering, or force them to leave.

"If we let them stay, we'll all die," one of the protesters said. "They've all got smallpox, I tell you. They'll kill us all."

"The ones with smallpox have already died. Now they need food, water, and someplace to stay warm and rest for a while before continuing on. These are human beings after all; men, women, and children who have been forced from their homes," John Henry Woodward said. "Have you met any of them? Spoken with any of them? They aren't savages, they are civilized, and in many cases, educated people. We can't turn our backs on them!"

Woodward's impassioned plea won the day, and through spring and into early summer, he, and the other citizens of Cape Girardeau, nursed the sick, even as many of the most ill among them continued to die, including Otahki, the daughter of Chief Bushyhead.

One of those most active was John Henry Woodward's daughter, Elizabeth. Elizabeth had become aware of a letter that one of the Indians had written to the president of the United States, copies of which had circulated around Cape Girardeau.

Dear Mr. President Jackson,

It is with some hesitancy that I address this letter to your eminence, aware as I am of my incompetency; and certain that you would not be well entertained by the address of a Cherokee. But having been ordered to emigrate west of the Mississippi river, and this move to be made in the dead of winter, I believe it proper to make a few remarks to express my views and make known my feelings as to living under the degrading influence of laws which are passed without one Indian voice considered.

For all these many years we have been good neighbors. We have not made war against you, we have not raided your farms and communities, we have lived in peace with you, and traded with you, and taken your names and many of your ways. And yet you have come with soldiers to say that we must remove ourselves to a land that we do not know.

It can only be hoped that the relocation of our nations, what you call the "civilized tribes," (though our civilization thrived upon this continent long before the arrival of the white man) will result in a final peace for our people, and once settled there, we will never again be forced to undertake a trail which results in the death of so many.

Respectfully yours, James Sixkiller

A Cherokee

So intrigued was Elizabeth by the letter, that she made it a point to look up James Sixkiller. When first she saw him, she was struck by his appearance. There was nothing about his clothing that would suggest he was an Indian, and she believed he was the most handsome man she had ever seen. He was, as Elizabeth knew from his letter, an educated and well-spoken man. James was also a natural leader among his people and worked with the citizens of the town to coordinate their efforts in helping the beleaguered Indians.

"Both my parents died on the other side of the river," James told her. "And now, my sisters are very ill, and I am worried about them."

"I will do what I can to help you with them," Elizabeth promised, and over the next three months, Elizabeth and James spent a lot of time working together. Then, even as his two sisters and the others recovered and there was less need for them to be working together, they continued to spend time together.

One evening, as the finishing repairs were being made on the wagons and carts that would be needed to continue their westward move, James and Elizabeth walked down to the river's edge. They stood there in silence for a moment, listening to the sound of the river, and looking at the gleaming reflection of the moon in the water.

"Elizabeth, you have shown yourself to be a woman of unusual strength, compassion, honor, and courage. I wonder if you have enough courage?"

"Enough courage?"

"To come with me, when we leave."

"James," Elizabeth said in a quiet, almost choked voice. "Are you asking me to marry you?"

"I know it is asking a great deal of you. I am Indian, you are —"

"I am the one who is going to marry you," Elizabeth said, interrupting James in mid-sentence.

"Will your father be all right with this?"

"I am twenty-one-years old," Elizabeth said. "I will make up my own mind."

"Elizabeth, no, please," John Henry Woodward said. "You have no idea what you will be getting yourself into. You'll be ostracized by your friends, he will, too. Indians and whites don't marry."

"Papa, you said yourself that they are human beings. They are civilized. Before this — this abominable Indian Removal Act, James and his family were wealthy farmers. If he owned a farm here in Cape Girardeau County, you would think him quite the catch."

"But that's just it, child. He doesn't own a farm in Cape Girardeau County. If he did, even though he is Indian, I would give you my blessings. But, Elizabeth, you will be hundreds of miles from here, that is if — if you survive the trip. Look at how many of

16

them have died, and they are only halfway there. Your mother and I may never see you again."

"I love him, Papa," Elizabeth said. "I want your blessings, but, I am going to marry him, and I am going to go with him."

"I can't give you my blessings," Woodward said. He lowered his head and pinched the bridge of his nose. "But neither will I make any effort to stop you. Marry him if you must."

"Thank you, Papa. Oh, thank you!"

One week later they were married in the Old McKendree Methodist Church. Elizabeth saw what her father meant when he told her that she would be ostracized by many of her friends. Only one of her friends came to the church to see her married. The attendance for James wasn't much better. His two sisters, Emma and Millie came. So did John Bushyhead.

"I confess that it had been my hope that you would marry Otahki," Bushyhead said. "But I respect Elizabeth for everything she did for our people, how she tried to save Otahki, and how she did save your sisters. Some may hold bitterness for the whites, for what they have done to us. But I do not. Your father is dead, so in his place, I give you my blessings."

When the Cherokee left Cape Girardeau, Elizabeth Woodward, now married to James Sixkiller, went with them.

CHAPTER TWO

James and Elizabeth Sixkiller, with now just under 600 of the original 1,000 who had left with their particular group remaining, crossed Missouri, then went through a corner of Arkansas, before entering Indian Territory. They were a confused and weary people when they finally came to the end of their trail in March 1839. The journey of a thousand miles had taken six months, in the hardest part of the year. Over 4,000 of the 16,000 Cherokee who started the journey died along the trail, to be buried in unmarked graves in strange and alien soil, thus giving birth to the name "Trail of Tears."

Once settled in the new territory though, the Five Civilized Tribes who were ultimately involved in the removal showed the tenacity, ingenuity, and work ethic that had served them well back East. They started farms, ranches, and towns. One such town was Sequoyah, started by James Sixkiller and the men and women who had come with him.

In 1842, Elizabeth bore James a son, whom she named John Henry, after her father. John Henry was her third child, but the first to survive past infancy. As the boy increased in years, he was taller, stronger, and faster than his contemporaries. He made friends easily, but there was one who was jealous of him and because of that, there was often friction between the two.

The two should have been friends; they shared a heritage which ought to have brought them together. Just as John Henry Sixkiller was half white, so too was Willie Buck. In Willie Buck's case it was his father who was white, a trader who had married a Cherokee woman in order to receive head rights.

Growing up, there had been a few fights between them, but the worst one occurred because of Sasha Quiet Stream. Sasha was no longer a child, but not yet a woman. She was fourteen years old, and already showing what a beautiful woman she would grow into. John Henry heard her calling for help one day, and responding to the call found Willie Buck trying to tear off Sasha's clothes. He pulled him off her.

"Come on, John Henry, I was just having a little fun," Willie Buck said. "Wouldn't you like to see what she looks like under that dress? Why, I bet she's tittied up just real good."

"Stay away from her, Willie Buck. If I see you bothering her again, you'll be sorry."

"Ha! Big hero," Willie Buck said, but he left without challenging John Henry.

Sasha was crying, and trying to cover that part of her body that had been exposed by Willie Buck's brutal assault.

"Here," John Henry said, removing his shirt and handing it to her. "You can put this on."

"He might come back," Sasha said.

"No, he won't. And if he does, I'll be here for you. Come on, I'll walk you home."

They walked together for a few minutes without speaking, the silence between them interrupted only by Sasha's smothered sobs. Finally, they reached the small house where Sasha lived. She started to take his shirt off and give it back to him.

"You don't need to give it to me now," John Henry said. "You can give it to me later."

"Thank you," Sasha said, then she smiled, the first smile since the incident.

"He's right, you know," she said.

"What?"

"Willie Buck said you are a hero. He was right. You are a hero. You are my hero."

John Henry laughed. "Nothing heroic about it. Anyone else would have done the same thing."

"But nobody else did. Only you."

"Well, I'm glad I was there at the right time."

"He was right about the other thing, too."

"What other thing?"

Sasha blushed. "Never mind," she said. She turned to go into the house. "I'll wash the shirt before I give it back to you."

John Henry returned to his own house to get another shirt and it wasn't until then that he realized what Sasha meant when she said he was right about the "other" thing. And he knew why she blushed.

"Wouldn't you like to see what she looks like under that dress? Why, I bet she's tittied up just real good."

When John Henry was fully grown, he had a muscular build and stood six feet tall, weighing in at 175 pounds. He had his father's dark hair, and his mother's blue eyes, so that it often surprised people when they learned that he was half Indian.

Like his father, John Henry got an education, first in the schools that were established in the Indian Territory. Then, with his enrollment arranged by his maternal grandfather, John Henry attended Washington University in St. Louis.

He left college without graduating in 1861 when the War Between the States started. The Cherokee allied themselves with the Confederacy and Stand Watie, a Cherokee, became a brigadier general in command of the American Indian Cavalry. James Sixkiller was appointed to the rank of colonel in command of the Second Cherokee Mounted Rifles, and John Henry was a lieutenant in his father's regiment.

Part of John Henry's task was to fill the ranks of his company by recruitment, and one of the men he tried to recruit was Hector Crow Dog.

"You want me to be in your company and salute you, and say sir to you like a good soldier, do you?" Crow Dog asked.

"That's what an army is all about."

"Well, no thank you, no. I'll fight against the Yankees, but I'll find my own way to do it. I've got a cousin up in Missouri by the name of Bill Anderson and I aim to go join up with him. He's riding with Quantrill."

"Quantrill isn't a soldier," John Henry said. "He's nothing more than an outlaw. If you go with him, you are likely to wind up hanging from a tree."

"I don't have to worry about anything like that," Crow Dog said. "I gave Sam Blackhorse a dollar to read my fortune, and I asked him right out if I was ever goin' to hang, and he told me I wasn't."

"Ha," John Henry said. "Blackhorse passes himself off as a medicine man, just so he can fleece the white men. I can't believe you fell for it."

"Well, no matter. I ain't joinin' your army. I reckon I'll just see you after this here war is over."

John Henry's first military action took place at Pea Ridge, Arkansas. When the Second Cherokee Mounted Rifles came on the field, they were taken under fire by Union batteries. As soon as they arrived, they were met by a messenger from General Pike.

"Colonel Sixkiller, the general's regards, sir, and he asks that you position your men to receive a cavalry charge he expects shortly."

"John Henry, take ten men and reconnoiter to the east," James ordered.

John Henry nodded. Then selecting his men, he went on the scout to the east. Suddenly, his ten men were attacked by a company-strength unit of Colonel Nemett's Union Cavalry. There was shouting, slashing, and shooting, during which mounted men from each side became so intermixed that command and control was impossible. The battle became a series of individual fights, and in one encounter, John Henry barely managed to avoid what would have been the killing thrust of a Yankee saber before taking his adversary down with one pistol shot. Upon hearing the shooting, James brought his regiment up quickly, and the Federal troops, now outnumbered, withdrew from the field.

A few months later, the Second Cherokee Mounted Rifles came upon a grisly scene just outside Lamar, Missouri. Here, thirty bodies were lying out in the sun. All males, the youngest looked to be no older than thirteen and the oldest was clearly in his seventies. The odd thing about it was the makeup of the group. Not one of the bodies were of the age one would normally expect to find in an army unit.

There were several men wandering through the bodies, clearly taking anything of value from them, in some cases, even their clothes. A mustachioed man came toward Colonel Sixkiller. He was the only one wearing a uniform of any kind, and it was gray and gold, with the collar insignia of a Confederate colonel. The colonel was stroking his mustache as he approached.

"Are you the commanding officer of this unit?" the approaching colonel asked.

"Yes. I am. This is the Second Cherokee Mounted Rifles, and I am Colonel James Sixkiller. And you, sir?"

"I am Colonel William Clarke Quantrill, and these are my men. Oh, they aren't wearing pretty uniforms, I'll grant you that. But as for fighting spirit, sir, I will put them up against any unit in the entire Yankee army. Or any unit in the Confederate army, for that matter."

"Quantrill, are you responsible for this?" James Sixkiller asked.

"Responsible? Responsible? That seems to me like an ill-chosen word, carrying with it the onus of foul deeds. I would prefer to say that we met these men on a field of battle, and we prevailed."

"They are nothing but old men and young boys," James protested. "What field of battle are you talking about?"

"They were Unionists, sir, and the battle takes place on the field of ideas," Quantrill said. "Any Unionist killed is one less enemy."

■ ■ ■ ■

John Henry walked away from the discussion his father was having with Quantrill. He was afraid that if he stayed there much longer, he would wind up saying, or doing something he would regret.

"John Henry!" someone called, and looking in the direction of the shout, John Henry saw Hector Crow Dog. "Have you come to get a glance at the real fighting men?"

"You were a party to this?" John Henry asked, the tone of his voice clearly showing his disgust with it.

"I was, and I'm proud of it," Crow Dog replied, as he took in the field of dead bodies with a broad sweep of his hand.

John Henry shook his head in disgust, and walked away.

"You go march with your tin soldiers, and leave the real fighting to us!" Crow Dog called after him with a loud and raucous laugh.

"Lieutenant," James called out to John Henry.

"Yes, sir?"

"Get the word out to the other officers. We are going to leave this" — James paused and looked back toward the body-strewn field, and the raggedly dressed men who composed Quantrill's Raiders — "this — battlefield." He set the word apart, twisting it on his tongue to show his distaste in referring to it in such a way.

John Henry was a captain by the time the war ended, and he returned home scarred, body and soul. He, and the other veterans of the losing side of the war, licked their wounds and got on with their lives. Soon, the industriousness of John Henry and his father had the ranch productive once more.

Then one day James and John Henry drove one hundred and fifty head of cattle to Coffeeville, Kansas to sell to Adam Bowser, a cattle broker. Although James could have gotten thirty-five dollars a head had he driven them all the way to Kansas City, he settled for thirty dollars a head, believing it was worth it to close the deal so close to home.

"Forty-five hundred dollars, Mr. Six-killer," Bowser said. "That's a lot of money to be carrying in cash. Are you sure you wouldn't rather have it in a bank draft?"

"I prefer cash. Drafts are sometimes difficult to negotiate down in The Nations."

"I understand. Very well, cash it will be. Come on down to the bank with me and

I'll get the money."

"Edodah," John Henry said, using the Cherokee word for father. "While you are doing that, I am going to the general store to get some things for *etsi.*"

"All right, I'll meet you at the shoe store. I'm going to get a new pair of boots."

CHAPTER THREE

Homer Tilghman was a very ugly man with an oversized nose and a pock-marked face. His looks weren't helped any by his right eye, which had such a droop to it that it was almost closed. At the moment he was standing at the customer's table in the bank, ostensibly writing out a deposit slip, but in reality, checking to see how difficult it would be to rob the bank.

He paid little attention to the two customers, a white man and an Indian when they came in. But when he saw the white man withdraw a great deal of cash and give it to the Indian, he decided it would be easier to rob one man than the bank. He left the bank, then stepped around the corner. Pulling his gun he waited in the little narrow space between the two buildings until the man with the cash started to mount his horse. That was when Tilghman stepped out onto the boardwalk behind the man.

The man had just started to put his foot in the stirrup when Tilghman shot him in the back. When he fell, Tilghman reached down into his inside jacket pocket and took the money.

"Well now," Tilghman said, smiling down at him. "This is a day of luck, ain't it? Good luck for me, bad luck for you. Oh, and I'll be taking your horse, too. You ain't goin' to be needin' it now."

Earl Cook's barbershop was just across the street from the bank. He was cutting the hair of Loomis Depro, who was the stage-coach agent.

"Damn, Loomis, did you see that? Homer Tilghman just shot that man down."

"Yeah, I saw it. It was Tilghman, all right. But who is the man that got shot?"

"I'm not sure but I think he may be one of those two Indians who brought some cattle in to sell," Cook said.

Depro took the cover off, then stood up. "You can finish cutting my hair later, Earl. Right now I expect Sheriff Dobson will be wanting to talk to us."

John Henry was in the general store, buying things for his mother that weren't always available in Sequoyah.

"I'll take three bars of that Pears Fragrance Soap," John Henry said, pointing to the soap.

"Oh, yes," the store clerk said as he reached for it. "I'm sure you will love this soap."

"It is for my mother," John Henry said, pointedly.

"Yes, indeed, sir, and that is what I meant," the clerk replied.

A young man with a star pinned to his shirt came into the store.

"Deputy Burns, I'll be right with you," the store clerk said.

"You ain't the one I come to see," the deputy replied.

"Oh?"

"I come to see this feller. That is, if you are one of them two Injuns that come into town to sell some cows."

"I am," John Henry replied. "Is there something I can do for you?"

Deputy Burns squinted. "You sure you are one of them two Injuns? You sure don't look Injun."

"I assure you, I am Indian. My father and I came into town and sold one hundred and fifty head of cattle. Now, what is this all about?"

"Oh. That man was your pa, huh?"

John took a quick breath as he felt a sense of dread come over him. "What do you mean, was?"

"I'm sorry to have to tell you this, Mister, but your pa is dead. He was shot down and robbed by a man named Homer Tilghman."

"How do you know who did it? Is Tilghman in jail?"

"No, he got away, but was seen and identified by at least five witnesses. So we are dead certain it was him."

"Where is my father now?"

"He was lyin' in the street in front of the livery, but Sheriff Dobson figured that wasn't very respectful, so he's got him over in the hardware store. That's where our undertaker has his office."

When John Henry hurried over to the hardware store, he saw his father lying out on one of the tables. He wasn't covered and several citizens of the town were just coming by to gawk.

"They say he is Injun, and when you look close, why, you can see that he is. Only he sure don't dress like an Injun."

"Well, how do you want him to dress?"

"He can dress any way he wants, don't mean nothin' to me. I was just sayin' he is

dressed more like a white man than an Injun."

"Get out of here," John Henry said to the
two men who were arguing over his father's
body.

"What? Look here, you can't just throw
me out of here," one of the two men said.

"Maybe he can't, but I can," Sheriff Dobson said.

"You got no right to —"

"Get out of here, now!" the sheriff said
forcefully. "Or by damn I'll throw the both
of you in jail for trespassing!"

"Well, I'll be . . ." one of the men started,
but the other grabbed his arm.

"Come on, Dempster. I think the sheriff
might actually do it."

The two men hurried out, then Sheriff
Dobson turned toward John Henry. "Mr.
Bowser said that father and son had come
to sell him the cows. You must be the son."

"I am."

"Well, I guess you heard, the man that did
this is named Homer Tilghman, and he has
left town."

"Which way?"

"Those who saw him leave said he was
going south. That figures. He's half Indian,
so more'n likely he figures if he can get into
the Indian Territory, we can't come after

him," Sheriff Dobson said. "I expect the best thing we can do now is get word down to the Indian police."

A small, very thin man with no hair and a pencil-thin mustache approached. "Excuse me, sir, but are you the next of kin?" he asked.

"Yes, I am the son."

"What disposition will you want of his remains?"

"I plan to take him back home."

"Very good, sir. I will get him ready for travel."

After receiving condolences from many, John Henry bought a buckboard, hitched his horse, Iron Heart, to it, then put his father, now lying in a pine coffin, in the back. What should have been a triumphal return, with the largest profit the ranch had ever earned was, instead, a somber ride back.

John Henry comforted his mother as much as he could. Then, after his father's funeral, he declared that he was going after Homer Tilghman.

"John Henry, no," Elizabeth pleaded. "Let the police do that."

"The police will do it," John Henry declared.

■ ■ ■ ■

Tahlequah was the capital of the Cherokee Nation. It was here that the Cherokee National Council met, and it was here that the Lighthorse Company, as the Indian police called themselves, had their headquarters.

"I remember you, John Henry," Captain Charles LeFlores said. "You were in your father's regiment. How is James doing?"

"My father is dead, slain by a man named Homer Tilghman."

"Tilghman? Yes, I've heard that name. He's been evading us now for nearly a year, darting back and forth between Indian Territory and Kansas."

"I will find him for you."

"You will find him?"

"Yes."

"And do what?"

"Whatever it takes."

"John Henry, you can't just take the law into your own hands, you know."

"I know. That's why I want you to swear me in as a policeman."

It took less than a week for John Henry, who was now a member of the Cherokee

36

Indian Police, to find his quarry. Tilghman was at a livery in the small settlement of Venita, arguing with the liveryman.

"This here horse is better'n any swayback nag you've got," Tilghman said. "I ain't givin' you no extra money. You should give me extra money for tradin'. But, I'm willin' to trade you dead even."

"I don't know, there's something fishy about this," the liveryman said. "If you think this horse is worth more'n anything I got, and if I'm bein' honest with you, it prob'ly is, why in Sam Hill would you be willin' to trade dead even?"

"Because it isn't his horse and he doesn't want to be caught with it," John Henry said. He had walked up on them quietly, and his words startled both of them. "He stole that horse."

John Henry had no difficulty in recognizing Tilghman, not only from the description he had been given, but also because he knew his father's horse.

"You're crazy!" Tilghman said. "I've had this horse for more'n five years."

"Have you?"

Tilghman rubbed the horse behind his ears. "I raised him from a colt."

"Mister, take the horse over there," John Henry said to the liveryman. "We will let the horse decide."

"Sounds like a good idea to me," the liveryman said, leading the horse about twenty feet away.

"Call him to you," John Henry said.

"Come here, horse. Come here," Tilghman called.

"You've had the horse since he was a colt, and you haven't given him a name?" John Henry asked.

"He doesn't need a name. He's just a horse," Tilghman replied. "Come here, horse. Come here."

The horse didn't move.

"Come on, you dumb horse! I'm calling you!"

"The horse isn't moving," the liveryman said.

"I can see that the son of a bitch isn't moving!" Tilghman said, angrily. "That doesn't mean anything."

"*Ehena na Galegi,*" John Henry said. Then he repeated it in English. "Come here, Blacksnake."

Blacksnake whickered, nodded his head, then trotted over to John Henry. He lowered his head so John Henry could pet him.

"Mister, were you tryin' to sell me a stoled horse?" the liveryman asked.

"I didn't steal it. I bought it. Only I just

bought it, which is how come the horse wouldn't come to me when I called it."

"I thought you said you raised him from a colt," the liveryman said.

"I just said that 'cause I didn't know who this man was, or what he wanted."

John Henry showed Tilghman his badge. "I am a policeman. And you are under arrest for killing my father."

Tilghman looked over at John Henry with an expression of surprise and fear.

"What? You're crazy! I told you, I bought this horse."

"Did the man you bought the horse from also have one eye that droops like yours?"

Tilghman stared directly at John Henry. It was obvious now that this man wasn't going to just go away.

"You aren't going to go away, are you?"

"Not without you, I'm not."

"If you were smart, you would turn around now, and leave me about my busi—" Then, midway through his sentence, and without any forewarning, Tilghman's hand suddenly dipped toward his gun.

"He's going for his gun!" the liveryman shouted, but his warning wasn't necessary. John Henry was ready for him, and his own pistol was out and booming before Tilghman could even bring his gun level. A stain of red spread across his chest, and he got a surprised look on his face, as if shocked that John Henry had beaten him, even though he had started his draw first.

Tilghman gurgled a curse as the blood rose in his throat, then dribbled from the corners of his mouth. He fell backwards, landing in a freshly deposited pile of horse apples. His arms flopped out to either side of him, the unfired gun dangling from a crooked, but stilled finger. It had all happened so quickly that the first indication to any of the citizens of the town that something was happening was the boom of John Henry's gun.

John Henry stood there for a long moment, the gun still in his hand, smoke curling up from the end of the barrel.

Two weeks later, John Henry was standing in Captain Charles LeFlores's office as twenty-one-hundred dollars, all that remained of the stolen money, was counted out to him.

"I'm sorry that this is all there is left," Captain LeFlores said.

"It's better than a total loss."

"I guess so. So, what are you going to do now?"

"I don't know. Get a seed bull and some

heifers and start over, I guess." John Henry took off his badge and held it out toward Captain LeFlores. "I thank you for giving me the opportunity to do this, legally."

LeFlores didn't take the proffered badge.

"You don't need to give that back to me. You could stay on with the police."

"Why would I want to do that?"

"I can't answer that. Only you know why you might want to do something. But I can tell you why I want you to stay. I think you would make a fine police officer, John Henry. Probably the finest on the force. And Lord knows we could use you. What about it? Would you consider becoming a full-time policeman?"

"I don't know."

"I tell you what. Today is Friday, take the weekend to think about it. I have an opening, and it's yours if you want it. But let me know by Monday, would you?"

"All right," John Henry said. Again, he held out the badge, and again LeFlores refused it.

"Keep it over the weekend. As of now you are still a member of the Indian Police. If you don't want to remain a member, you can resign on Monday."

John Henry sat by the dying campfire staring out over the flickering light into the shadows beyond. He had been riding alone all day, thinking of the offer made to him by Captain LeFlores, and now that day had come to a close. Darkness was gathering about him, and the silence of the night was ideal for such contemplation. A soft breeze fanned the glowing embers, lifting sparks, white ashes, and a thin column of smoke to curl upward into the darkness.

Behind John Henry, Iron Heart whickered, and shifted his stance.

"Am I being too quiet for you, Iron Heart? Well, I need the quiet. I have a lot of thinking to do."

The choices were clear-cut. Either he turned down Captain LeFlores's offer and made a go of the ranch, which would be a more difficult task now that he was alone, or take LeFlores up on the offer and, for all intent and purposes, be a wanderer.

Oddly, it was the latter thought which most appealed to him. Ever since he came back from the war, he had felt a sense of impermanence. He had stayed with the ranch out of a sense of obligation to his father. But with his father gone, he no longer felt that sense of obligation. He knew that his mother was here only because she had come here with his father, but John Henry also knew that the ranch meant nothing to his mother except for her connection to it through the man she loved. She liked the house, but John Henry could make enough money as a policeman to keep her in her house, and to see to her needs.

A trapped gas bubble in one of the logs was ignited by the flames making a loud pop and emitting a little shower of sparks. The glowing red sparks drifted up on a column of heated air until they joined the stars, red and white pinpoints of light in the black vault of darkness. John Henry stretched out beside the fire to sleep on his question. He was sure he would have the answer by the time he awoke in the morning.

"I am glad you have decided to join us," Captain LeFlores said when John Henry told him of his decision. "But I never doubted that you would."

"How is it that you were sure, when I wasn't?" John Henry asked.

"I know this business," Captain LeFlores said. "And if ever there was a man born to be a law officer, it was you. As our grandfathers used to say, John Henry, our people will be singing praises and telling stories of your exploits for many years to come."

CHAPTER FOUR

From the *Cherokee Advocate:*

John Henry Sixkiller
Subdues the Vann Gang

It has only been three years since John Henry Sixkiller became a member of the Cherokee Indian Police, but in that three years he has made a record of service so sterling that even newspapers in the States have extolled his virtues.

Sixkiller's most recent accomplishment is worthy of more accolades than can be heaped upon him by this newspaper, though we will try, in all sincerity, to do just that. And nothing would accomplish this task better than to present you, the reader, with an account of his most recent experiment.

On the month previous, Arnold Vann, Jacob Proxmire, Sylvester Malone, and Kerry Leach robbed a store in Tahlequah.

Taking two hundred dollars from the hard-working store owner, and shooting down and killing two of the store clerks, the Vann gang made good their getaway.

One might have thought that the robbers were so successful in their operation that they would never be caught, but they did not figure on the resourcefulness or bravery of John Henry Sixkiller. Captain Sixkiller located the outlaw gang and engaged them, with the result that three of the outlaws were killed and one, Arnold Vann, was brought to justice.

Captain Sixkiller has been rewarded for his service by being appointed chief sheriff of the Cherokee Nation. He has won the respect and admiration of all law-abiding people of the nation, Cherokee and White alike.

Willie Buck was sitting in the outhouse as he read the story about John Henry Sixkiller. When he finished the story, he tore the page from the newspaper and used it.

"This is what I think of you, John Henry Sixkiller," he said, chuckling as he thought about how he was using the newspaper.

Like John Henry Sixkiller, Willie Buck had gone to war, but unlike John Henry Sixkiller, Willie Buck had joined the Union

Army. He took part in only one battle, then deserted soon after, and managed to find his way back into Indian Territory. Once back in Indian Territory, he formed a group of raiders who called themselves the Indian Independence Council and, declaring war against both the North and the South, managed to profit by pillaging Yankee towns in Kansas, and Rebel towns in Arkansas. By war's end, Willie Buck had enough money to go into business, smuggling liquor into The Nations.

He had a few run-ins with the Indian Police, including one with John Henry, who caught him with an entire wagon load of liquor. John Henry confiscated the wagon, brought Willie Buck into Tahlequah, where he was fined one hundred dollars, and his liquor, worth over five hundred dollars, was destroyed. The enmity between the two that had started when they were but boys was greatly intensified with that action.

Shortly after John Henry was appointed Chief of the Cherokee Indian Police, events were occurring in Washington, D.C., that would have a profound impact on his life. It was an act granting five sections per mile for the construction of a railroad to the southern border of Kansas. Additionally, the act read that construction was authorized "from the southern boundary of Kansas, south through the Indian Territory, with the consent of the Indians, and not otherwise, along the Valley of the Grand and Arkansas Rivers."

Judge Levi Parsons of New York, the chief executive of the Missouri, Kansas & Texas Railway, chose as his general manager and field commander for the KATY, as the railroad was called, Colonel Robert Stevens. Stevens chose Otis Gunn as his chief engineer. He wanted a very special man to be his chief of construction, and he had been told that John Scullin was such a man. He went to St. Louis to meet with Scullin.

It was early morning, and Stevens was standing at the window of the hotel, looking down upon the Mississippi River. There were at least two dozen boats docked along the cobblestone bank, consisting of side paddlers, stern-wheelers, and even a couple of screw-propelled boats. Most were freight-carrying boats and goods were being off-loaded from some and loaded onto others. At least one of the docked vessels was a passenger-carrying boat, and people were going aboard for their journey. There were two more boats out in the river, one fighting the strong, downriver current to make a landing, the other taking advantage of the five-mile-per-hour current to move rapidly downstream, headed for Cape Girardeau, New Madrid, Memphis, Vicksburg and, eventually, New Orleans.

Stevens envied those who were in the riverboat business. Their right of way was already laid out for them, the wide, navigable Mississippi River. All they needed was a boat to put in the water. Stevens wanted to do the same thing with trains, establish a network of freight and passenger service that moved as efficiently across land as the boats did on the rivers. But in order to do that, he not only had to purchase the rolling equipment, but track also had to be laid. It was that, the laying of the track, that had brought him to this hotel in St. Louis.

Stevens met John Scullin at the Landing Restaurant for breakfast. Scullin was a big man, at least six feet, three inches tall, with red hair and beard, and weighing, Stevens guessed, about two hundred and forty pounds.

Scullin had come highly recommended to Stevens. "Nobody in the West," Stevens was told, "can handle the wild, rollicking Irishmen who make up the railroad construction crews like John Scullin."

"You would be Mr. Scullin?" Stevens asked.

"Aye, m' bucko, and were you told to look for the biggest and ugliest son of a bitch in the room?"

Stevens laughed. "Something like that," he said.

"Tell me about the railroad you are building, laddie."

"If we succeed, the rewards will be enormous. First, we will have access through Indian Territory to Texas and on to the Rio Grande. In addition, we will be given title to more than three million acres of some of the finest farming and ranching land in the entire country. And, as an officer of the railroad, you stand to profit handsomely for any success we may have. And that, of course, depends upon how our construction goes."

"If 'tis only a matter of concern about the construction, you need not concern yourself, Colonel. Sure 'n' the construction will be done."

"There is a one more thing that you should know."

"And what would that be?"

"We are in a race."

"A race?"

"Yes. A one-hundred-mile race to the

49

border against James Joy and his boys. Whoever reaches the border first will be given the right to take their tracks across Indian Territory."

"I see," Scullin said. He split open a biscuit and covered it with butter and jam before taking a bite.

"And what you are sayin' m' bucko, is that, to the victor goes the spoils." He spoke the words even as he was chewing his food.

"Yes. That is exactly what I'm saying."

"But the spoils, sure 'n' they're well worth running the race for," Scullin said.

"Oh, indeed they are, Mr. Scullin. So, are you in?"

"Aye, Colonel," Scullin replied. "I'm in."

"Do you think you can keep the graders out of the way of the track layers? And do you think you can lay a mile of track a day?"

" 'Tis a mile a day you are wanting, is it? Sure, m' bucko, I'll give you that and more."

"I'll have the contract drawn up for you," Stevens said.

"A contract is good," Scullin said. "But I like to take the measure of any deal by a handshake." He reached across the table, his big hand open. "Would you be for shakin' my hand, Colonel?"

"Aye, Mr. Scullin," Stevens said, smiling as he adapted Scullin's Irish brogue.

" 'Twould give me great pleasure to shake your hand."

As the meeting between Colonel Robert Stevens and John Scullin was taking place in St. Louis, three hundred fifty miles to the southwest, in the small settlement of Spavina, Indian Territory, Emil Walks Fast, Edward Lean Bear, and Damon Straight Arrow were just coming into town. Though the permanent population of Spavina was small, it was a busy trading center for this part of the Cherokee Nation and this morning half-a-dozen wagons were parked along the streets. The board sidewalks were full of men and women, Indian and white, looking in the windows of the shops as they hurried to and fro.

"There's the bank over there," Walks Fast pointed out. The bank was a rather flimsy-looking building, thrown together with mismatched boards and leaning so that it looked as if a good stiff wind would knock it over.

"It doesn't look like much of a bank," Lean Bear said.

"What do we care what it looks like on the outside? It is what is inside the bank that counts. Come. Let's take the money and get out of here," Straight Arrow suggested.

"Not so fast," Walks Fast said, holding up his hand. "First, we need to scout out the town. Straight Arrow, you go up that side of the street and take a look around. Lean Bear, you do the same thing on this side."

The two men rode slowly down the entire length of the town, then they turned their horses and rode back.

"What does it look like?" Walks Fast asked.

"I didn't see anyone that might cause us a problem," Straight Arrow said.

"I didn't either," Lean Bear said. "It looks clear to me."

"All is ready," Walks Fast said. "Lean Bear, you come with me. Straight Arrow, you stay outside and hold the horses."

Walks Fast and Lean Bear swung down from their horses and handed the reins over to Straight Arrow, who stayed mounted. He held the reins of all three horses with his left hand, while in his right he held his pistol, though he kept it low and out of sight.

When Walks Fast and Lean Bear stepped inside the bank, they saw a woman and a little girl sitting across the desk from a bank officer. There was one bank teller behind the cage, but he didn't even look up as the two men entered.

Walks Fast and Lean Bear pulled their pistols.

"This is a holdup!" Walks Fast shouted. "You, teller, empty out your bank drawer and put all the money in a bag!"

Nervously, the bank teller began to comply, emptying his drawer in just a few seconds.

"What are you trying to pull? There isn't much money here," Walks Fast said as he looked at the money given him by the teller.

"That's all there is," the teller insisted.

"I don't believe you! You are lying!"

"I swear to you, I am telling the truth!"

Walks Fast looked toward the desk where the bank officer, the woman, and the little girl were all reacting in fear to the situation.

"You!" Walks Fast called to the bank officer. "I know there is more money than this in the bank. Open your vault!"

"I'm just a loan officer. I don't have the combination to the vault," the man replied.

"You're lying!" Walks Fast said. He pointed his pistol at the bank officer. "Open that vault!"

"Help!" the bank officer shouted, starting toward the door. "Help! The bank is being robbed!"

Walks Fast and Lean Bear both started

shooting at the fleeing bank officer.

The little girl went down and her mother screamed.

Thinking the robbers were distracted, the bank teller pulled a gun from the shelf below the teller's window and fired. His bullet hit Lean Bear, but before he could fire a second time, Walks Fast whirled around and shot the teller.

Clutching the sack of money in his hand, Walks Fast ran through the front door.

"Let's get out of here!" he shouted as he got mounted.

"What was all the shooting? Where is Lean Bear?" Straight Arrow called back.

"Lean Bear is dead."

"But I have his horse!"

"Leave it!"

By now the townspeople had heard the shots and realized what was going on.

"The bank!" someone shouted. "They're robbing the bank!"

Walks Fast slapped his legs against the side of his horse and the horse bolted ahead. Straight Arrow dropped the reins to Lean Bear's horse and followed him

One of the townspeople had armed himself, and he ran out into the street, shooting wildly. Walks Fast returned fire, and the man fell back, bleeding from a chest wound. The rest of the townspeople began screaming and running for cover.

Across the street someone came running from a hardware store carrying a rifle. He fired at the two robbers, missing them, but hitting Straight Arrow's horse. Straight Arrow leaped from the back of his animal as it went down. There were several horses tied to hitching rails, reacting nervously to all the shouting and shooting. Straight Arrow ran to the nearest one and swung into the saddle.

"Hey! That is my horse!" someone shouted, coming out of the apothecary. Straight Arrow shot at him, driving him back inside.

The local Indian policeman, an older man, was just now reaching the scene, having run the entire length of the street from the police office. He was carrying a rifle and he raised it to his shoulders. But before he could pull the trigger, Walks Fast shot the policeman, who fell with a red, bleeding hole in his forehead.

The two men galloped toward the end of town, where they saw several armed men coming toward them, already shooting. Realizing they couldn't go that way, Walks Fast and Straight Arrow turned off the street, then galloped through a schoolyard. The children screamed as the two bank robbers galloped through the playground. The schoolteacher ran to push a little girl out of the way. She saved the little girl, but Straight Arrow ran her down and she lay, unmoving, on the ground behind them as they galloped away.

By the time the townspeople regrouped and mounted, Walks Fast and Straight Arrow were two miles out of town. With the police officer dead and no one to lead them, the pursuit quickly fizzled out. The would-be posse turned to the gruesome business of tending to their dead: three men, one little girl, and the schoolteacher. There was a fourth dead man, but that was one of the bank robbers and he was buried within the hour, without benefit of a coffin.

CHAPTER FIVE

John Henry and Sasha Quiet Stream halted beside the lake, among windblown willows. The moon reflected back a huge silver orb from the surface of the water. John Henry dismounted, then helped Sasha down. It was the gentlemanly thing to do, though Sasha certainly needed no help in dismounting.

"The horses need water," John Henry said as he led both of them to the edge of the lake.

The night was warm, and as Sasha stood there, looking out at the splash of silver the moon spilt on the surface of the water, she recalled some time from her youth, when she would go into an inviting stream. It seemed so appealing now, offering the promise of cooling her heated body.

Sasha looked over toward John Henry and saw that he was standing next to the horses, watching them drink. Smiling as she yielded to the appeal offered by the lake, she walked down to the edge, then, with her bare feet, stepped out into it. At first, she meant only to wet her feet, but as she got into it, the temptation to go deeper grew stronger, so she moved farther out, feeling her dress grow wet as the cool lake water climbed above her knees, then to her waist, then higher.

She looked back at John Henry, and seeing that he still had not seen her, swallowed a laugh over the trick she was playing on him.

When the horses had drunk their fill, John Henry led them away from the water and tied them off to a low-hanging branch.

"I think we can sit here for a while and . . ." John Henry stopped in midsentence and looked around, startled that he didn't see Sasha. "Sasha? Sasha, where are you?" His call reflected some concern.

"I am here," Sasha replied in a soft, throaty voice.

"Where?"

Sasha laughed, the laughter like the sound of a swiftly moving brook over stones. "John Henry, do you mean you don't see me?" she teased.

John Henry looked toward the sound and

saw, in the silver spread of moonlight on the surface, only Sasha's head protruding above the water.

"What are you doing in there?" he asked. "Did you fall in?"

"No, I walked in. I was hot, and the water looked cooling," Sasha said. She started toward the shore then, gradually emerging from the water as she walked. Near the edge she slipped and would have fallen, had John Henry not reached out his hand to her.

Using his hand to steady her, she emerged from the lake dripping wet.

She smiled at John Henry, enjoying her little joke on him, until she saw his eyes studying her with passionate intensity. At first, she wondered what he was looking at — then she was aware of an extraordinary coolness on her breasts, a breeze against the dampness. Glancing down, she saw that the action of the water had caused her dress to become almost transparent, and John Henry's gaze was resting upon her breasts, clearly visible through the wet cloth. Quickly, she crossed her arms across her chest.

"John Henry, you are staring," she said.

"Yes, I suppose I am," John Henry replied, making no effort to look away.

"Please, I am growing uncomfortable."

Smiling, John Henry began unbuttoning his shirt.

"What . . . what are you doing?"

John Henry took his shirt off and handed it to her. "Here," he said. "This will help you restore some modesty."

"I fear it is too late for that," Sasha said.

"If not modesty, then a little dignity," John Henry suggested.

Sasha chuckled, then put the shirt on. "This is the second time you have defended my — dignity — with your shirt," she said.

At first, John Henry didn't know what she was referring to, then he remembered the incident, so many years earlier, with Willie Buck.

"Come," he said. "I'll take you back home."

"John Henry, you are a good and decent man, and you have done the honorable thing, saving me from my own imprudence. I thank you for that."

"Now is not the time for us, Sasha."

"When will be the time?"

"Sasha, I am in a dangerous profession. I could be killed at any time. If we were to be married, it wouldn't be fair to you."

"John Henry, do you think I would grieve your death any less because we are not married?"

John Henry put his hands about her waist preparatory to lifting her into the saddle. But before he did, he leaned forward and kissed her.

The kiss was soft and undemanding.

"And, what of us now?" Sasha asked when he drew his lips from hers.

"We shall see what we shall see," John Henry answered.

It was just after dark when Walks Fast and Straight Arrow rode into the town of Verdigris, butt-weary from the long ride down. Walks Fast and Lean Bear had been to Verdigris many times before, but this would be Straight Arrow's first visit to the town. They had fifty dollars apiece from the bank job in Spavina. In most towns fifty dollars would be considered a lot of money, but Walks Fast was quick to point out that their money wouldn't go far here.

"You can get a whore for a dollar anywhere else," he explained. "Here, they'll cost you three dollars."

"Why so much?" Straight Arrow wanted to know.

"There is no law here."

"There is law everywhere."

"Not here. Why do you think Lean Bear and I have spent so much time here? It is because there is no policeman who stays here. The people in the town don't want law. They want people like us."

"Why?"

"So they can charge much, and we won't complain," Walks Fast said.

Verdigris was dark except for the patches of light that spilled out into the street from the windows and doors. The town was noisy with drums and bells. Laughter and loud voices filled the night air, and occasionally a gunshot would ring out, though for the most part the gunshots were in boisterous fun and nothing more.

A woman was leaning over the balcony banister, wearing nothing but an undergarment and it was cut low enough to expose the tops of enormous breasts. Her breasts were large because she was large. "Hey, why don't you two boys come on up here?" she invited. "I'll take both of you on for the price of one."

With her red hair, pasty-white complexion, and flat, twangy accent, she was a definitely a white woman.

"Have you ever had a white woman?" Straight Arrow asked.

"Yes," Walks Fast answered.

"How was she?"

"She was white," Walks Fast said without

elaboration. He had been with Willie Buck's Indian Independence Council Raiders then, and they had raped two white girls when they sacked the small town of Kibler, Arkansas. After they finished with the two girls, Willie Buck ordered that they be killed.

Because it was illegal to sell liquor anywhere in The Nations, smuggling whiskey into Indian Territory had become quite a profitable operation. The smuggling was done almost entirely by whites, many of whom had married Indian women in order to give them status as residents of Indian Territory.

The lawless town of Verdigris was more than half white, and more than a quarter Mexican. Even though it was a town in Indian Territory, Indians made up the minority of the population. It was partly because of this makeup that there was no representative of the Indian police in the town. And because it was a lawless town, it made no attempt to hide the trafficking in liquor. Like just about any town anywhere else in the West, Verdigris had a saloon. Unlike many of the other saloons throughout the West, though, the entry to this saloon was not through bat-wing doors, but through a hanging blanket. Inside, the bar was noisy with conversation, nearly all of it in English, but some in Spanish. Nowhere did they hear Cherokee being spoken. There was no piano, but a Mexican was sitting on a stool in the back of the saloon, strumming a guitar.

There was a pretty Mexican girl standing at the end of the bar and she smiled when she saw Walks Fast.

"Walks Fast. You have come back to Elaina! I knew you could not stay away from me!"

Walks Fast went up to her and put his arm around her. "Come, Elaina. We will go upstairs."

"Do you have money?" the girl asked.

"Yes, I have money." Walks Fast took some money from his pocket and showed it to her.

"All right," the girl said to Walks Fast. "If you have money to spend on me, then I will go with you." Teasingly, she put her hand in his hair and twisted a strand of it around her finger. "If you want me," she added, coquettishly.

"You come with me and I will show you how much I want you," Walks Fast said, pulling her with him as he walked over to the bar to buy a bottle.

Because the policeman had been killed in

Spavina, John Henry Sixkiller, who was now the chief sheriff of the entire Cherokee Nation, took responsibility for the case.

"They killed three men: Rodney Gilbert, the loan officer; Homer Foster, the bank teller; and our policeman, Clyde Running Horse, who was a good man," Dan Norton said. Norton was the mayor of Spavina. "They also killed Alice Clemons, who was the schoolteacher, and little Sally Shoemaker."

"Did anyone recognize the men who did this?" John Henry asked.

Norton smiled. "Yes, we know exactly who did it. Several witnesses have identified them. It was Emil Walks Fast and Damon Straight Arrow. Do you know them?"

"Yes, I know both of them. They are often with Edward Lean Bear."

"They won't be with Lean Bear anymore," Norton said. "Lean Bear was with them when they pulled the job, but he was killed by one of the bank customers. I hope you find them, and I hope they hang for what they did here."

"I will find them, and they will hang. They were sentenced to hang six months ago, but they escaped jail on the very day they were to be executed."

"Is that a fact? Well, if they have already

been convicted, then they know what is in store for them if they are caught. That means they aren't going to come in easy. Be very careful," Mayor Norton cautioned.

John Henry started his search by interviewing those who had witnessed the crime. Of the actual robbery, only Wanda Shoemaker, the woman who was in the bank at the time, could give direct testimony. She had lost her daughter and had seen the two bankers killed. Spavina was a town that was still grieving. They were lamenting the death of all the victims, but the town was particularly upset by the killing of the little girl and the schoolteacher.

John Henry visited with the widow of Clyde Running Horse, comforting her as best he could.

"He was a good man," she said. "It is not good that he would be killed like this. The men who did this, Walks Fast and Straight Arrow, are evil men. I hope they are found and punished."

"I will find them, and they will be punished," John Henry promised.

After leaving Running Horse's widow, John Henry walked down to what had been the police office. There he met Leon Barker. Barker was a white man, a former

66

sheriff from Missouri who had settled in the Indian Territory. He had no official standing, though he was acting as a law officer until someone else could be assigned to replace Clyde Running Horse.

"I thought you would be sending us someone," Barker said. "I didn't know you would come yourself."

"Clyde Running Horse was a good man," John Henry said. "I felt the need to come myself."

"Yes, sir, well I'm glad you did. I'll just get Clyde's things out of here and over to his widow, and the office is all yours."

"I understand one of the robbers was killed."

"Yes. Lean Bear, his name was. He was killed by Glen Black, who was one of the two men who was killed in the bank."

"Where is Lean Bear now?"

"Oh, we've already buried him. Planted his ass in a hole outside of town."

"Did he have anything on him?"

Barker smiled. "I told the others that you would want to look at the stuff. Yes, he did, and I've got it all right here."

Barker opened a drawer and took out a cloth bundle. He unrolled the cloth and showed the contents to John Henry. Barker had two silver dollars, a half dollar, three quarters, and a dime in money. He had a bone whistle, a black, round rock, and a brass coin of some sort. John Henry turned the coin over in his hand, examining it closely, trying to figure out what it was.

Barker chuckled. "You don't know what that is, do you?"

"I've never seen anything like it."

"It's a whore's chit."

"A what?"

"It's a chit that whores give out. It's good for one visit."

"I've never seen such a thing."

"You haven't spent a lot of time around whorehouses, have you? Anyway, they are mostly in places like Kansas, Colorado, Wyoming, New Mexico. About the only one place in The Nations that you might find something like that would be in Verdigris."

"Verdigris," John Henry said. "Yes, I have heard of that place. I have never been there, but I have heard of it."

"What have you heard about it?"

"I have heard that it is an evil place."

"You have heard right, my friend," Barker said. "There is no law in Verdigris."

"That is where they will go," John Henry said.

In Verdigris, Walks Fast and Straight Arrow

68

had befriended three white men. Dan McGuire, Barry Appleby, and Ken Crader were in the Indian Territory because they were wanted on murder charges back in Kansas. The three men were talking about a bank they wanted to rob.

"The bank is in a place called Greysons, about thirty miles east of here," Appleby said.

"That's in the Osage Nation," Walks Fast said.

"You think the banks in the Osage nation don't have any money?" McGuire asked. "I happen to know that this bank has a lot of money. At least twenty thousand dollars."

"How do you know it has so much money?"

"Because I seen it in a newspaper. They was braggin' about how much money they had. Robbin' that bank is goin' to be as easy as takin' candy from a baby."

"If you think it is going to be so easy, why haven't you robbed it?" Straight Arrow asked.

"Maybe you ain't noticed but we are white men," Crader said. "As soon as we ride into town, everyone is going to notice us. But if we rode in with a couple of Injuns now, why folks would just think we are doin' some business."

"And we are goin' to do some business," McGuire said, laughing. "Yes, sir, we are goin' to do a lot of business with them."

"What do you think, Walks Fast?" Straight Arrow asked.

Walks Fast stroked his chin. "Nothing is easy," he said. "We thought the bank in Spavina would be easy. But Lean Bear was killed, and we only got a hundred dollars."

"I'm tellin' you, this one will be easy," Appleby said. "And it has a hell of a lot more than one hundred dollars."

"All right," Walks Fast said. "We'll do it. But I'm going to stay here a few more days, spending money and enjoying myself."

"We can wait," McGuire said.

CHAPTER SIX

As John Henry rode toward Verdigis, he recalled a conversation he once had with Captain LeFlores about the town. "We don't keep a policeman there because less than a quarter of the population of the town is Indian. We have no jurisdiction over the white people who are there, and the town is too small to have a U.S. Marshal there," Captain LeFlores explained.

"What has happened to it? How can a town survive with no law?" John Henry asked.

"It can't survive," LeFlores replied. "There is no longer any stagecoach or mail service into the town. They have no representatives on the governing council. It's as if the town didn't even exist and I think most people wish it didn't exist."

"I would think that a place like that would be a haven for outlaws who want to hide out," John Henry said.

"It is. But I think the general consensus is now, as long as they stay there, they aren't bothering anyone else. We have sort of assumed an informal, 'we won't bother you, if you won't bother us,' attitude. Not exactly the best way to handle it, I admit. But that's the way it is."

It was approaching nighttime, but not quite dark as John Henry rode into the small town of Verdigris. Verdigris, more than any other settlement in the Indian Territory, was a town that came alive at night. As John Henry rode into town, he didn't have to look for the saloon. All he had to do was follow the noise.

He passed a building that had a sign advertising itself as a stagecoach depot, and he remembered LeFlores telling him that no stagecoach line serviced Verdigris anymore. Curious, John Henry stopped, dismounted, then went over to the building to look around. The front door was hanging by a single hinge, and when he looked inside he saw the nothing but dirt and cobwebs. A schedule board still hung on the back wall, but whatever information there had been on it was now so faded as to be unreadable.

In front of the abandoned stagecoach depot was a well and, looking down into it,

John Henry saw that it was no more than fifteen-feet deep and completely dry.

His curiosity satisfied, John Henry re-mounted and continued his ride on through town, headed for the saloon. He knew, without a doubt, that if Walks Fast and Straight Arrow were in town, they would be at the saloon.

Walks Fast and Straight Arrow had been in Verdigris for almost two weeks now, and Straight Arrow discovered that Walks Fast was right about everything being more expensive here. A shot of whiskey was ten cents anywhere else, but here it was a quarter for one glass.

Straight Arrow had been relatively frugal with his money, whereas Walks Fast was anything but frugal. Walks Fast talked about the bank job they were going to pull over in Osage Country where "we'll have all the money we might ever want or need. I say let's have a good time until this money runs out." Following his own advice, Walks Fast was, at the moment, upstairs with Elaina. This was his twelfth visit with her in as many days.

Straight Arrow walked up to the bar. "What have you got to eat today?" he asked.

"Steak, beans," the bartender answered.

"Eggs?"

"Yes. We have eggs."

"I want a steak and some eggs," Straight Arrow said. "And let me have a pitcher of beer."

Straight Arrow took the pitcher of beer from the bartender and walked over to a corner where he found an empty table. He sat down with his back to the wall and began drinking his beer. As he drank his beer, he studied some of the pictures that decorated the wall of the establishment. One picture in particular caught his attention. It showed a man on a horse riding alongside a thundering herd of buffalo. The horse had no saddle and the Indian was controlling him with his knees only. He was holding a bow and the string was pulled back as he rode alongside one big bull. There was already one arrow sticking out of the buffalo.

The Indian was obviously not a Cherokee, for though the Cherokee had hunted buffalo and deer since coming to Indian Territory, they had never done so in such a way. Still, it made Straight Arrow feel good to imagine himself as that Indian.

John Henry knew both Straight Arrow and Walks Fast on sight, and as soon as he stepped into the saloon, he saw Straight Arrow sitting alone at a table in the back of the room. He saw, also, a Mexican man carrying a plate of food toward the table.

"Is that food for Straight Arrow?" John Henry asked.

"Sí, Señor."

"I'll take it to him," John Henry said, taking the plate from the waiter.

As Straight Arrow continued to study the picture, a plate of steak and eggs was put on the table in front of him, but he was too absorbed by the picture to bother to look up. He reached for the steak and picked it up in his hands.

"We pride ourselves on being civilized," John Henry said. "And here you are, Straight Arrow, eating with your hands. Haven't you ever heard of a knife and fork?"

Gasping, Straight Arrow looked up to see that the person who had just delivered his food was not the bartender, but someone who was wearing a badge and holding a pistol in his hand. The pistol was pointed toward him.

"Sixkiller?"

"Good, I see you remember me. That means there is no need for an introduction. Go ahead and take a bite," John Henry said. "I wouldn't want to disturb a man before

75

he was finished eating his supper."

Straight Arrow just sat there staring wide-eyed at the man who had confronted him.

"Go ahead, Straight Arrow, eat," John Henry said again.

Straight Arrow raised the steak to his mouth, then suddenly dropped it and made a mad grab for his pistol. But John Henry was quicker and he brought his pistol down hard on Straight Arrow's head. Straight Arrow wound up facedown on the table.

John Henry bent down to take Straight Arrow's pistol. Then he dragged the outlaw's limp, unconscious form over to one of the supporting posts where he propped him up, and putting one arm to either side of the post, put the handcuffs on.

The guitar music, laughter, and conversation had all come to a stop when John Henry knocked Straight Arrow out. Most of the other patrons looked on in curiosity, making no comment until they saw John Henry put on the handcuffs.

"Hey, wait a minute! What are you doing?" someone called. The person who called out was, as were most of the people in the saloon, a white man.

"What does it look like? I'm putting this man under arrest for murder and robbery," John Henry replied easily.

"No, you ain't. There ain't no law here in Verdigris, and we don't want any. So if I was you, I'd get them cuffs off that man and get out of here while you still can."

John Henry looked up at the speaker. "Who are you?" he asked.

"The name is McGuire, and I'm the man that's goin' to run your ass out of Verdigris. Who the hell are you?"

"The name is Sixkiller. John Henry Sixkiller. I am Chief Sheriff of the Cherokee Nation, and I am taking this man to jail."

"I don't care who you are, I say you ain't goin' —"

John Henry pulled his pistol and shot McGuire in the leg. McGuire let out a cry of pain, grabbed his leg, and fell to the floor.

"Son of a bitch!" he shouted.

John Henry reached down and pulled McGuire's pistol from his holster, then removed all the shells. Walking over to the front door, he tossed the pistol out into the street. After that, he returned to the table where Straight Arrow had been sitting. The untouched steak had fallen back onto his plate and John Henry cut off a generous piece of it and stuck it into his mouth. Then he picked up the pitcher of beer and took several swallows before he set it back down. The rest of the saloon continued to watch him in silence.

Returning to the bar, he glanced down at McGuire, who was sitting up now, groaning in pain and holding his hand over the bullet hole in his leg.

"You shot me in the leg, you son of a bitch!"

"Yeah, I did," John Henry replied, his voice as calm as if telling the time of day. John Henry looked over to the bartender. "There were two of them," he said.

"I don't know, I haven't been paying any attention."

"Really? They have been here for several days but you haven't noticed them? Do you think a bullet in your leg would help you remember?"

The bartender looked down at McGuire, who was sitting on the floor, leaning back against the bar with his hand over the bullet hole in his leg, moaning in pain.

"The other man's name is Walks Fast," John Henry continued. "Walks Fast and this man, Straight Arrow" — he pointed to the man who was sitting on the floor, cuffed to a support post — "murdered four people back in Spavina. One of them was a woman schoolteacher, and the other was a little girl. Now, where is Walks Fast?"

■ ■ ■ ■

Upstairs, Walks Fast was sitting on the foot of Elaina's bed drinking whiskey when he heard the shot.

"What was that?"

"I think it was nothing," Elaina said. "Always there is shooting here."

"No, I think it was something more."

Walks Fast moved to the door of the room, opened it, then looked down. From here, his view of the floor was restricted, but he could see the mirror behind the bar, and in the mirror he saw John Henry Sixkiller talking to the bartender.

"Sixkiller," he said aloud.

"*¿Qué has dicho, cariño?*"

"Come here."

"*¿Qué?*"

"I said, come here!" Walks Fast repeated, his words harsh and demanding.

Elaina, who was wearing only a chemise, came to him. Suddenly, he grabbed her, then, opening the door, pushed her out onto the landing in front of him. He stepped up to the railing, then called down.

"Sixkiller!" he shouted.

John Henry looked up toward the sound and saw Walks Fast standing there, holding a pistol to the head of a young woman.

"Let my friend go!"

John Henry made no effort to move.

"You heard me! Let him go, or I will kill this woman."

"Please, Señor, let him go!" Elaina begged.

"Ha!" McGuire said. "He's got your ass in a crack, don't he? What are you going to do now, you son of a bitch?" McGuire asked.

"I'm going to let Straight Arrow go," John Henry said.

John Henry walked over to Straight Arrow and leaned down to open the handcuffs. Looking back toward Walks Fast, he saw that moving over to the post to which Straight Arrow was attached had greatly improved his position with regard to the angle he had on Walks Fast. From this angle there was more of Walks Fast exposed than there was of the woman.

"Hurry it up!" Walks Fast ordered.

John Henry drew his pistol and fired. Elaina screamed, but she wasn't hit. John Henry's shot had been deadly accurate, and Walks Fast pitched over the railing, turned one-half flip, and landed on his back on a table that was occupied by four cardplayers. Cards and chips went flying as the men, with shouts of anger and alarm, jumped up and moved away from the table.

John Henry, with the smoking gun still in his hand, crossed over for a closer look at Walks Fast. It didn't take much of an examination to see that he was dead.

"*¡Señor, cuidado!*" Elaina shouted.

Heeding the warning, John Henry looked around to see that McGuire had gotten another gun from somewhere, and he was aiming it at John Henry.

"You son of a bitch!" McGuire shouted as he pulled the trigger.

The bullet from McGuire's gun fired past John Henry's ear, coming so close that he could feel the wind of its passing. John Henry returned fire and McGuire, who had gotten to his feet despite the wound in his leg, fell back with a bullet in his heart.

Putting his pistol back in its holster, John Henry returned to the post where Straight Arrow was attached. He freed his prisoner from the post, then cuffed his hands again, cuffing them in front, so Straight Arrow could ride.

"What are you planning on doing with that man, Sheriff?" someone asked.

"First thing tomorrow morning, I'm going to take him back to Tahlequah."

"Yeah? Where are you plannin' on keepin' him tonight? Maybe you didn't notice, Mr.

Indian Sheriff, but we don't have a jail in this town."

"I will improvise."

"Do you think you'll make it to Tahlequah alive?"

"Oh, I'll get there alive," John Henry said. He nodded toward his prisoner. "But if anyone tries to stop me, he won't."

When John Henry rode away from the saloon, Straight Arrow was mounted on his own horse, but secured by means of a rope noose around his neck. John Henry's end of the rope was tied around his saddle horn, and by this method he rode the full length of the single street in Verdigris.

He recalled the question one of the men in the saloon had asked him. "Where are you plannin' on keepin' him tonight? Maybe you didn't notice, Mr. Indian Sheriff, but we don't have a jail in this town."

John Henry said that he would improvise, and now, as he contemplated what to do with Straight Arrow, he thought about the well. When they reached the old, abandoned stagecoach office and well, he stopped.

"Whoa," he said.

"What are we stoppin' here for?" Straight Arrow asked.

"Get down," John Henry ordered.

Moving gingerly because of the noose around his neck, Straight Arrow dismounted.

"You didn't answer my question. What are we stoppin' here for?" Straight Arrow asked again.

"We are going to spend the night here."

"Here? Where?"

"Down in the well," John Henry said. "At least you are."

"The hell you say! I'm not going down into that well."

"You have a choice. You can go down into that well, and I will take you back alive. Or you can refuse to go down into the well, and I'll take you back dead."

"I'll go down into the well," Straight Arrow said. He walked over to look down into it. "But how am I goin' to get down there?"

"That's easy. I'm going to lower you with this rope."

"What?" Straight Arrow asked, his eyes growing big in fright. He lifted his cuffed hands to the noose around his neck.

John Henry chuckled. "Not that way," he said. "Widen the noose until you can slip it down around your waist."

Straight Arrow did so, then John Henry lowered him.

"You'd better work that rope off you so I

can pull it up," John Henry said. "Otherwise, I won't be able to get you out of there in the morning."

John Henry recovered the rope. Then, with Straight Arrow safely down in the well, he walked up to the abandoned depot building and took the door down. Because it was hanging by a single hinge, it was easy to remove. Then, carrying the door back to the well, he laid it across the top. That done, he spread his bedroll out on the door.

Within a few minutes, he was sound asleep.

It was the middle of the night when John Henry was awakened by a nudge from Iron Heart's nose. Opening his eyes, he didn't see anything, but he did hear someone talking.

"You're sure they're here?"

"Yeah, I saw him put the Injun down in the old dry well."

Drawing his pistol, John Henry slipped down from the door and knelt behind the well. He saw two men come into view a moment later.

"You men looking for something?" John Henry called.

"What the hell!"

"Drop your guns and get out of here."

84

"You got no right to tell us to —" Whatever he was going to say was interrupted by the sound of John Henry's pistol being cocked.

"All right, all right, we're goin'."

"Leave your guns here," John Henry said.

The two men dropped their guns, then turned around and disappeared into the night.

CHAPTER SEVEN

John Henry pulled Straight Arrow up from the well just after first light the next morning.

"I see that you met Appleby and Crader," Straight Arrow said.

"Who are Appleby and Crader?"

"They are friends of mine."

"You don't have any friends."

"They were here last night. I heard you and them talking. What happened to them?"

"Nothing. I just convinced them to go back to town. Come on, we have a long ride ahead of us."

Once more John Henry had Straight Arrow mounted on his horse with a rope around his neck.

They had been underway for the better part of two hours when they crossed a stream. Straight Arrow stopped.

"What are you stopping here for?" John Henry asked.

"I never pass up a chance to fill my canteen with water."

"You are going to pass it this time. Keep going."

John Henry knew why Straight Arrow wanted to stop. There were two men riding parallel with them, and stopping at the creek would give the men the opportunity to make their ambush.

They rode on for another mile before Straight Arrow stopped again.

"Why are you stopping here?" John Henry asked.

"Can't you tell? My horse is going lame."

"I don't see anything."

"Maybe you can't see it, but he's favoring his right foreleg. I can feel it."

"Keep going."

"This is a good horse. If I ride him lame now, what am I going to do for a horse in the future?"

"You don't have a future," John Henry said.

"We've got to stop, I tell you, and give my horse a rest."

John Henry looked over to his left without being obvious about it, and saw the two riders slipping through a notch in the hills, moving so quietly and expertly that only someone who was specifically looking for them would have noticed.

"All right, we'll stop here for a few minutes."

"There's no need now. I think he may just have picked up a rock in his shoe, but now he's thrown it. He's not limping anymore."

Evidently, Straight Arrow had also seen the two men and now that the two men had gotten ahead of them, he wanted to ride on, to lead John Henry into the ambush that was being planned.

"We'll stop here," John Henry said. "I'm going to have you wait while I check ahead."

"Wait? You're going to have me wait here?"

"Yes."

"Yeah, you go ahead and check it out. I won't go anywhere." Straight Arrow smiled broadly.

"Oh, I know you won't."

"What do you mean?"

"You'll see."

"You can't leave me here like this, you son of a bitch!" Straight Arrow shouted in fear and anger a few minutes later as John Henry rode on ahead.

"I would be quiet if I were you," John Henry called back to him. "You don't want to spook your horse now, do you?"

Straight Arrow was sitting on his horse, now with his hands cuffed behind his back.

The rope around his neck had been thrown over the limb of a tree and tied off. Should his horse decide to run away from under him he would be hanged.

John Henry left the trail he had been following, then rode over to the trail where the two would-be ambushers were riding. It didn't take him long to catch up with them. They were behind a rock out-cropping, watching the path John Henry would have been coming on, had he not stopped. He couldn't be certain, because it had been dark, but he believed these were the same two men he had encountered last night. He did recognize them from having seen them in the saloon back in Verdigris, and he believed, based upon what Straight Arrow had said, that they were Crader and Appleby. Though of course, he didn't know which was which.

John dismounted, pulled his rifle from the saddle sheath, then walked up behind them. He approached them very quietly, stopping when he was less than thirty feet behind them.

"What the hell is keepin' 'em?" one of the two men said.

"Don't be so damn anxious. They'll be here in a minute."

"Straight Arrow won't, but I'm here now,"

John Henry said.

"What?" The two men whirled around, shocked by hearing the voice from so close behind them.

"Drop your guns."

The two men, who were carrying rifles, complied.

"And your holsters."

"We ain't got nothin' in our holsters. You took our guns last night."

"So I did," John Henry said. "You, take off your shirt." He pointed to the larger of the two men.

"What for?"

John Henry raised the rifle to his shoulder and aimed at the man. "I'm not going to ask you again," he said.

Once the man took off his shirt, John Henry directed that they put the two rifles on the shirt.

"Tie it up into a neat bundle for me," John Henry ordered, and the men did as he directed.

"Now, get out of here."

The two men started toward the horses they had tied to a nearby tree.

"Leave the horses. You're walking."

"The hell you say," one of the two men said angrily. "We're out here in the middle of nowhere. There ain't no way I'm goin' to leave my horse."

"You can walk out of here alive, or stay here dead, I don't care which. But you're not going to ride out of here."

"I think the son of a bitch means it, Crader. You seen what he done to McGuire last night."

"Good thinking, Mr. Appleby," John Henry said.

"What? How the hell do you know my name?"

"A medicine man told me."

"You're lyin'."

"Indians never lie. I thought you knew that," John Henry said with a smile.

"Let's get out of here," Crader said.

John Henry watched the two men until they were out of sight. After that, he operated the lever, jacking all the shells out of the rifles, then slammed the rifle barrels against rocks until they were bent so badly that they could never be fired again. That done, he untied the two horses, slapped them on the rump, and sent them running.

When he returned, Straight Arrow was sitting perfectly still, exactly as he had left him. He untied the rope from the tree, then had Straight Arrow get down so he could remove the handcuffs and recuff his hands in front so he could ride.

"What happened to them?" Straight Arrow asked. "Did you kill them?"

"They decided to go back to town," John Henry replied.

When the two men rode into Tahlequah late that afternoon the entire town was turned out to meet them.

"Did they give you much of a fight, John Henry?" someone called.

"Hey, Straight Arrow, I'm glad they caught you, you murdering son of a bitch!"

Straight Arrow gave no reaction to the taunts from those who had gathered alongside the street. Instead, he stared ahead, glumly, and when they reached the jail, Captain LeFlores was standing there on the porch to meet them.

"Hello, Straight Arrow, welcome to Tahlequah," Captain LeFlores said. "Or in your case, I suppose I should say welcome home."

"You go to hell, LeFlores," Straight Arrow snarled.

"Now, is that any way to act toward the man who is going to be your host for a while? Or for at least until we hang you."

"I hope you got somethin' to eat in there," Straight Arrow said. "This son of a bitch ain't give me nothin' to eat all day long."

Straight Arrow started toward the front door of the jail house, but Captain LeFlores reached out his hand to stop him.

"Uh-uh, Straight Arrow, you won't be goin' in there," he said.

"What do you mean?"

"Boyette, take him over to the courtyard and put him in the holding cell," Captain LeFores said.

"The holding cell? What do you mean the holding cell?" Straight Arrow asked, in dread. "Don't I get a trial? You can't hang me without a trial."

"You've already had your trial," Captain LeFlores said. "You were tried, convicted, and sentenced to be hanged, before you escaped. There's no need to try you all over again."

CHAPTER EIGHT

The town of Emporia, Kansas, which lay in the forks of the Cottonwood and Neosho rivers was almost blanketed in the swirling dust kicked up by the heavy traffic of countless riders and wagons. The hitching rails all along the main street were full, and the livery stables and horse lots were jammed with saddled horses. Wagons and buckboards and carts were parked everywhere there was space, and cowhands and frontiersmen mingled with the townspeople and the handful of soldiers from Fort Riley.

Judge Levi Parsons was there meeting with Robert Stevens, John Scullin, and Otis Gunn. Parsons was president of the newly constituted KATY Railroad Line. Stevens was his general manager, Scullin his superintendent of track, and Gunn his construction manager. There were others there as well, men Parsons had invited who might be potential investors.

Stevens gave the first report.

"Since I have taken over as general manager, good progress has been made. The month before I assumed the position, only five miles of track were laid. Now, we have regularly scheduled freight and passenger service running from Emporia to Junction City."

"Thank you, Bob, you've done a very good job," Parsons said. "But as you, Mr. Scullin, and Mr. Gunn already know, this is only the start."

Parsons addressed the investors he had invited.

"Gentlemen, after much negotiation, the Cherokee have granted permission for a railroad to be built through their land. I propose to push the KATY down through Indian Territory and all the way through Texas to the Mexican border. This will open Kansas City, St. Louis, and Chicago to the lucrative cattle shipping market."

"Judge Parsons, I have been told that only one railroad can proceed through The Nations," one of the prospective investors said.

"That is true," Parson replied. "And I intend for the KATY to be that railroad."

"But what about the Border Tier Line? Isn't it also building south, to the Kansas border?"

"It is."

"Then how is it to be resolved as to which railroad will have the right to go through Indian Territory?"

"The right of passage through Indian Territory, gentlemen, will be awarded to the railroad which first reaches the border between Kansas and the Indian Territory."

"Then what you are saying is, we are in a race."

"That is exactly what I'm saying," Judge Parsons replied. "And I'll say it again: it is a race that I intend for the KATY to win."

Within a matter of days of the KATY Railroad meeting in Emporia, James Joy was having a meeting of the Border Tier Line in Kansas City. James Joy owned several railroads, including the Border Tier Railroad, the line that he was pushing from Kansas City down to the Kansas and Indian Territory border.

"There is no way I intend to let that upstart KATY Line beat us. Parsons has grandiose schemes of eventually connecting to the transcontinental railroad to give him connections to the west coast.

"We are already to the West Coast.

"Parsons wants to build through to Chicago. We are already there, and with our railroad that goes through Chicago, we have connections to New York and Philadelphia as well.

"By opening our railroad through Indian Territory, and through Texas to Mexico, we will control the most important railroads in the world! And when that time comes, using only the Joy Lines, one will be able to traverse this nation from the Atlantic to the Pacific, and from Canada to Mexico. And much of that travel will be on one of my railroads.

"And here is the thing, gentlemen. By necessity, Judge Parsons will be working on a shoestring. I, on the other hand, intend to put as much money as is necessary to make certain that our railroad is the first one to the Indian Territory border."

"Mr. Joy, why don't you just buy the KATY out? That way, there will be no need for a race to the border. You will have the only railroad," one of the men asked.

"Why should I waste the money to buy him out?" Joy asked. "All we have to do is beat him to the border, and his railroad will be worthless. If I really wanted it then, I could pick it up for pennies on the dollar. No, sir, gentlemen, as I said, I intend to beat him to the border."

"Here, here!" one of the others in the

room shouted, and the others applauded.

Joy reached for his glass and held it up. "Gentlemen, I give you the Joy Lines, from coast to coast, and from Canada to New Mexico!"

The others, enthusiastically, joined the toast.

Two hundred miles south of Emporia, in the Indian Territory town of Sequoyah, the Two Hills Mercantile store was not yet open for business, but Mary Two Hills was folding blankets and putting them on the table. Colorful blankets were always a good product in Sequoyah, for the Indians and for the whites. Mary, and her husband, Harold, owned the Two Hills Mercantile, which was the biggest, and most successful store in town.

Harold was posting bills on the bulletin board, not only advertising his own goods and wares, but, because everyone came into the mercantile, others advertised with him.

FOR SALE
Fine Pony
For riding or for pulling a cart
See Mr. Crabtree

Miss Imogene Parks
Announces she will give
Piano Lessons
To qualified students

WANTED
For <u>Robbery</u> and <u>Murder</u>
1000 Dollars
For
Abe and Darrell Karnes

"Do you know what we should get, Harold?" Mary asked.

Harold was just posting a flyer advertising a new supply of wallpaper.

"What should we get?"

"I think we should get in a supply of fine lace."

"Lace? Why such foolishness? Lace, indeed."

"I've had two or three ladies enquire. I think it would be a good —" Mary halted in mid-sentence when she looked up and saw two men coming in.

"The store isn't open yet," Mary said.

"You don't say," one of the men replied.

"Here," Harold said. "How did you get in here? I thought I had the front door locked."

"Show him, Darrell," one of the men said. The other man held up a little piece of metal and smiled at him.

"Darrell picked the lock. He's just real good at that. Ain't that right, Darrell?"

"That's right, Abe."

Harold gasped. He had just posted their flyer on his bulletin board. "Darrell and Abe? You are the Karnes brothers!"

"That we are. And now that you know who we are, well, I reckon we won't be havin' any trouble with you, when we tell you to empty your cash box."

"You've got no right to come in here like this!" Harold said.

"Oh, yeah, this gives us the right," Abe said, holding up his pistol. "Now empty out that cash box."

"I'll do no such thing."

"You want to see your woman killed?" Abe pointed his pistol at Mary.

"No, no, don't hurt her. I'll give you the money," Harold said. He pulled a box from under the counter and opened it, then handed the money over.

"What is this?" Abe said. "There's not even fifty dollars here. Are you telling me this is all the money you have? A big store like this?"

"I make a bank deposit every night," Harold said. "This is just the money we'll need for making change today."

"You son of a bitch! You are holding out on me!" Abe shouted. "I told you what would happen!"

Abe shot Mary, and she went down without a sound.

"Mary!" Harold cried. With a loud shout of anger, Harold grabbed an axe handle and started toward Abe. He raised the handle, but that was as far as he got before Darrell shot him.

"That son of a bitch was comin' after me with an axe handle!" Abe said.

"Come on, Abe, let's get out of here while we can."

"He was lying. I know there is more money here," Abe said. "Let's look around."

"No, we don't have time! Come on, let's go! Someone for sure has heard the shooting."

Abe saw a jar filled with horehound candy, and he picked it up.

"You can't ride with that jar. Just grab a handful and stick 'em in your pocket," Darrell said.

Abe grabbed several hands full and stuffed the candy down into both his pockets, then, with a laugh, he threw the jar down so that it broke, causing shards of glass and pieces of candy to spread all over the floor. Then, putting a piece of candy in his mouth, he followed his brother out the front door.

After the two men left, Harold managed to get to his feet for just a moment. Reaching toward the bulletin board he tore off the wanted flyer for the Karnes brothers, then he fell back. He was able to pull himself across the floor until he could just reach out and touch Mary. He grabbed her hand.

"Mary," he gasped.

"This is just how we found them, John Henry," Lee Carson said. "They was layin' together like this, Harold holdin' on to Mary's hand. They must'a died that way."

"And Harold was holding on to this piece of paper," Eddie Webb said. He showed the paper to John Henry. "I figure he must've been just about to put it up when whoever done this came in."

John Henry looked at the piece of paper and saw that the corners were torn off. Looking at the bulletin board he saw a small, triangular piece of paper with an irregular tear. Removing the triangle, he held it up to the torn corner of the wanted flyer.

"No," John Henry said. "He wasn't about to put it up, it was already up. He tore it off to tell us who the murderers were."

"You think it was the Karnes brothers?" Lee Carson asked.

"I would bet my life on it."

"They are white," Eddie Webb said. "That means we are going to have to go over to Tahlequah to get the U.S. Marshal."

"You do that," John Henry said. "In the meantime, I'm going after them."

"You can't do that, John Henry. You are the chief sheriff of the Cherokee Nation. You can only deal with Indians."

"I'm going after them," John Henry said again.

When John Henry stepped back outside the store, he saw something on the ground right in front of the step.

"Well, you didn't just break the jar, did you?" John Henry asked under his breath. "You took some with you."

John Henry walked slowly up and down the road as the other citizens of the town, now aware of the double homicide, were going toward the Two Hill Mercantile store to satisfy their morbid curiosity.

John Henry was at the north end of the town when he saw what he was looking for. There, lying in the dirt, was a piece of horehound candy. He hurried back to his horse, then rode north, out of town.

Ten minutes later John Henry found another piece of candy about a mile from the town. Finding this piece was very significant because this far out of town there were now only two sets of hoofprints to follow, and the little piece of candy connected them to the shooting in town.

John dismounted and studied the hoofprints. There was a nick in the shoe of the right foreleg of one of the two animals, and that nick left a small "V" shape in the side of the shoe. Now he would be able to follow them with, or without, finding any more pieces of the candy. But the candy had done its job.

"I don't know which one of you boys has a sweet tooth," he said. "But I'm glad you do."

CHAPTER NINE

Darrell Karnes lay on top of a flat rock looking back in the direction from which they
had just come. He saw the rider doggedly
following the trail.

"Is he still there?" Abe asked.

"Yeah," Darrell growled. He climbed back
down from the rock and ran his hand across
the stubble on his unshaven cheek. "He's
still there."

"Who is that fella that's trailin' us?" Darrell asked.

"I don't have any idea. But he's trackin'
us like a damn Injun. Maybe he's an Injun
policeman."

"What the hell is he chasin' us for? The
Injun police don't have any authority over a
white man."

"You want to tell him that?" Abe asked.

"No, I reckon not."

"Yeah, well, I don't plan to say nothin' to
him about it neither," Abe said. He pointed

back down the trail. "But I'll say this. He is one trackin' son of a bitch. We've done tried ever' trick there is, from followin' the crick beds, to doublin' back on him, and there ain't none of it worked. He's still back there, trailin' us as easy as if there was road signs put out tellin' him which way we was a'goin'."

"What can he do to us when he gets here? Like I said, he ain't got no authority over us."

"Whether he's got 'ny authority over us or not, it don't matter," Abe said. "He's been stickin' to us like a tick on a dog's ass, and I'm gettin' tired of it."

"So, what are we goin' to do about the son of a bitch? He's already showed us that we sure as hell can't shake him off," Darrell growled.

Abe looked back toward the rider. "This trail takes a pass through Coody's Bluff just up ahead. S'pose we ride through it, then double back, and one of us will get on either side of the pass. Then, when he starts through, we'll have him in a cross fire."

"Yeah," Darrell said. "Yeah, that's a good idea."

"We better get a move on," Abe said. "We need enough time to ride through it, then come back and set up the ambush."

"All right, let's do it," Darrell said.

John Henry knew every inch of this land. He knew that the pass through Coody Bluff was deep and narrow, and that once a person committed himself to it, there would be little to no opportunity to maneuver, in case someone started shooting at him. He could see the tracks of the men he had been trailing though, and he knew they had gone right through here.

Why would they do that? Why would they put themselves in such a confined area?

One reason, he knew, was that this pass was the shortest way out of Indian Territory through to Coffeeville, Kansas. John Henry stopped at the mouth of the path and took a drink from his canteen while he studied it. He had tracked them all the way from Sequoyah, and there had been no deviation in their trail. He was sure they were going into Kansas. But, was that the only reason they had come through this pass? Or did they figure to draw him in, then set up an ambush for him?

John Henry pulled his long gun out of the saddle holster. Then, leading his horse, he started climbing the pass. The floor of the pass was covered with wash gravel, and the horse's hooves fell sharply on the stones, making enough noise to let anyone know he was here, and that he was coming through.

The pass made a forty-five degree turn to the left just in front of him, so he stopped. Right before he got to the turn, he slapped his horse on the rump and sent it on through.

There was a sudden explosion of gunfire as the Karnes brothers opened up on what they thought would be their pursuer. Instead, their bullets whizzed harmlessly over the empty saddle of the riderless horse.

From his position just around the corner from the turn, John Henry located both of his ambushers. There was one on each side atop of the walls that flanked the pass.

The firing stopped and, after a few seconds of dying echoes, it grew silent.

"What the hell?" one of them shouted across the draw to the other. "Where did he go, Darrell? Did we shoot him off his horse?"

Grabbing onto roots to help himself, John Henry, concealed from view by the turn in the gully, climbed up to the top. As soon as he reached the top, he looked north, toward the direction from which the shooting had come. He saw a man on one knee, leaning out over the edge of the bluff, looking down into the pass.

"Do you see him, Abe?" Darrell called.

"I don't see hide nor hair of him," Abe answered.

"Where the hell is he?"

"I'm right here," John Henry said calmly, now no more than sixty feet from his would-be ambushers.

"What the hell? How did you get here?"

"I walked," John Henry said. "Drop your gun and put up your hands."

"Darrell, drop to the ground, I've got a shot!" Abe shouted from the other side, and looking across the gully, John Henry saw someone drawing a bead on him with a rifle.

John Henry dropped to one knee as Abe fired, and the bullet cracked through the air as it passed just over his head. John Henry fired back and Abe grabbed his chest, then pitched forward, falling over the edge and down into the pass about sixty feet below.

"You son of a bitch! You killed my brother!" Darrell shouted, scrambling to recover his gun.

"Don't do it!" John Henry called out to him, but Darrell didn't listen. Instead, he raised his rifle to his shoulder, and John Henry had no choice but to fire.

Darrell Karnes fell on his back, his arms thrown to either side of him. John Henry approached, then looked down at him. He could tell by the opaque look in the eyes that the man was dead. Nevertheless, he kicked him once, just to make sure.

Although white settlers were not allowed in Indian Territory, they could be there under the classification of "traders." And the term, traders, covered a broad spectrum, including hotel keepers, livery stable operators, barbers, draymen, grocers, and suppliers of saddles, carbines, ammunition, wagon tongues, kitchen knives, sunbonnets, calico dresses, tobacco, and snuff.

Whites could not own land, but they could lease land from the Indians on a year-by-year basis, so that, in essence, they did own it. Also, many whites married Indians, thus becoming members of the tribes and granted full rights of citizenship within the Indian Territory.

Indians and whites alike turned out when John Henry came riding into Tahlequah with the two bodies thrown belly down over their saddles. Technically, the Indian police had no jurisdiction over the whites who lived with them so there were, in addition to the Indian police, white lawmen, Deputy U.S. Marshals, who handled crimes involving whites. Because the Karnes brothers were white, John Henry took them to

110

the office of the white Deputy U.S. Marshal who, already alerted, was standing out in front of his office.

"What do we have here, Sixkiller?" Deputy U.S. Marshal Dennis asked.

"These are the men who murdered Harold and Mary Two Hills," John Henry said. He swung down from his saddle and stood there, holding the reins to his horse, Iron Heart.

"Well now, we aren't going to ever know that, are we?" Dennis replied. "They didn't get their time in court."

"That was their decision, Marshal. I attempted to bring them in, but they wouldn't have it that way. They shot at me, so I shot back."

"Are they white, or Indian? You brought them here, so I'm assuming they are white."

"Yes, they're white."

"Then what were you doing trying to bring them in in the first place? They are white men. You are an Indian policeman; you have no authority over them."

"The Indian half of me tracked them, Marshal. But it is the white half of me that brought them in. You might say that I was making a citizen's arrest."

"Who are they?" Dennis asked, stepping down from the porch to examine them.

111

"You'll recognize them."

Dennis grabbed one of the bodies by the hair, then lifted the head.

"Son of a bitch," he said. "It's Darrell Karnes." He stepped over to the other horse and examined that body as well. "And his brother Abe."

"I believe they are wanted men," John Henry said.

"You're damn right, they are wanted. Not only here in The Nations, but in about half the states in the West. And you say they murdered Harold Two Hills and his wife?"

"Yes. I tracked them from the Two Hills Mercantile to Coody's Bluff."

"That was quite a job of tracking. Probably headed for Kansas, I would say," Dennis said.

"That's what I figured."

"Well, I can't say I'm sorry to see 'em brought in, belly down like this. But there's goin' to have to be a hearing as to whether or not your killin' 'em was justified."

"In whose court? Indian court, or white man's court?"

"White man's court in Fort Smith," Dennis said.

"When is the hearing?"

"More'n likely within the next two weeks. I'm not going to have to come get you, am

I, Sixkiller? You'll show up?"

"I'll be there," John Henry promised.

Leaving the sheriff's office, John Henry went to the trading post and bought bacon, beans, coffee, corn meal, and flour. Then he took his purchases to his mother's house.

"John Henry!" his mother said, greeting him warmly when he came into the house. She saw the packages he was carrying. "John Henry, you don't have to bring me gifts when you come. Just having you here is gift enough."

"That's not it," John Henry said. "I thought maybe you would make some beans and corn bread for me."

John Henry's mother laughed. "Of course, I will. But I'll have to put them on to soak. It'll be tomorrow before I can fix them."

"That's fine, *Etsi,* I can wait." *Etsi* was Cherokee for mother.

"John Henry, Sasha has been over to see me several times," Elizabeth said.

"Has she?"

"She is such a sweet girl. She has been a big help to me."

"I'm glad."

"She thinks a lot of you," Elizabeth said, smiling at her son.

"I think a lot of her as well."

"So?" Elizabeth pressed.

"What do you mean, so?"

"John Henry, you know what I mean. You aren't getting any younger, you know. Most men your age, and many who are younger, are married. Don't you think that is something you should consider?"

"It wouldn't be fair to Sasha for me to take her as a wife."

"Why would you say such a thing? What isn't fair to the poor girl is to keep her dangling like this."

"I'm not keeping her dangling. I've told her that my job will keep me away a lot of the time."

"Do you think she wouldn't understand that?"

"And, there is always the chance that . . ."

"That what? That you could be killed?"

"Yes."

"John Henry, do you think I didn't worry about your father, and you, when you went away to war?"

"I'm sure you did, but . . ."

"But nothing. You are not giving Sasha credit for being the strong woman she is. If a wife can handle her husband going to war, then a wife can certainly handle her husband being a policeman. Besides, if something like that is going to happen, it's going to happen. Who would ever have thought

114

that James would be killed as he was? James wasn't a policeman, he was a rancher and businessman."

"Etsi . . . Mom . . . I know that you want only what is best for me, and I know that you think Sasha would make a good wife. I think she would, too. I'm just not ready to make that move, yet."

"Let me ask you this, John Henry. Suppose Sasha married another man? It could happen, you know. She is a beautiful and intelligent young woman with much to offer any man who might want to take her as his wife. Suppose that happened. How would you feel?"

John Henry was quiet for a long moment.

"I . . . I would hope that it would be a happy marriage for her."

Elizabeth smiled. "But you wouldn't be all that happy about it, would you?"

John Henry didn't answer.

"You can't keep her dangling forever," Elizabeth said. "I will invite her over for beans and corn bread tomorrow."

"Mom, I'd rather you not do that."

"I'm not inviting her for you, John Henry. She is my friend, I am inviting her for myself."

CHAPTER TEN

Even though John Henry thought he would be uncomfortable with Sasha as a dinner guest, he actually found that he enjoyed her company. Sasha was all smiles as she shared some good news with Elizabeth and John Henry.

"I have been hired as a schoolteacher," she said.

"Oh, Sasha, that is wonderful," Elizabeth said. "But, does that mean you will be leaving Sequoyah?"

"No, that is the best part. I'll be staying right here."

Elizabeth glanced over at John Henry and thought she saw relief on his face that Sasha would not be leaving.

"You make the best beans, Elizabeth," Sasha said. "You will have to teach me how to make them."

"There's nothing to it — you just soak them overnight, then cook them about five hours with a big piece of fat pork, some onions, and a few cut-up potatoes. They are John Henry's favorite, you know."

Sasha looked over toward John Henry and was surprised to see him crumbling some corn bread into a glass of milk.

"What are you doing?" Sasha asked.

"I like corn bread in milk," John said unabashedly.

"I've never heard of such a thing. I must try that," Sasha said.

Elizabeth laughed. "Believe me, dear, all you will be doing is wasting corn bread. You won't like it. Honestly, I don't know how John Henry can eat it that way."

Sasha broke up a piece of corn bread into her milk, then spooned some of it into her mouth.

"Oh!" she said. "Oh, this is delicious! I don't know why I've never heard of this before."

John Henry looked at her in surprise. "Wait a minute, you mean you actually like it? You aren't saying that just to be nice to me?"

"No, I really like it," Sasha said.

Elizabeth started to clear away the dishes from the table, and Sasha stood quickly.

"Let me help," Sasha said.

"Oh, there's no need for you to help,"

Elizabeth said. "Why don't you two young people go into the living room where you can visit? I'll take care of this."

"My mother is about as subtle as a sledge-hammer," John Henry said.

"She means well," Sasha replied with a smile.

John Henry and Sasha went into the living room. John Henry sat in a chair rather than on the sofa. Though Sasha said nothing, John Henry could tell by the expression on her face that she would have preferred he sit on the sofa so she could join him.

"My mother is trying to —"

"I know what she is trying to do," Sasha replied. "She has mentioned it to me several times."

"How do you feel about that?"

"I feel that you are the one who has to make a decision, not your mother."

"Sasha, please don't think that I am averse to the idea of marriage. I'm like everyone else, I want to find a good wife, and have a family. And of all the people I know, I've never met a woman who I think would make a better wife than you. It's just that, well for a while anyway . . ."

"You want to continue being a hero," Sasha said. The words were neither sarcastic nor challenging.

"Well, I wouldn't say that."

"Why not? You are a hero, John Henry. Don't you know that every young boy in the Territory looks up to you, and considers you a hero. But I'm not surprised. You have always been my hero, ever since the day you rescued me from Willie Buck."

John Henry chuckled. "Anyone who might have come along that day would have done the same thing. I just happened to be in the right place at the right time."

Like Willie Buck, Hector Crow Dog, returned from the war unable, or unwilling, to become a law-abiding citizen. While riding with Quantrill's Raiders, Crow Dog had developed a taste for murder and robbery, and it was a taste he continued to satisfy when the war was over. John Henry had not seen Crow Dog since the war, because Crow Dog had not returned to Indian Territory. He carried on most of his nefarious activity in Kansas. That activity soon made him one of the most wanted outlaws in all of Kansas.

He was waiting at a bridge outside Coffeeville for the night stagecoach to Sedan. The coach had running lamps with mirror reflectors that cast twin light beams forward. The lamps helped Crow Dog track the coach as it was approaching, but he knew they would not be putting out enough light to see him, unless he was standing in the road, right in front of them.

Crow Dog could hear the driver whistling and calling to his team as the coach got closer. Then, just as it slowed to pull up onto the bridge, Crow Dog jumped up from the side of the road.

"Hold it right there!" he shouted. "Throw down the mail pouch!"

The driver stopped, but the guard jumped up and pointed his shotgun at Crow Dog. He pulled the trigger, but the shotgun misfired.

"Ha!" Crow Dog shouted. He fired twice, the flame pattern of the two shots painting the side of the coach like two flashes of lightning.

Moses Garret was one of the passengers inside the coach. Garret was a Deputy U.S. Marshal, but tonight he was riding as a passenger on the way back to Sedan. As soon as he heard the demand to stop, he knew immediately what was going on, and putting his finger across his lips to caution the others to be quiet, he slipped out of the door on the opposite side of the coach from the robber. With his pistol in hand he came around the back of the coach just as Hector

Crow Dog was climbing up to retrieve the mail pouch.

Crow Dog had put his pistol back in the holster and, so intent was he on the task of getting the mail pouch, he didn't see Garret come up behind him. His first indication that Garret was there, was when Garret spoke to him.

"Come back down here," Garret said.

Crow Dog started to move his hand toward his pistol, but stopped when he heard Garret cocking his own pistol.

"Oh, yeah," Garret said easily. "Go for your gun. It'll be a lot easier taking you back dead than it will alive."

When Crow Dog reached the ground, even before he turned around, Garret brought his pistol down hard on Crow Dog's head, knocking him out.

"Mr. Parkinson?" Garret called to the other male passenger in the coach. "Help me load him into the luggage boot. I'll handcuff him in there."

Hector Crow Dog's crime spree had come to an end, and because he had stolen U.S. Mail, it became a federal crime. Crow Dog was tried in Judge Isaac Parker's court, and despite the long-ago promise of the medicine man that he would never be hanged, he was found guilty and sentenced to be hanged.

Thus it was that when John Henry arrived at Fort Smith for his hearing, he got there just in time to see Crow Dog about to be hanged. Crow Dog was standing on the gallows, his legs tied together, and his arms lashed to his side.

U.S. Marshal John Sarber was standing beside the prisoner, sweating under the hot sun. There were several hundred spectators, standing in the same sun looking up at the gallows. There was one black cloud in the sky, but it wasn't large enough to provide any relief from the sun. Outside the walls of the fort, over a hundred buckboards, spring wagons, and saddle horses bore witness to the distance so many had traveled to watch this hanging. Several had come the day before and spent the night on the ground so they would be here to see the hanging of Crow Dog, the man who had become infamous for murdering and plundering in Kansas, Arkansas, Colorado, and the Indian Territory.

"Look at those dumb people standin' there in the hot sun, sweatin' like a run-out horse," Crow Dog said.

"You're standin' in the same sun," Marshal Sarber said.

"Yeah, but you forget, I ain't goin' to be here much longer," Crow Dog replied with a loud, raucous laugh.

Crow Dog was of muscular build, though he was quite short, standing only about five feet, four inches tall. As he looked out over the crowd he was surprised to see John Henry.

"Well, look here. If it's not my old friend John Henry Sixkiller," he called down from the gallows. "Come to watch your old friend die, did you, John Henry?"

"Looks like I got here just in time, Hector," John Henry said.

"Hey, John Henry, do you remember I told you once I wasn't never goin' to hang?" Crow Dog said.

"I remember."

"That's because Sam Blackhorse told me I wasn't never goin' to hang. You remember him, don't you? The old medicine man?"

"I remember him," John Henry replied.

"Yes, well I wish I could see the old son of a bitch now. I paid him a dollar to tell me I wasn't goin' to hang, and here I am, about to. I'd get my money back, that's what I'd do," Crow Dog said, then he laughed again. "Of course, that dollar wouldn't do me much good now, would it? Still, I'd like to have it in my pocket when I swing.

Maybe when I get to hell, I could buy myself a nice cold beer."

"You got any last words, Crow Dog?" Marshal Sarber asked.

"I come here to die. I didn't come here to make a speech."

Crow Dog looked at Sarber, then out at the crowd, which consisted of men, women, and children, white, black, and Indian. He looked at John Henry again, then smiled.

"I'll just bet you wish you was standin' up here so's you could pull the lever, don't you, John Henry?"

"You put yourself there, Hector, when you killed that driver and his shotgun guard."

"I suppose I did, but it seemed the thing to do at the time. *Da gi yo `we ga. Ko `hi i ga-ge `ga,*" Crow Dog said. "I am tired. Today I am going home."

"*Donada `govi* — good-bye," John Henry replied.

"Say, didn't you say you was going to hang me?" Crow Dog asked Sarber.

"That's what I intend to do," Marshal Sarber replied.

"Then what the hell are you waiting around for? You don't want to disappoint all these people now, do you? They came to see a good show, and I'm the star. So let's quit all this foolin' around and get it done."

Sarber looked over at the hangman and nodded. The hangman pulled the lever and Crow Dog's neck jerked to one side as he fell down to the end of the rope.

Then, by an eerie coincidence, just as the trapdoor opened under Crow Dog's feet, a tremendous clap of thunder shook the earth, completely drowning out the thudding sound of the opening trap. The black cloud that had been hanging above the fort, not large enough to blot out the sun, had managed to shoot down a bolt of lightning. The lightning struck Crow Dog as he fell, causing sparks to fly from his body.

Many among those who had gathered to watch the hanging now called out in shock and fear, the children cried, and some of the women swooned.

Hector Crow Dog's body hung at the end of the rope, still smoking from the lightning bolt.

"I'll be damned," John Henry said. "The old medicine man was right after all. Hector Crow Dog was killed by the lightning bolt before he reached the end of the drop."

CHAPTER ELEVEN

Judge Isaac Charles Parker was thirty-five-years old when he took the bench in the federal court in Fort Smith, making him the youngest federal judge in America. Despite the heat of the day, he was wearing a suit, vest, and tie. Dark-haired, and with a dark and well-trimmed Vandyke beard, he sat behind the bench without robes because this was a hearing, and not a trial. There was no jury present.

"Your Honor," Howard Gibson said as he addressed the court. Gibson was the federal prosecutor in the United States Court for the Western District of Arkansas. "The United States Government, by these presents, makes the case that John Henry Sixkiller has exceeded his authority in apprehending two white men, Darrell and Abraham Karnes. That is a felony violation, and, in the course of this felony violation, John Henry Sixkiller did shoot, and kill, both men. In that they were killed during the commission of a felony, a case could also be made for first-degree murder."

"Are you asking that Mr. Sixkiller be tried for first-degree murder?" Judge Parker asked.

"No, Your Honor," Gibson replied. "At the most, I would ask for unlawful manslaughter. However, I am willing to withhold even that charge if the defendant would agree to plea to the unlawful exceeding of his authority."

"Are you willing to make that plea, Mr. Sixkiller?" Judge Parker asked.

"I am not, Your Honor, for such a plea would necessitate my removal as a policeman in the Cherokee Nation," John Henry replied.

"Very well, Mr. Gibson, you may make your case."

"Your Honor, if I may?" Marshal Dennis said, interrupting the hearing.

"Yes, Sheriff, what is it?"

"I have spoken with Marshal Sarber. I made a proposal to him that he agrees with. And with your cooperation, it could take care of the situation that we dealing with now."

"And what is that proposal?"

"I propose, Your Honor, that you swear in

John Henry Sixkiller as a U.S. Marshal. That way he will be able to deal with criminals, whether they be Indian or white."

"Would you be willing to serve as a U.S. Marshal in my court?" Judge Parker asked John Henry.

"Yes, Your Honor, I would consider it a great honor to serve as a U.S. Marshal in your court," John Henry replied.

"That won't do any good, Your Honor," Gibson interrupted. "We are dealing with a case that happened two weeks ago."

"Suppose we make Mr. Sixkiller's appointment retroactive?" Judge Parker suggested.

"Retroactive?"

"Yes. We could appoint him as a U.S. Marshal effective one month ago. That way, his tracking, apprehending, and shooting in the act of apprehending, would no longer be an issue."

Gibson nodded, then smiled. "Your Honor, in that case, the prosecution will drop all charges."

"John Henry Sixkiller, raise your right hand, please."

John Henry did as requested.

"Repeat after me: I do solemnly swear that I will faithfully execute the Office of United States Marshal, and will to the best of my ability, preserve, protect, and defend the Constitution of the United States, so help me God."

John Henry repeated the oath.

"Marshal Sarber, do you have a badge for our newest marshal?"

"I do, Your Honor."

"Pin it on him. Marshal Sixkiller, you are now an officer of the United States Court for the Western District of Arkansas. Don't do anything to embarrass us."

"Thank you, Your Honor, Marshal Dennis, and Marshal Sarber. I will do all I can to see that none of you regret this appointment," John Henry said.

Later that day, Marshal Sarber and all the deputy marshals celebrated John Henry's appointment.

"You are one of us now," Sarber said. "You have a federal commission, which means you aren't limited to the Indian Territory. You can go anywhere in the country and make arrests."

"That's good to know," John Henry said.

"But because you are appointed by the U.S. Court for the Western District of Arkansas, you will bring your prisoners to Fort Smith," Sarber added.

"I understand."

"By the way, you do know what they say about Fort Smith, don't you?" Jim Messler, one of the deputy marshals, asked.

"No, what do they say?"

"There is no Sunday west of St. Louis, and no God west of Fort Smith."

Coffeeville, Kansas

When Vernon Simmons, Pete Fuller, Kit Darrow, and Injun Joe Pipestem rode into town, few of the townspeople paid any attention to them. They rode right down through the middle of the street, a habit that was developed over the years they had spent on the outlaw trail. By keeping to the middle of the street, it lessened the chances of someone suddenly appearing from behind a building to ambush them. All four men were wanted, not only in Kansas, but in Missouri and Arkansas as well.

They rode in between the First National Bank and Derris Drugstore to reach the alley behind the bank. There, they tied their horses to a fence that bordered the backyard of Ely Bowman's house.

Vernon Simmons, who was at one time a deputy sheriff in Coffeeville, and the acknowledged leader of the outfit, disguised himself with a false mustache and goatee. Accompanied by Fuller, Darrow, and Pipestem, he entered the First National Bank.

The bank teller looked up from behind his cage as they came in and, recognizing them, knew at once that this was trouble. He tried to cover it with a nonchalant attitude.

"Hello, Vernon. What can I do for you?"

Fuller laughed. "I told you that disguise wouldn't do you no good," he said.

Simmons pulled the mustache and goatee beard off, then dropped them into a wastebasket.

"I reckon you know what you can do for us, Harrigan," Simmons said. Simmons and the others pulled their pistols from their holsters and pointed them toward the teller and the cashier.

"Is this a robbery?" Harrigan asked.

Simmons smiled. "Well, now, you got that right the first time. Yeah, this is a robbery. Empty those bank drawers and put the money in this bag."

Harrigan began very deliberately taking the money out of the drawer and putting it in separate stacks on the counter in front of him.

"Hurry it up," Simmons ordered.

"I can't be too fast. I have to count it."

"Count it? What the hell do you have to

131

count it for?" an exasperated Simmons asked.

"Don't you want to know how much you are getting?"

"I'll count it later. Just drop the money down in the sack like I told you."

"Simmons, someone is coming," Darrow said.

"Who?"

"Looks like it might be Deputy Kelly."

"That's the son of a bitch that took my place. Step out front there and throw a shot at 'im."

Darrow stepped out front and shot at Deputy Kelly. Kelly went down.

"I got 'im!" Darrow said.

"Let's get out of here!" Simmons shouted, tossing the bag of money to Darrow as the four men dashed out the back door of the bank. As they were untying their horses, two men appeared, having come from the space between the bank and the drugstore.

Simmons and the other three bank robbers turned their guns on the two men and shot them down.

"What the hell? Neither of them was armed," Darrow said.

"Then it was their dumb mistake for running back here," Simmons said.

At that moment, Luke Baldwin came out

132

of the back door of Isham's Hardware Store. Injun Joe shot him, and he fell dying in the alley. Mounting, the four men rode at a gallop down the alley where they killed two more of Coffeeville's citizens. Leaving the alley they came out into the middle of the street, where Charles Brown fell.

By now the shooting had alerted everyone in town, and at least a dozen men were on the street firing at the bank robbers. Darrow was hit and he fell from his horse, still clutching the bag of money.

"Our money!" Simmons said. He started to dismount to recover it, but the shooting grew even more intense.

"Vernon! Leave it! We got to get out of here!" Fuller shouted.

Simmons hesitated only a moment, then he remounted and the three men galloped out of town. Behind them they left seven dead, and the sack of money they had taken from the bank. That very day word was sent, by telegram, to Judge Parker in Fort Smith, Arkansas, advising him of what the newspapers would call: CARNAGE IN COFFEE-VILLE.

It didn't take John Henry long to get his first assignment. On the very day he was sworn in as a U.S. Marshal, he was sent out to bring in . . . dead or alive . . . Vernon Simmons, Pete Fuller, and Injun Joe Pipestem.

"Yeah, I know exactly where they are," Sheriff Miller said when John Henry went to Coffeeville to start his hunt for them. "They hang out around Bird Creek down in The Nations. They know as long as they stay down there, that there ain't nothin' I can do about 'em, 'cause they are out of my jurisdiction. You bein' a U.S. Marshal though, means you can go down there. Do you know the Bird Creek area?"

"Yes," John Henry replied. He knew Bird Creek like he knew the back of his hand. He had fished and hunted there from the time he was a boy.

In Bird Creek, John Henry went to speak to Red Moon, who was mayor of the town. "The two men with Pipestem are white men. You have no authority over them," Red Moon said, when he learned that John Henry was looking for the people who had murdered Harold and Mary Two Hills.

"I have this authority," John Henry said, showing Red Moon the badge he had recently acquired.

"You are a U.S. Marshal?"

"Yes."

"Yes, I see that you are given much power with that badge. I will make no trouble for you as you look for them. It is my wish that you can find these men, for they are evil, and have killed Indians as well as whites."

"You can help me," John Henry said.

"What can I do?"

"Let it be known that I am looking for them. Let it be said that when I find them, I will take them back so that Judge Parker can hang them. If enough people know this, soon the men I am looking for will know it as well, and I will not have to find them, because they will come looking for me."

"Yes," Red Moon said. "That is a good plan."

By John Henry's second night out, he knew that his plan had worked because there were three men trailing him. He knew, also, that they would not confront him directly, but would make their move tonight when he camped out.

That night, he drank his coffee and ate a piece of jerky. Then he laid out his bedroll. He put the piece of canvas down, then the blanket, then the saddle, trailing the stirrups down along the blanket. Finally, he covered the saddle with another blanket and put his hat at the head.

When John Henry was through, he moved about twenty yards away, slipped down into a little depression, and looked back upon his handiwork. The fire was burning low, the area smelled of coffee, and his horse stood quietly in the dark. His hat on the bedroll covered what appeared to be the head, while the saddle gave the blanket the dimensions of a sleeping man. Satisfied with the illusion he had created, John Henry settled back to wait.

CHAPTER TWELVE

"You know the son of a bitch is goin' to have to bed down somewhere, and when he does, we've got him," Simmons said. "All we have to do is locate his camp, sneak up on him in the night, and shoot the son of a bitch while he's sleepin'."

"Yeah," Fuller agreed. "Let's do it and be done with it."

It was Injun Joe who discovered the campfire first. He found it, not by sight, but by smell. "I smell smoke," he said, pointing. "There's a campfire on the other side of the water."

The three men crossed the creek, moving as slowly and as quietly as they could. Then Fuller stopped. "Would you look at that? Why the hell would he build a fire like that? It's almost like he is wanting us to find him."

"No, it's 'cause he's lookin' for us, and didn't figure on us lookin' for him," Simmons replied, laughing out loud. "We done it, boys! We've got 'im!"

"He's a cocky son of a bitch, ain't he?" Fuller said. "I mean, buildin' a fire like he don't have no fear of nothin' in the world."

"Yeah, well, why don't we just see how cocky the son of a bitch can be with a couple of bullets in his gut?" Simmons suggested.

The three men dismounted and tied off their horses, then they crossed the creek on foot.

"You two stay back here," Fuller whispered.

"Why?"

"He belongs to me."

"Be careful," Pipestem said. "That is John Henry Sixkiller."

"What is that supposed to mean?"

"I know John Henry Sixkiller. He will be a hard man to kill."

"How hard can it be? He's asleep now."

"It is said that when he sleeps, he can still see," Injun Joe said. "Many have tried to kill him, but all have failed."

"No offense, Injun Joe, but you're talkin' about Injuns that have tried to kill him, and Injuns like to do things that's honorable. Now me, I don't give a damn about bein' honorable. I just want the son of a bitch dead, and it won't bother me none at all to shoot the bastard while he's asleep."

"Yeah, well quit gabbin' about it and do it," Simmons said. "As long as the son of a bitch is dead, I don't care how you kill him."

Simmons and Injun Joe waited down by the river as Pete started toward the campfire, a small, dim blaze that was now some fifty yards away. They watched until Pete was completely swallowed up by darkness.

It had been a long, tiring trail. As a result John Henry, who was tired, dozed off several times during the night. But even while he was asleep, he was alert, and when, while approaching the campsite, Pete's foot dislodged a pebble, John Henry was instantly awake. By the light of the moon, John Henry saw someone approaching the "sleeping" saddle.

John Henry raised his gun and watched and waited.

The night intruder pulled his pistol out and pointed it toward the bedroll. He took careful aim, then fired twice. The muzzle flash of his pistol lit up the night, the booming sound of the shots echoed back from this hills.

"Vernon! Vernon, I got him!" Fuller shouted.

"Sorry, friend, but you missed," John

Henry called out from the dark.

"What the hell?" Fuller shouted, spinning around and blazing away in the direction of the sound of John Henry's voice.

John Henry returned fire, using the flame pattern of Fuller's muzzle-blast as his target. John Henry fired only once, but that was all he needed. Fuller dropped his gun, then crumpled.

"Pete! Pete!" Vernon called from the darkness. "What's happenin', Pete?"

"Fuller's not going to answer you, Simmons," John Henry said. "I just killed him. I think you and Injun Joe Pipestem had better come on in and give yourselves up."

"Like hell we will!" Simmons called back from the darkness.

John Henry heard, but could not see, the two men running over rocky ground. He knew when they hit the creek because he heard water splashing. He looked toward the sound, tying to see them, and though he couldn't see them, he could see the little fluorescent feathers of white water kicked up by their feet as they splashed across the shallow stream. John Henry fired a couple of times in the general direction of the white splashes, but the two were too far away and it was too dark for him to have a real target.

Once Simmons and Injun Joe reached the

other side of the creek, the white splashes disappeared, and John Henry could no longer see them. He could hear them though, through the scrape of iron horseshoes on hard rock as they rode away.

John Henry had not been able to track them when he was first given the mission of bringing them in, but he could track them now, because he was able to pick up their tracks from the creek.

Long before he got there, John Henry could see the community of Doster. The tracks of the two men he was following had led him here to this little town that lay baking under the sun, hot, dry, dusty, and as brittle as tumbleweed. Before leaving his campsite, he had filled his canteen at the stream and now, with the town in front of him, he allowed himself to drink the final few swallows. The water was warm, but his tongue was swollen and dry so that any moisture, regardless of temperature, was welcome. And, although he was drinking tepid water, he could almost taste the cool beer he would have once his job was done. Alcohol was not allowed in The Nations, but John Henry had developed a taste for beer and had one whenever the opportunity presented itself.

John Henry hooked his canteen back onto

the saddle pommel, then urged the two horses, the one he was riding and the one he was leading, forward. The horse he was leading was carrying Pete, belly down across the saddle. If the horse had any reaction to its rider being dead, he didn't show it.

The buildings in the town had collected the day's heat and they were now giving it back in waves so that Doster seemed to shimmer in the distance. A dust devil was born in front of him, propelled by a wind that felt as if it were blowing straight from the fires of hell. A jackrabbit popped up, ran for several feet, then darted under a dusty clump of fescue sedge.

It took another ten minutes to reach the town after he first saw it, and he rode in slowly, sizing it up with wary eyes. It was a town with only one street and a dozen or more ramshackle buildings that fronted the street. The unpainted wood of the few buildings was turning gray and splitting. Hitching poles lined either side of the street and the horses thereon tied nodded and stamped at the flies. There was no railroad coming into the town, but there was a stagecoach station with a schedule board announcing the arrival and departure of two stagecoaches per week. The town appeared to be isolated, inbred, and stagnant.

John Henry rode past the buildings, checking each of them over as he passed. There was a rooming house, a livery, a smithy's, and a general store that said DRUGS, MEATS, GOODS on its high, false front. There was a hotel and restaurant, too, and, of course, the ubiquitous saloon . . . this one called the Kansas Prairie Saloon. Across the street from the saloon was the city marshal's office.

John Henry rode up to the hitching rail in front of the jail, dismounted, then looked up and down the street. He knew that coming into town with a body thrown over a horse would attract some attention, and evidently it did. A few buildings away a door slammed, while across the street an isinglass shade came down on the upstairs window of the hotel. A sign creaked in the wind and flies buzzed loudly around the piles of horse manure that lay in the street.

John pushed open the door. There was no one at the desk, but he saw someone sleeping on the bunk of one of the three cells. The door to that cell, like the door to the other two, was standing open. Except for this one, all the cells were empty. John Henry had left the door to the building standing open, and a gust of wind blew it shut with a loud bang.

"What? What?" the man in the cell said, awakened by the loud pop. He sat up on the bunk and saw John Henry standing just outside the cell.

"Who are you?" he asked. "What do you want?"

"I'm looking for the town marshal."

"Yeah? Well, you found him. I'm Marshal Dawes."

"You're taking a chance, aren't you, Marshal Dawes? Sleeping in the cell, I mean. What if someone came in here and slammed the door shut on you?"

"I've got the keys," the marshal said. "What are you lookin' for me for?"

"Marshal, I am United States Marshal Sixkiller and I . . ."

"Sixkiller? Is that an Indian name?"

"Yes, I'm Cherokee."

"You don't look like no Indian."

"My mother is white."

Marshal Dawes stroked his jaw and stared at John Henry. "U.S. Marshal, huh? Well, what brings you to Doster, Marshal?"

"I've got a body for you," John Henry said.

"A body? Where?"

"Belly down across his horse," John Henry answered. "He's tied up out front."

"Who is it?"

John Henry saw a poster with Pete Fuller's

144

name and picture, and he tore it down. "This man."

The town marshal, who was bald headed and overweight, came out of the cell poking his shirt down into his trousers. "The hell you say. Pete Fuller, huh? He's a bad one. Did you kill him?"

"Yes."

"Well, good riddance, I say. What do you want me to do with him?"

"Get a notary to validate who it is, then get him buried."

"What? You want the town to bury him? Who's goin' to pay for that? Maybe you didn't notice, but this town ain't all that large. We don't have a lot of — what you call — disposable income."

"You can keep his horse and tack," John Henry said. "That should cover it."

"All right," Marshal Dawes said. "That seems about right. What are you goin' to do now? You'll be goin' back down into The Nations?"

"No, the other two men who were with Fuller are here in town now. I'm going after them."

"There's two more of 'em, you say?"

"Yes. Vernon Simmons and Injun Joe Pipestem."

"Damn!" Marshal Dawes said, his eyes

opening wide. "That's a couple of bad ones. And they are here, you say? In my town? How do you know they are here?"

"Because I tracked them here, and I intend to arrest them and take them back to Judge Parker to be hanged."

"Hanging Judge Parker," Marshal Dawes said. He nodded. "Yes, sir, you take them boys back to him, and he'll hang 'em all right. Uh, would you be wantin' — that is, are you askin' me to come help you arrest 'em?"

"No."

"That's good. Don't get me wrong, I mean, if I thought you really needed help, I'd come along with you, though I don't know how legal that would be. I mean, me being nothin' but a town marshal and them two boys wanted by the state and federal government means I ain't really got no right to be messin' with 'em."

"I'll handle them myself," John Henry said.

"Well, if they're in town, it's a guarantee that they'll be down at the saloon. Either that, or in the cathouse, which turns out to be the same thing, since a couple of the girls that's workin' there is the town's only whores."

"John Henry Sixkiller is here," Injun Joe said. "He just rode in down at the marshal's office. He'll be comin' down here next."

"What's he doin' up here? He's an Injun policeman, ain't he?"

"I think that is true," Injun Joe said.

"Then I ain't worried about him. He's got no authority over us here."

"I think for a man like Sixkiller it will not matter whether he has the authority or not," Injun Joe said.

"Yeah, maybe you are right. All right then, we'll be waitin' for him," Vernon said. "Start blasting away as soon as he sets foot on the porch."

Vernon and Injun Joe both moved up to the front door and, with guns drawn, looked down toward the marshal's office.

"You have a back way out of this building?" John Henry asked Marshal Dawes.

"Yeah, I do, but I keep it locked."

"Unlock it. I'd just as soon not be seen going down to the saloon. I take it the saloon has a back door."

"Yes, and it isn't locked, because the privy is out back."

147

"Thanks."

Marshal Dawes unlocked the back door to the jail house and John Henry stepped outside.

"Good luck," Dawes said.

John Henry nodded in reply to the sheriff's best wishes, then moved quickly up the alley, which was lined with at least five privies, all of which were competing with each other with their odiferous emanations. When he reached the back door of the saloon, he pulled his pistol, then stepped inside.

The back door was shielded by the piano, which wasn't being played at the time. That allowed John Henry a moment to peruse the room. There were three men standing on one side of the bar, and the bartender on the other side. There were two other men sitting at one of the tables, and a man and a bar girl sitting at another table. There were three more tables that were empty. Everyone in the saloon was staring at the two men who were standing up front, just inside the swinging bat-wing doors. Both had pistols drawn, and were looking outside.

John Henry took a few more steps into the saloon, so far not noticed by any of the others in the saloon, all of whom had their attention riveted upon the two armed men standing up by the front door. John raised his pistol, pointed it at the two men, then called out.

"Vernon Simmons, Injun Joe, drop your guns!"

"What the hell?" Vernon shouted, spinning around.

"Don't do it!" John Henry warned, cocking his pistol and aiming it directly at Vernon.

Injun Joe was the first to drop his pistol and put his hands up. Then, seeing that he would have to face John Henry alone, Vernon dropped his pistol as well.

"That's real smart of you boys," he said. "Now, let's take a little walk down to the jail."

"You got them, did you?" Marshal Dawes asked nervously, as John Henry brought the two men in. "Good, I was getting a little nervous waiting, wondering what was going on. I was about to come down there and offer you my help if you needed it."

"As you can see, I didn't need it."

"So, what do we do with them now?" Marshal Dawes asked.

"We'll keep them here, in your jail, until Fort Smith sends a prisoner transport van for them."

"Here? You are going to keep them here?"

Dawes asked. "But, do you think that's wise? I mean, them being federal prisoners and all? This is just a small city jail."

"Where else would you suggest I keep them? In the hotel?"

"No, I, uh, I guess it will be okay to keep them here."

"I'll sleep in the next cell," John Henry said.

"Yeah, yeah, that would probably be a pretty good idea. I mean, in case they try to escape or something," Marshal Dawes said, relief obvious in his voice.

"Will you be all right with them until I get back?"

"Get back? Get back from where?"

"I put in a lot of miles today, hot, dry, dusty miles. And I intend to have a beer."

"I thought Indians couldn't drink."

"Indians can't, but that's all right. It just means more beer for the white half of me," John Henry said with a chuckle.

CHAPTER THIRTEEN

"What do mean, my brother is in jail?" Milton Simmons said.

"I mean he is in jail," Abner Turner said. "Him, and that Injun he runs with."

"Injun Joe."

"Yeah. Well, they was both in here, but that Injun marshal, the one they call Six-killer, took 'em both down to the jailhouse."

"He's just one man. I can't see one man bein' able to do that. Not with Vernon and Injun Joe both."

"Vernon and Injun Joe didn't have no choice in it," Turner said. "Sixkiller come in through the back door with his gun already drawed. If Vernon or the Injun had tried anything, he would'a shot 'em both."

"Why didn't you do somethin'?"

"There weren't nothin' I could have done except maybe got the two of 'em kilt. You didn't want that, did you?"

"Well, I can tell you right now, my brother

ain't goin' to stay in no jail," Milton said.

"Sumbitch," Turner said quietly. "There he is now."

Turner nodded, but did not point at the tall, powerfully built man who had just come in. John Henry stepped up to the bar, and the bartender moved down to him.

"Did you get the two boys put away for the night?" the bartender asked.

"I did."

"What'll you have?"

John Henry took a nickel out of his pocket and put it, with a snap, on the bar.

"No, sir," the bartender said. "This first beer is on me. I figure puttin' away those two characters is worth a beer in anybody's saloon."

"Hey you!" Milton called out. "You, the Injun standin' at the bar! What are you doin' up here with the white people? Don't you know Injuns aren't welcome up here? Why don't you go back down into The Nations where you belong?"

"Why don't you have a beer on me?" John Henry replied.

"I don't want a beer on you, you son of a bitch. You're the one who just put my brother in jail."

John Henry turned toward him and studied him for a long moment.

"You don't appear to be an Indian, so I'm guessing Vernon Simmons is your brother."

"You're guessing right."

"What can I do for you, Mr. Simmons?"

"You can let my brother and Injun Joe out of jail."

"I don't think so," John Henry said. "Your brother and Mr. Pipestem murdered six people. I'm taking them back to Fort Smith to hang."

"No, you ain't goin' to do that." He moved his hand in such a way as to take in Turner. "As you can see, there's two of us and only one of you," Milton said. "And you ain't standin' behind us the way you was when you got the drop on my brother."

From behind the bar came the sound of hammers being pulled back on a shotgun, and looking toward the bar, John Henry saw the bartender pointing the shotgun at Simmons and Turner.

"You are sounding most quarrelsome, Mr. Simmons. And I don't like quarrelsome people in my saloon."

"You think you are scarin' me with that scattergun?" Milton asked. "I know damn well you ain't willin' to shoot me just 'cause I'm quarrelsome."

"Maybe he isn't, but I am," John Henry said.

"You are what?"

"I'm willing to shoot you."

There was neither anxiousness nor fear in John Henry's voice. There was no expression of any kind, other than a cold statement of fact.

"Hah!" Turner said. "You ain't thinkin' very straight, are you? You was behind Vernon and Injun Joe. You're right here in front of us."

"Shut up, Turner," Milton said sharply. He continued to stare at John Henry. "I think the son of a bitch means it."

"I do mean it. Now, drop your gun belts," John Henry ordered.

Milton hesitated.

"Now!" John Henry repeated, the word loud and reverberating through the saloon. By now everyone present was watching the drama that was being played out in front of them.

"Do what the marshal says," the bartender said, raising the shotgun to his shoulder.

First Milton, and then Turner, unbuckled their pistol belts and let them fall to the floor.

"Now step back away from them," John Henry ordered.

"Look here, Marshal, this is gettin' a little out of hand now," Milton said. "Like you said, let's just stop this now. I reckon I'll take that beer after all."

John Henry nodded at the bartender, who put his shotgun away, then drew two beers and set them on the bar.

Suddenly, Milton spun away from the bar toward John Henry. He had a pistol in his hand and an evil smile on his face.

"Did you think I was really dumb enough to drop my gun unless I had another?" he asked. "Turner, pick up the other guns."

With a big smile on his face, Turner retrieved the two belts and holsters. He strapped his on, then pulled his pistol and pointed it at John Henry, holding it there as Milton started to strap on his own gun.

"Now here is what we are going to do," Milton said, laying his second pistol on the bar as he began strapping on his holster. "We're goin' to go down to the jail, and you are goin' to turn my brother and Injun Joe loose."

"You wouldn't listen to me, would you?" John Henry replied. "You could have enjoyed your beer, then walked out of here free men. Now you are both under arrest."

"What?" Milton asked, barking a laugh. "Why you dumb son of a bitch! We got the drop on you, and you are telling us that we are under arrest?"

"You have your choice," John Henry said calmly. "You can either come down to the jail with me now, or . . ." He let the last word hang.

"Or what?"

"I'll kill you both."

Milton laughed again. "Let me get this straight. Your gun is in your holster, Turner and I are both holding our pistols on you, but you are going to kill us both. Is that right?"

"Yes."

"Then, Injun, you'd better start killin', 'cause I've had about enough of you. I'm goin' to count to three, and if you ain't started toward the jail to let my brother and Injun Joe out, you're the one that's goin' to get kilt. One, two . . ."

In a draw that was so fast that his hand was a blur, John Henry pulled his pistol and fired two times. The shots were so close together that most thought he had shot only once, until they saw Turner down and Milton leaning back against the bar, his hand covering a bleeding belly wound.

"You . . . didn't . . . let . . . me get to three," Milton said.

"Yeah. Sometimes I cheat," Sixkiller said.

Milton slid down to the floor, sitting against the bar. Then he fell over, his head hitting a filled spittoon, turning it over and spilling the expectorated tobacco juice on his face.

He didn't feel it.

One hundred and fifty miles northeast of Doster, in the town of Emporia, Kansas, Octave Chanute, the chief construction engineer for the Border Tier Line was standing in the station, waiting for the afternoon train to arrive. He wasn't alone; train activity in and out of Emporia was still an exciting enough event to cause more than half the town to be at the depot to watch the arrivals and departures. Chanute had a legitimate reason for being at the station because he was meeting with James Joy, the president of the Border Tier Railroad.

"Here it comes!" someone shouted, though as the oncoming train had now rounded "half-mile curve," there was no need to announce its approach, because everyone could see it. It was a behemoth with smoke rolling up thickly from the stack, then laying a long black line over the length of the train. Steam was gushing from the actuating cylinders on either side of the engine and the large puffs could be heard rolling toward them.

Finally, the train roared into the station,

with the engineer applying the brakes to bring it to a stop at exactly the right place. Once the train stopped, there was a loud hiss as excess steam was vented. The train was still, but it wasn't quiet. Chanute was standing close to the engine, and he could hear the water percolating in the boiler. The pressure relief valve was opening and closing in great gasps, as if the locomotive were some living beast, gathering its breath from a long run. Overheated bearings and journals popped and snapped as they began to cool.

The first car behind the express car, a highly polished mahogany that attracted the attention of everyone, was the private car that belonged to James Joy.

"Have you ever seen anything so beautiful?" one of the platform spectators asked.

"Never. It must be the private rail car of someone very wealthy."

As the arriving passengers began leaving the train, the conductor came up to Chanute.

"Mr. Chanute?"

"Yes?"

"Mr. Joy asks that you join him in his car."

"Very well, thank you."

"This way, sir," the conductor said, leading him back to the entrance to Joy's private car. Chanute was well aware that he was the object of everyone's attention as he stepped up onto the entry platform. He knocked on the door and Joy opened it.

"Mr. Chanute, very good of you to meet me at the depot," he said. "Please, come in."

Chanute had heard of Joy's private rail car, but this was the first time he had ever seen it. The floor was covered with a deep red carpet. There was a bed at the front of the car, not a small bunk as was found in the sleeper cars, but a full-size bed. The walls were paneled with cherrywood, and the light fixtures were of real gold. Against the left wall of the car, there was a highly polished liquor bar. Right across from the bar was a small dining table with two chairs, and, moving back from the table were two larger, overstuffed leather chairs. A sofa was just across from the two chairs, creating a conversation area. Between the sofa and chairs was a low table which was covered with maps and papers. It was obvious that Joy had been working during the long train ride back from New York.

Joy stepped over to the bar and poured two drinks, then came back to hand one of them to Chanute.

"Thank you," Chanute said.

"Have a seat."

Chanute sat in the chair indicated and Joy sat on the sofa.

"How did the trip to New York go?" Chanute asked. "Did you find more investors?"

"Not for the Border Tier, I'm afraid."

"No?"

"It seems that the investors think that running a railroad through Indian Territory is not very smart. On the other hand, they are all lining up to invest in railroads in the Western states, so all isn't lost."

"Perhaps not in the long run it isn't lost," Chanute said. "But it doesn't do much for the project we are working on now."

Joy smiled, and took another sip before he responded.

"Not necessarily. We can still do this, it is just going to require a bit of manipulation, is all."

"What sort of manipulation?"

"Here is what I want you to do. I want you to inspect the tracks between Garrison and Blaine, and find enough fault with them that they have to be pulled up and then put down again."

"What? Why would we want to do that?" Chanute asked. "I've been over those tracks, there is nothing wrong with them. And don't forget, we are scheduled to start operation over that line, soon."

"Mr. Chanute, you and I both know that we will make no money on that line for at least three years. Tear it up, I tell you. We'll put it back after we reach the border of the Indian Territory."

"Mr. Joy, you are a smart man, so I know you have some reason for this."

Joy smiled. "I do, indeed. As I told you, it has been difficult to raise money for the Border Tier Railroad, but for all the other railroads, I am getting investments to the tune of forty-six thousand dollars per mile. It is twenty-three miles between Garrison and Blaine. That comes to just over one million dollars, and for that track, I'll have no trouble getting money from investors."

"I still don't understand. Tear up the track, then get money to rebuild it. It doesn't make sense."

"It does, if you realize that the money we'll be getting for the Garrison to Blaine stretch will be diverted for use for the Border Tier Line."

"I'll be damned," Chanute said. "Like I said, you are a smart one, all right."

CHAPTER FOURTEEN

John Henry met the prison wagon when it arrived in Doster. There were two men with the wagon, the driver, Bert Rowe, and the shotgun guard, Travis Calhoun.

"Hard trip?"

"Took us ten days, making thirty-five miles a day. We didn't have to camp out none," Rowe said. "Spent last night in Arkansas City."

"What about going back? Did you make arrangements with all the local law to use their jail for a night?"

"Where there was a jail, we did. At least three of the towns don't have a jail. When we pass through there, our prisoners will just have to stay in the wagon. It won't be a problem — we've had to do that before."

"All right," John Henry said. "Let's go get our prisoners."

Marshal Dawes was more than happy to turn the prisoners over to John Henry for transportation back to Fort Smith.

"I don't mind tellin' you, gettin' rid of these two is a relief," he said. "Mostly, all I have to deal with is a few drunks. I haven't been real comfortable having a couple of murderers in my jail."

"Not to worry anymore, Marshal, we're taking them off your hands," John Henry said.

Marshal Dawes opened the door to the cell and John Henry stepped inside with the two prisoners.

"Hold your hands out here, Simmons," he said. "I'll slip these wrist manacles on you."

"How far will you be takin' us?" Simmons asked.

"To Fort Smith. It'll be about ten days."

"Ten days? You plan to keep us cooped up in that wagon for ten whole days?"

"Yeah," John Henry answered.

John Henry locked the cuffs on Simmons's wrist, then signaled for Injun Joe. Injun Joe stood up, and held his hands out.

On the third night out, they stopped in front of the jail in Winfield, Kansas. John Henry took the two prisoners inside where they were met by Sheriff James Finely.

"Well, I'll be damned," Sheriff Finely said when he saw the two prisoners. "I knew we were going to put up a couple of prisoners for the night, but I didn't know one of them would be Vernon Simmons."

"You know him?" John Henry asked.

"Yeah, I know him. Everyone in Cowley County knows him. Three years ago he and his brother hit the Dumey farm, about five miles south of town. They killed Chris Dumey and his ten-year-old son, then they raped and murdered Dumey's wife and fourteen-year-old daughter. We've had wanted bills out on both of them ever since. Vernon and Milton."

"Well, you can take down the ones on Milton," John Henry said.

"How so?"

"Because the son of a bitch killed him, that's why," Vernon Simmons said. "He killed my brother in cold blood, and there ain't nobody done nothin' about it."

"I wouldn't have done anything about it if I had seen him strangling him in his sleep," Sheriff Finely said. "What have you got Simmons on?" he asked John Henry. "Something that is likely to get him hanged?"

"Double murder."

"Good. If it was anything less, I was goin' to get the judge to grant an injunction against you taking him any farther."

"An injunction wouldn't have done any good," John Henry said. "This is a federal prisoner. I'm taking him to Fort Smith, and he'll hang there."

That night, John Henry, Bert Rowe, and Travis Calhoun were having dinner at the Palace Café when a nervous-looking deputy came in.

"Marshal Sixkiller?"

"Yes?"

"You better come quick, Marshal. There's a crowd gathered out in front of the sheriff's office, and they say they're goin' to take Simmons out of jail and hang him."

John Henry wiped his mouth with a table napkin, then stood up from the table.

"Thanks, Deputy."

"I'll come with you," Calhoun said.

"I will, too," Rowe offered.

"No, you stay here and finish your supper," John Henry said. "Travis and I can handle this all right."

John Henry and Travis Calhoun followed the deputy sheriff outside, then walked quickly down the street toward the jail. Even before they got there, they could hear the shouts.

"Bring that murderin' son of a bitch out

here, or we're comin' after him!" someone yelled.

"I've got a rope!"

"Bring him out here, Sheriff Finely! We aim to hang the bastard!"

When the deputy, John Henry, and Travis Calhoun got close, they could see the crowd, a dark mass gathered around the front of the jail and spilling far out into the street. John Henry figured there must be at least a hundred here. They were still shouting, and one of them was brandishing a rope, which was already made into a hangman's noose.

"Sheriff said to go around back," the deputy said. "The door is locked, but I've got the key."

"All right," John Henry said.

Because it was dark, and because the attention of the crowd was directed toward the front of the jail, nobody saw the three men cut in between the barbershop and hardware store to get to the alley behind the sheriff's office.

The deputy opened the door, and John Henry and the others stepped inside.

"Hey!" Simmons called. "You've got to protect me! You've got to keep me from that lynch mob."

"Really? Why?"

"Why? Because you are a U.S. Marshal, that's why. It's your duty to protect me while I'm in your custody."

"Why don't I just let you go now?" John Henry suggested. "You wouldn't be in my custody anymore."

"You can't do that!" Simmons said, fright constricting his voice. "You can't turn me over to a lynch mob!"

John Henry walked into the front of the jail where Sheriff Finely was standing to one side of the window, peering out between the shade and the window.

"Do you know any of those men, Sheriff?" John Henry asked.

"Yes, I know all of them. They are my friends and neighbors. They are good men, really. It's not like them to form a mob like this. But ever' one is still riled up by what Simmons and his brother did."

"Do you think that if you went out there as a friend, and a neighbor, you could talk them out of this?"

"No, sir, to be honest with you, I don't think I could. I told you, after what Vernon and his brother, Milton, done, there ain't nobody in this town feeling kindly toward them, even me. And truth be told, if I wasn't wearin' this star right now, I would more'n likely be out there with 'em."

"You've got a good view there: Who in the front row is the most dangerous?"

Sheriff Finely looked again. "I would say that would be Bull Blackwell. He's the one in the front, holding the rope."

John Henry walked over to the gun rack and took down a double-barrel shotgun. Breaking it down, he saw that the breaches were empty.

"Where are your shells?"

"Right over there, top drawer," Finely said, pointing to a stand-up filing cabinet.

John Henry took two shells out of the drawer, then with a knife he opened up one of the shells and dumped the "buck and ball" out onto the floor. They made a loud thump as they hit the floor, then rolled away.

With the same knife, he cut a piece of rope, then pushed it down into the shotgun shell casing.

"Give me that bottle of ketchup," he said, pointing to what had been left of the prisoner's supper.

Travis Calhoun handed him the bottle, and John Henry poured it into the open shell casing around the bit of rope. After that, he loaded the gun, putting the rope shell in one barrel, and the live shell in the other. He snapped the barrels closed, then looked over at Calhoun.

"You ready?" he asked.

Calhoun had a tight expression on his face, and he answered with a quiet, but determined, "Yes."

"Open the door, Sheriff. And close it behind us," John Henry ordered.

Sheriff Finely nodded, then did as John Henry asked. John Henry and Calhoun stepped out on the front porch, and the surprise of actually seeing someone come from the jail caused everyone to grow quiet.

John Henry stood there for a long moment, holding the shotgun with the butt of the gun resting on his right hip, the barrel pointing up.

"Who are you?" the man Sheriff Finely had identified as Bull Blackwell asked.

"I am United States Marshal John Henry Sixkiller. And those two men in there are not the sheriff's prisoners. They are my prisoners, and I am taking them on through to Fort Smith."

"You can have the 'breed!" one of the men in the crowd shouted. "We don't give a damn what happens to him. But you ain't goin' nowhere with Simmons. We aim to haul his ass out of that jail and hang him right here in the middle of town."

"Are you in charge of these men, Blackwell?" John Henry asked.

It was easy to see where Blackwell got the nickname Bull. He was a big man, with a round, bald head that sat upon his shoulders with no visible neck.

"Yeah, I'm in charge of these men."

"Tell them to go home."

"I ain't tellin' 'em shit!"

Without another word, John Henry pointed the shotgun toward Blackwell and pulled the trigger. The gun roared, and the muzzle flash lit up the night.

Blackwell's stomach turned red and he grunted and went down. The others shouted in alarm, and John Henry turned the shotgun toward them.

"I've got one barrel left," he said. "Who's next?"

The crowd turned then and ran away in panic and confusion.

Sheriff Finely and his deputy came out onto the front porch. By now the crowd had scattered and, groaning in pain, Blackwell got to his feet. He looked down at himself, then rubbed himself with his hand.

"What the hell? What did you shoot me with? There ain't no holes in my stomach! Where'd all this blood come from?"

"Sheriff, I would feel better if you would keep Mr. Blackwell in jail overnight, at least until after we leave tomorrow."

Looking on the ground Blackwell saw a short coil of rope. The rope was red. He picked it up.

"You shot me with a piece of rope?" Blackwell smelled the red on the rope, then touched his tongue to it. "Ketchup? You put ketchup on a rope and shot me with that?"

"Yeah."

Blackwell shook his head. "What would you have done if everyone had charged you? You couldn't stop them with a piece of rope."

John Henry pointed the shotgun toward the sheriff's sign, a small board that dangled down from the porch roof. He pulled the trigger and again, there was a roar and a bright flash of light from the muzzle blast. Half the sign was torn away.

"I had a live round in the second barrel."

It took eight more days for the prison wagon to make it through to Fort Smith, Arkansas, stopping at towns along the way. Each night, the prisoners would be put in the local jail, and each morning they would be returned to the wagon, which had a steel reinforced floor and roof, and bars around all four sides. It wasn't that uncomfortable for them inside: They had bedrolls, they had a chamber pot, and they were given something to eat, three times a day.

The arrival of such a wagon to Fort Smith wasn't that unusual an event, but it still brought several people out to watch as it rolled down the street, the two prisoners inside clearly visible behind the bars.

"Who you got there, Bert?" someone called from the street. Bert Rowe had been driving prison wagons for the last five years and was well known by everyone in Fort Smith.

"Hell, you don't need to ask. I know them two galoots," another said. "That's Vernon Simmons, and Injun Joe."

Rowe drove through the town and stopped at the gate to the prison. He waited at the gate until it was opened for him, then he drove through. John Henry rode in with him.

Rowe stopped, and set the brake, then crawled down to be met by a couple of prison guards.

Rowe opened the tailgate, and the prisoners crawled out.

"Marshal, if you'll go on in to see the warden, he'll give you a receipt for the two prisoners," the senior guard said to John Henry.

John Henry nodded, then walked across the yard to the main office, where he was greeted warmly by the warden.

"You'll be staying for the trial?" the warden asked as he made out the receipt.

"I have to. I'm a witness for the prosecution."

"Oh, yeah, that's right. Well, we've quarters for you here if you need them. I admit that they are empty cells, but they have a bed."

"Thanks, but no thanks. I will be staying at a hotel."

The warden chuckled. "I can't say as I blame you," he said, handing the signed receipt to John Henry.

CHAPTER FIFTEEN

The trial was held within three days after John Henry delivered the prisoners. Vernon Simmons and Injun Joe Pipestem were provided with a lawyer because they had no money to hire one. The lawyer did the best he could with uncooperative clients, and to the surprise of no one, both men were found guilty as charged. All that remained now was the sentencing, and that took place the very next day after the trial.

John Henry, who had testified for the prosecution during the trial, was present in the court the next day, waiting with the others for Judge Parker's arrival.

The back door to the courtroom opened, and the bailiff called out, loudly, "All rise!"

There was a scrape of chairs, a rustle of pants, petticoats, and skirts as the spectators in the courtroom stood. A spittoon rang as one male member of the gallery made a last-second, accurate expectoration of his tobacco quid.

"Oyez, oyez, oyez. This federal court for the Western District of Arkansas is now in session, the Honorable Judge Isaac Charles Parker presiding."

The gallery was limited to fifty spectators, and tickets for attendance were highly prized commodities. Most people agreed that Judge Parker's performances were the best show anywhere, not because of any particular showmanship, but because of his hard-nosed treatment of criminals. He had sentenced so many hardened criminals to hang that he was known far and wide as the "Hanging Judge."

A former United States Congressman from Missouri, Parker was a stern-looking man with a Vandyke beard and piercing blue eyes. He moved quickly to the bench, then sat down.

"Be seated," he said.

The gallery sat, then watched with interest as Vernon Simmons and Injun Joe Pipestem, their trial completed, were brought into the courtroom, bound and shackled. The evidence against them had been overwhelming and the jury had taken little time in returning a verdict of guilty on all counts. Now, all that remained was for Judge Parker to pass on their sentence.

"Bailiff, would you position the prisoners before the bench for sentencing, please?" Judge Parker asked.

"Yes, Your Honor."

The two men were brought before the bench. Injun Joe stood with his head bowed, contritely. Vernon Simmons smiled at the judge in arrogant defiance.

Judge Parker cleared his throat. "You men have been tried before a jury of twelve men, honest and true, for the murder of Harold and Mary Two Hills. You were ably represented by counsel —"

"Is that what that fella was? A lawyer?" Vernon interrupted. "I figured maybe it was someone you brung in from cleaning horseshit out of the stalls."

Judge Parker glared at Vernon, but he made no direct reply. "You have both been found guilty as charged. Had you not been found guilty of that murder, you would have been tried again, a total of five times for each of the murders you are known to have committed."

"We know all that. Get on with it," Vernon taunted.

The bailiff took a step toward Vernon, but Judge Parker nodded at him, and the bailiff stepped back.

"Additionally you, Mr. Simmons —"

"Why don't you call me Vernon, Isaac? Why, I feel as if we are old friends now," Vernon shouted.

When the gallery laughed nervously, Vernon turned toward them and held his arms over his head, with his handcuffed hands clasped. "It looks like I'm just surrounded by friends," he said.

"You ain't got no friends, you low-life murderin' son of a bitch!" someone from the gallery shouted.

"Order! Order in the court!" Judge Parker said loudly. He banged his gavel several times for order and when the gallery quieted, he glared at them.

"If there is one more demonstration I will clear the court and hang these men in private," he growled.

The crowd, not wanting to miss the spectacle of the hanging, fell silent.

"And now, Mr. Simmons," the judge continued. "As I was about to say, though you were only tried for the one murder, it is well known that you have killed others. Would you like to clear your conscience and confess to those other murders here, before this court?"

"Yeah, why not?" Vernon replied. "What are you going to do, hang me five times?"

"If that were possible, Mr. Simmons, you

may be assured that I would do so. Fortunately, one hanging is all it will take. I normally ask God to have mercy upon the souls of those I condemn to the gallows, but for you, Mr. Simmons, and you, Mr. Pipestem, I offer no such prayer. My sentence is temporal, but after it is carried out, you will be sentenced by a higher judge to a penalty that will be eternal."

"You go to hell, Judge," Vernon spat out.

"Interesting you should say that," Judge Parker replied. "For that is exactly where you are about to go." He picked up his gavel and rapped it sharply against the pad on his desk.

"I sentence you, Vernon Simmons, and you, Joe Pipestem —"

"My name is Billy Ray Pipestem."

"I beg your pardon?" Judge Parker replied.

"If I am to die, I want to die under my real name. I am not Injun Joe. My real name is Billy Ray Pipestem."

"I'll be damned, I've rode with you for two years, you never told me that," Simmons said.

"I've never died before," Billy Ray Pipestem said.

A nervous laugher spread through the courtroom, but was quickly silenced by a stern glance from the judge. The judge resumed his sentencing.

"I sentence you, Vernon Simmons, and you, Billy Ray Pipestem, to be hanged by the neck until you are dead. Sentence will be carried out at one o'clock tomorrow afternoon."

"Your Honor!" the court-appointed defense attorney said. "That leaves no time for appeal!"

"You should know, Mr. Dempster, that there is no appeal beyond me, short of the United States Supreme Court. The sentence will be carried out as ordered."

There was a buzz of whispered excitement throughout the court as everyone realized that tomorrow there would be a double hanging.

"Two! We're goin' to be hanging two at the same time! This will for sure make the papers back East!" someone said excitedly.

"Silence! Silence in the court," Judge Parker said, and again, he slapped his gavel against the pad. The gallery grew quiet. "Deputy Messler, escort the condemned men to the holding cells. Court is dismissed."

"Who'll have tickets to the hanging?" the clerk called.

"Me! I want one!" someone called.

"Save one for me!"

The two prisoners, their legs hobbled with an eighteen-inch chain, were, for the move back to the cells, chained together. As the deputy escorted them out of the court and to the holding cell, they had to move with an awkward gait. They shuffled out as crowds of people pressed around the clerk to get the little blue ticket which would grant them access to the side courtyard where the hanging would take place.

The holding cell was separated from the main jail. It was out in the side courtyard, less than fifty feet from the gallows itself. There, the condemned prisoners would be able to look through the barred windows and watch the crowd gather and the excitement grow as time for their execution approached.

The deputy took them out through the side door of the courthouse, then across the sun-baked, dirt-packed courtyard toward the little holding cell. It was quiet in the yard since, as yet, no spectators had been allowed around the gallows.

After he left the courtroom, John Henry walked down the street to the saloon. From the moment he stepped into the establishment, he was aware of the noise and the smells, not only of beer and whiskey, but of expectorated tobacco quids, pipe smoke, and body odor. He saw Marshal Sarber standing near the bar.

"Hello, John Henry," Sarber called out, cheerily. "Why don't you come and join me? Barkeep, a beer for my friend."

"Thanks," John Henry said.

"Has the judge talked to you yet?" Sarber asked as the beer was put in front of John Henry.

"Talked to me about what?"

"Oh, no, you aren't going to get me to steal the judge's thunder. The judge doesn't like to be upstaged, if you know what I mean."

John Henry lifted the mug to his mouth and took a long, satisfying drink of the amber liquid.

"You just upstaged him, didn't you? By telling me he wanted to talk to me?"

"Yeah, maybe I did. Anyway, what are you doing drinking beer? I thought Injuns couldn't be served liquor."

"This is the white part of me drinking beer," John Henry said. "The Indian part of me is back at the hotel, already gone to bed."

Marshal Sarber laughed. "That's a pretty damned good trick. Someday you'll have to tell me how that works."

■ ■ ■ ■

The next afternoon, there were nearly a thousand people gathered in the courtyard to watch the double hanging. Enterprising vendors were making the best of the situation, passing through the crowd to sell lemonade, beer, popcorn, and sweet rolls. In one corner of the courtyard, a black-frocked preacher stood on an overturned box, delivering a fiery sermon full of brimstone and perdition.

On the second floor of the courtroom, Judge Parker stood at the window of his chambers and looked down on the proceedings. John Henry was just behind him, lighting a cigar which he had extracted from a humidor on the judge's desk.

"You did well, Marshal Sixkiller, bringing these two men in," Parker said without turning away from the window. "Yes, sir, you did very well."

"Thank you, Your Honor."

"Step over here to the window, and you'll have a good view," Judge Parker invited.

"Does it ever bother you, Judge?"

"Does what bother me? Sentencing men to hang?"

"Yes. Does it ever bother you?"

"You have killed how many men, Marshal?"

"Twelve, if you count the ones I killed during the war."

"Does it ever bother you that you have killed twelve men?"

"The ones I killed in the war were not evil men, they were just soldiers, serving their side as I was serving mine. The only difference between us was the uniforms. But I've never killed anyone who wasn't trying to kill me."

"Do you think, John Henry, that any of the men I have sentenced to die, would have killed me, if they could?"

"I suppose they would."

"There is no supposing about it. They absolutely would. And I haven't condemned any man who hasn't been found guilty of a capital offense by a jury of his peers. So to answer your question, no, it does not bother me one bit."

John Henry stepped up to the window and looked down onto the courtyard below.

Down in the courtyard the two condemned men were led to the gallows. They were in the prison garb of a gray, collarless shirt and gray trousers. Their legs weren't hobbled, but their hands were handcuffed behind their back. John Henry saw Vernon

Simmons squirt out a stream of tobacco juice just as he reached the foot of the thirteen steps. He stopped there.

"Go on up now, Simmons," Marshal Sarber said. "You don't want folks thinking you couldn't die like a man, do you?"

"I'm the one that's about to die, Marshal," Simmons replied. "I don't need you tellin' me how to do it."

"Come on, Vernon," Marshal Sarber said more gently. "The longer you wait, the more time you have to think about it. Just get it done, and it'll be all over for you."

Simmons and Pipestem moved onto the scaffold, then both men were positioned under the noose. The clergyman who had been preaching fire and damnation now walked up to the two men.

"Vernon Simmons and Billy Ray Pipestem, since you both are soon to pass into an endless and unchangeable state, and your future happiness or misery depends upon the few moments which are left you, I require you to examine yourselves strictly, and your estate, both toward God and towards man, and let no worldly consideration hinder you from making a true and full confession of your sins, and giving all the satisfaction which is in your power to everyone whom you have wronged or injured, that you may find mercy at your heavenly Father's hand and not be condemned on the dreadful day of judgment."

"Now, why the hell should I want to do that?" Vernon asked.

"Why, to save your eternal soul, sir, as indeed, was the soul of the good thief saved by our Lord, even though the good thief, like our Lord, was dying upon the cross."

Vernon looked up. "This here ain't a cross," he said. "It's a rope."

"I beg of you, sir. Repent. Repent now, before it is too late."

"Go away, preacher. Let a man die in peace."

Suddenly Billy Ray Pipestem, who had been quiet until this moment, began chanting.

"Unequa dinelvdodi gaivladi."

"What are you doing?" the preacher asked.

"He's doin' his death song."

"Blasphemy!" the preacher said as, red faced with anger, he turned and walked quickly off the scaffold.

"Unequa dinelvdodi gaivladi."

"Do either of you men have any last words?" Marshal Sarber asked.

"Unequa dinelvdodi gaivladi."

Vernon laughed. "Sounds to me like Injun Joe is talkin' enough for both of us."

"All right. It is time," Sarber said.

"Sarber, you got 'ny friends in hell you want me to say hello to?"

"Probably quite a few," Marshal Sarber answered. He fit the noose. "When the trap opens, don't hunch up your shoulders. If you'll just relax, it will be better."

"Really? You want to tell me how the hell I can relax when I'm about to be hung?"

"Unequa dinelvdodi gaivladi."

When Sarber had the nooses on both men, he stepped over to the handle which would open the trapdoors. He glanced up toward the window where Judge Parker stood looking down. Parker nodded his head and the hangman pulled the handle. The trapdoor swung down on its hinges and the bodies dropped about five feet.

"Unequa dinelvdodi ga—"

"Well, it's done," Judge Parker said, turning away from the window. John Henry stood there for a moment longer watching the two men twist slowly as they hung there from the end of the ropes that had broken their necks.

Judge Parker poured himself a drink.

"I've got a job for you."

"In the Indian Territory?"

"Yes, out in the Cimarron Strip. There is

a man by the name of Lucas Redbone. Do you know him?"

"Yes, I know Redbone well. I had a few run-ins with him while I was with the Indian Police."

"Good, I'm glad you know him. There won't be any difficulty in you identifying him once you find him. I want you to bring him in, alive if you can. Dead if you have to."

"What has Redbone done now?" John Henry asked.

"It would be a better question if you asked me what he hasn't done. Murder, rape, robbery, you name it, he has done it. But the most recent thing he did was break a man named Ray Gibson out of jail. And he killed the jailer while he was doing it."

"All right, Judge. I'll find him for you."

"There was someone with Redbone when he broke Gibson out of jail, so there are three of them," Judge Parker said.

"I'll make sure I have at least three bullets in my pistol," John Henry said.

Judge Parker laughed. "You're my kind of marshal," he said.

CHAPTER SIXTEEN

When John Henry arrived at the farm, he saw two women tied to the base of the windmill. One was older than the other so that he thought, but wasn't sure, that they might be mother and daughter. Both were sitting at the base of the windmill with their heads to one side and their eyes closed. Lying on the ground in front of them were two bodies who might be father and son. The younger of the two looked to be around twelve or thirteen. He and the man had been shot multiple times, the blood around the bullet holes now baked black in the sun.

John Henry went to the women, then knelt in front of them. The faces of both women were red and sunburned. He reached out to touch the older woman and she jumped.

"You're alive," he said. Quickly, he cut her and the younger one loose.

"Water," the woman said, her voice scratchy.

The irony was that they were less than five feet from a trough that was filled with water brought up by the windmill, but of course they had not been able to get to it.

John Henry offered his canteen, first to the woman, then the girl. Both drank deeply.

"Who are you?" John Henry asked.

"Elizabeth Boydkin. This is my daughter, Lillian. That's my husband, Paul, and my son, Carl. Who are you?"

"I'm Marshal John Henry Sixkiller. Are you up to telling me what happened here?"

"There were three of them," she said. "They stopped here yesterday at about lunch, asking for something to eat. I fixed a meal for them and they visited with us for a while. Then one of them, Redbone his name was, grabbed Carl and held a gun to Carl's head. 'I'll be takin' what cash you have now,' he said. And he threatened to kill Carl if Paul didn't give him the money."

"Did you have any money?"

"We had about thirty dollars is all, but when Paul gave it to them, Redbone got mad, accused him of holding out on some of the money. He shot Paul, then he shot Carl. He demanded more money from me, but there wasn't any more. I thought he was going to kill us, too, but instead he dragged Paul and Carl out here, then tied Lillian

189

and me to the windmill so we could see them."

"Do you have a wagon and team? Or did they take your horses?"

"They took Paul and Carl's riding horses, but they didn't take the plow horses, and they are the ones we use to pull the wagon."

"Do you have any neighbors nearby where you and your daughter might go until you're feeling better?"

"There is the Russell farm. Their place is about three miles from here. Mr. Russell has two grown sons. They could take care of burying Paul and Carl for us."

"I'll hitch up the team."

"Give us a few minutes," Mrs. Boydkin said. "We'll need to get cleaned up a mite."

After John Henry dropped off the Boydkins at the Russell farm, he went back to the Boydkin farm to pick up the trail of Redbone and the two men who were with him. The trail was easy to follow because three of the horses had riders, and two didn't.

Lucas Redbone, Tyrone Rogers, and Ray Gibson were at the Big Turkey way station, a gray, weather-beaten building which had been abandoned, and now sat baking in the afternoon sun. A faded sign just outside the

190

door of the building gave the arrival and departure schedule of stagecoaches that no longer ran, for a line that no longer existed.

The roof and one wall of the nearby barn were caved in, but there was an overhang at the other end that provided some much-needed shade for their horses. Ray Gibson, a short man with a pockmarked face and a walrus style mustache was sitting on the front porch with his back against the wall. Redbone was a man of average size, clean shaven, but with long, black hair. He was inside the building, looking around at what remained of a once-busy passenger terminal.

Tyrone Rogers, who was of average size, and distinguishable by one eye which drooped so that it always appeared to be half closed, was outside, by the pump. A little earlier, he had taken the pump apart and now he was reassembling it.

Redbone stepped back out onto the front porch.

"Find anything interesting in there, Redbone?" Rogers asked from his position, bent over the pump.

"Not really," Redbone answered. He looked down at Gibson. "All right, Gibson, we busted you out of jail. You said you would make it worthwhile, so when are you goin' to do it? If your idea of worthwhile was robbin' the Boydkin farm, well, that ain't much. All we got from it was a lousy thirty dollars. Thirty dollars, which is only ten dollars apiece. We could do better than that working as cowboys for twenty dollars a month and found. At least cowboys got their food furnished for 'em."

"I met a feller in the jail last week, just before he got out. We didn't know each other durin' the war, but it turns out that our paths must'a crossed only we just never know'd it. I mean, me an' him had never run acrost each other before, but he know'd lots of the same folks I know'd. Like ole Bill Anderson, and George Todd. Hell, he even know'd Quantrill."

"They're all dead," Redbone said.

"I know they are dead. What's that got to do with anything?"

"It means we have no way of checking him out."

"He's all right," Gibson said.

"How do you know?"

"I can feel it."

"That's it? You feel it?"

"Yeah, I feel it."

"All right, so he rode with Quantrill. What does that mean?"

"After he found out I oncet rode with Quantrill, he said he trusted me, and he

192

asked me could I round up a couple more men for a job."

"What kind of job?" Redbone asked.

"That's what I asked him, and he said it was one that would let us make a lot of easy money. So I said, 'I'm always lookin' for an easy job.' But he says, 'It ain't like we're goin' to be takin' money from a baby. There's goin' to be some risks.' And when I asked him what kind of risks, he said it would be just like the risks we took when we was ridin' with Quantrill. Only this time, we'd get to keep a lot more money than the money."

"Did he say how much money?" Redbone asked.

Gibson shook his head. "He just said there was a lot of it. More'n any of us had ever seen before."

"What do you think, Tyrone?" Redbone asked.

"I think if there is a lot of money we'd better be getting an equal share," Rogers replied. "I mean none of this, he set up the job so he's gettin' most of the money. If we share equally in the risk, then we are going to share equally in the money."

"He didn't say nothin' 'bout whether the share would be equal or not. He just said there'd be lots of money," Gibson said.

"Equal," Rogers said again.

"What if he won't go along with that?" Ray asked. "I mean, it is his plan. He may figure he deserves more. And I don't want to pass up the deal, not if it means a lot of money."

Redbone smiled. "We'll do the job. And if he don't like the idea of an equal split, we'll just kill the son of a bitch and take his share. That is, unless he's some personal friend of yours and you don't want to see him kilt."

"Hell, I barely know the son of a bitch," Gibson said. "Yeah," he added with a big smile. "Yeah, I like the idea of killin' him, and takin' his share."

"Hey," Rogers called, smiling broadly as he began working the pump handle up and down. "Hey, you guys, look here! The pump is moving real smooth now! I think I fixed it."

"Don't do no good to have a working pump if there ain't no water down there," Gibson said.

"What do you think? That they pumped all the water out? There's water down there," Rogers said. "There's plenty of water down there." He started toward the barn.

"Where you goin'?" Gibson asked.

"To the horses. I'm going to get my canteen so I can prime the pump."

"Rogers, wait a minute! Do you think

that's a good idea?" Redbone asked. "If you use up all your water trying to prime this pump, there's no telling where we're going to find some more."

"There's water down there, Redbone. I can smell it. Only we ain't going to get it if the pump ain't primed."

"You use all your water up, don't think you're goin' to get any of mine," Gibson warned him.

"Hell, as I recall, it ain't your water anyway," Rogers called back. "I seem to mind that you was in jail. We had to dig up a horse and tack for you."

Rogers returned a moment later with his canteen. He unscrewed the cap and held it over the pump for a second as if trying to make up his mind, then he poured it in. The water glistened brightly in the sun, then gurgled as it all rushed down the pipe.

Rogers began working the handle. "It's comin'!" he said. "I can feel the pressure in the pipe!"

Redbone moved over to the pump, and even Gibson stood up to watch.

Suddenly the suction was broken, and the pump handle began to move easily again.

"Damn!" Rogers said.

"What happened?" Redbone asked.

"I don't know. The water was right there,

I know it. Then it just went away."

"I told you, you wasn't goin' to get no water out of that pump. It's a dry hole." Gibson said, moving back over to resume his position on the porch.

"Gibson, let me have your water."

"The hell you say."

"Give me your water, damn it! It was almost there. I need to prime the pump again."

"Well you ain't goin' to prime it with my water."

Redbone pointed his pistol at Gibson. "Like he said, it ain't your water. We just loaned it to you when we broke you out of jail. Give him your water."

"What if there ain't no water down there?"

"Then you ain't no worse off than you was before we broke you out of jail," Redbone said.

"It's there, I tell you. I just lost the suction, that's all."

"Give him your canteen," Redbone ordered.

"All right, all right," Gibson said. "I'll go get my canteen."

"And don't get any ideas about runnin' off. You promised us a payoff for gettin' you out of jail, and I aim to see that we collect."

"I ain't goin' to go nowhere. I aim to be

around to collect my share after we do that job."

Gibson went to get his canteen, then he came back and sat down on the edge of the porch. He reached down to pull up a straw, then stuck the end of it in his mouth. "I still think this is crazy. We're throwin' away good drinkin' water on the chance there might be some in that well."

Rogers took the canteen, then poured it into the top of the pump. Once again, he began pumping.

"Yes!" he said, after a moment. "Yes, it's coming!"

Redbone stood by watching with intense interest and even Gibson came over to see what was happening.

"Shit!" Tyrone Rogers shouted. "Shit, I need some more water to hold the suction. It's almost there, but I may lose it. I need more water!"

"Well, don't look at me," Redbone said. "You ain't gettin' my water."

"Come on, we're almost there."

Redbone sighed. "If I pour my canteen into that pump and we don't get no water, I'm goin' to shoot you."

"All right, all right, just get some more water. But hurry!"

Redbone ran to his horse, got his canteen,

then ran back.

"Pour it in while I'm still pumpin'," Rogers said.

"You crazy son of a bitch!" Gibson shouted. "You've used up ever' damn bit of our water!"

Ignoring him, Redbone began to pour as Rogers continued to pump.

There were more gurgling sounds as the water disappeared down the pipe. They watched as Rogers continued to pump, the only sound being the squeak and clank of the pump handle and piston.

Redbone pulled his pistol and pointed it at Rogers. "I told you I was going to shoot you if you didn't get water!" he said angrily.

"Wait! Wait!" Rogers said. Suddenly a big smile spread across his face. "Get ready," he said. "Here it comes!"

At that moment, water began pouring out of the mouth of the pump. For the first few seconds, the water was red with rust, then it cleared.

"Look at that!" Rogers said. "What did I tell you? There's all the water you need. And it's goin' to taste a hell of a lot better than that warm piss for water we had in our canteens."

CHAPTER SEVENTEEN

John Henry had been on the trail for three days when he found what he was looking for. He had traced Lucas Redbone and the others into a canyon.

Actually, he was pretty sure of its location even before he found it, because he had already looked up every other valley and draw within thirty miles of the Boydkin farm and this was the only place left that they could be. Then, when he started exploring this canyon and saw that it had a narrow, easily guarded entrance, he knew he was in the right spot. After that there was nothing for him to do but just dismount and let Iron Heart eat grass while he sat in the shade and kept watch for a while.

It was mid-afternoon when two riders finally exited the canyon. One was short, with a bushy, walrus mustache. The other was an average-sized man, with one eye that was half closed. The description of these two men fit perfectly with the way Mrs. Boydkin had described them.

"Well now, I thought you might show up sooner or later," John Henry said under his breath. He was so close that he could hear them as they were talking.

"I tell you, Tyrone, this may not be the smartest thing we've ever done," Gibson said. "What's Redbone goin' to think when he wakes up from his nap and sees that the two of us have gone?"

"When we come back with a side of beef, he won't say nothin'," Rogers said. "You think he ain't about as tired of eatin' dried jerky as we are?"

"Yeah, I guess so," Gibson replied. "But I still don't know if this is such a good idea. I mean us doin' a job on our own."

"What job would that be?" Rogers replied. "It ain't like we are out rustling cows or somethin' like that. We're goin' to find us one cow, that's all. And we ain't even goin' to move it. We're goin' to kill it on the spot, then butcher it and take back only the choice pieces. We'll be back before sundown and have beef in our bellies before we go to sleep."

The two men continued their conversation, but they rode out of earshot so that John Henry was no longer able to follow what they were saying. It didn't matter. Just from what he heard, he knew that they were acting on their own, and that Redbone wasn't right behind them.

John Henry hurried back to his horse, mounted, then rode parallel with the two riders while taking precautions so as not to be seen. He put his horse into a ground-eating gallop and easily raced ahead of them. Then, a few minutes later, he suddenly appeared on the trail just ahead of the two riders. Startled by his unexpected appearance, both horses reared and Gibson and Rogers had to fight to stay mounted, and bring their animals under control.

John Henry sat his saddle calmly, patting his own horse on the neck so that it wouldn't become excited by the antics of Gibson and Rogers's mounts.

"You two men going somewhere?" John Henry asked easily.

"Who the hell are you?" Rogers shouted. "What do you mean, jumpin' out in front of us like that? Where'd you come from?"

"Whoa, now, that's an awful lot of questions," John Henry said.

Rogers started toward his gun. "Mister, I'm going to . . ."

"You are going to sit there quietly," John Henry said, finishing the sentence. John

Henry cocked the pistol he was already holding in his hand. The metallic sound of the clicking gear as the cylinder rolled into position was cold and frightening, and it stopped Rogers before he made a mistake. Rogers dropped his hand by his side, making no effort to go for his gun.

"There, now, that's more like it," John Henry said. "The two of you undo your gun belts and hand them to me."

Rogers and Gibson did as they were ordered.

"Thanks," John Henry said, hooking the gun belts across his saddle pommel.

"What do you want with us?"

John Henry waved the barrel of his pistol in a motion to indicate they should get going. "I want you to come back to Sequoyah with me."

"You think we're going to ride back to Sequoyah with you just because you asked?" Rogers asked.

"It's your choice. You don't have to go back if you don't want to."

"What do you mean?"

"I'm looking for Lucas Redbone. If I take the two of you back to Sequoyah now, I'm going to lose him. I'd rather just shoot the two of you, so I don't lose Redbone."

"Ha! You're bluffing, Marshal. The truth

is, right now, you don't know whether to scratch your ass or pick your nose," Gibson said. "We've got you in a bind, don't we?"

"Oh, I'm not in that much of a bind," John Henry said. "I'm not going to scratch my ass or pick my nose. I'm just going to kill the two of you and be done with it."

John Henry raised his pistol and aimed it at Rogers's head.

"No, no!" Rogers said, holding up his hands. "We'll come with you!"

"Without giving me any trouble?"

"We won't give you any trouble at all, I promise."

John Henry held the pistol in position for several long seconds, as if trying to make up his mind whether he should just shoot them now, and get on with his search for Redbone.

"Please, Marshal, don't shoot! We'll go with you! We'll go!" Rogers said.

It was nearly sundown by the time John Henry herded his two prisoners back to Sequoyah. A shimmer of sunlight bounced off the roofs and sides of the buildings, painting the town red as he prodded his horse and prisoners down the street toward the office of the Deputy U.S. Marshal.

John Henry rode straight to the jail, then

dismounted and signaled for his prisoners to do the same. He and the prisoners tied their horses to the rail. Deputy Marshal Bill Ferrell met them just in front of the door.

"Well, John Henry, I see that you've brought me some business," Ferrell said. "Come on in, boys. I think you're going to like it here."

"You think you're going to keep us here, do you?" Gibson asked as he and Rogers were led into the jailhouse. "As soon as Redbone finds out where we are, he's going to come in here and take this town apart. You just mark my words."

"You have that much confidence in Redbone, do you?" Ferrell asked. He opened the door to one of the cells, and gave the two men a shove. "Well, then, we'd better keep you where he can find you, don't you think?"

"I'm tellin' you, Deputy, you're makin' a very big mistake," Gibson said again.

"Is that a fact? Well, I'm due a mistake," Deputy Ferrell said. "I was five years old when I made my last mistake. That was thirty years ago." He slammed the door behind them, then turned the key in the lock.

"This is a mistake you ain't likely to walk away from," Gibson said ominously.

"What did they do?" Ferrell asked John Henry as he walked over to rehang the key on the hook on the wall.

"You can ask Mrs. Boydkin and her daughter that. I'm sure she'll identify them."

"Good Lord. Are these the men who killed Mr. Boydkin and his son?"

"I'd bet a year's pay that they are. Mrs. Boydkin can verify it for us."

"I'll get Mrs. Boydkin and her daughter to come into town tomorrow," Ferrell said.

"Good enough. Now I'm going after Red-bone."

"Yeah, he's a bad one all right. Oh, before you leave, you got a telegram from Judge Parker. He sent it to you in care of me, because he figured you would be checking in here from time to time."

"Where is it?"

"In my desk drawer. Just a moment, I'll get it for you."

"Hey, Deputy! What time do we eat around here?" Rogers called.

"You'll eat next Wednesday," Deputy Ferrell called back. "No, wait a minute. We fed the prisoners this Wednesday. I guess you won't be eating until Thursday."

"What?" Rogers called back, the tone of his voice reflecting his despair. "You ain't goin' to feed us for a week?"

Deputy Ferrell laughed out loud and Rogers, realizing he was the butt of Ferrell's joke, swore at him.

John Henry took the telegram.

MARSHAL SIXKILLER, PLEASE RETURN TO FORT SMITH EARLIEST. THE COURT HAS NEW ASSIGNMENT FOR YOU. PARKER

After reading it, John Henry folded up the telegram and stuck it in his pocket. "I guess Redbone is going to have to wait for a while."

"Oh?"

"I've been called back to Fort Smith."

Eagle Hill, Arkansas, was a typical western town, flyblown, with a single street lined on both sides by unpainted false-fronted buildings. It could have been any of several hundred towns in a dozen western states. The most substantial building in Eagle Hill was Nippy's Saloon.

Under the soft, golden light of three gleaming chandeliers, the atmosphere in Nippy's Saloon was quite congenial. Half a dozen men stood at one end of the bar, engaged in friendly conversation, while at the other end, the barkeep stayed busy cleaning glasses. Most of the tables were filled with farmers, draymen, and storekeepers, and they were telling tall tales and flirting with the bar girls who were flitting about the saloon like bees from clover blossom to clover blossom.

It was the middle of summer but the two heating stoves had not been taken down. They were cold now, but when someone got close enough, there was a distinctive aroma of wood smoke from the stoves' winter activity. Mixed with the scent of retired wood smoke were the smells of liquor, tobacco, women's perfume, and the occasional odor of men, too long at work, and with too few baths.

At the moment, John Henry, who had taken advantage of the hotel's bathing room, was now enjoying the ambience of Nippy's Saloon. He was engaged in a game of stud poker with five players he had befriended, including the deputy city marshal, the doctor, the owner of the newspaper, and two of the community's merchants.

"I believe it is your bet, Marshal Sixkiller," the deputy marshal said.

John Henry looked at the pot, then down at his hand. He was showing one five, and two sixes. His down-card was another five.

He had hoped to fill a full house with his last card, but pulled a three, instead.

"Well?" the deputy asked.

It was easy to see why the deputy was anxious. He had John Henry beat, with the three jacks he had showing.

"I fold," John Henry said, closing his cards.

Two of the other players folded, and two stayed, but the three jacks won the pot.

"Thank you, gentlemen, thank you," the deputy said, chuckling as he raked in his winnings.

After a couple of drinks at the bar and a few flirtatious exchanges with one of the bar girls, John Henry went next door to the hotel, then upstairs to his room. He lit the lantern and walked over to the window to adjust it to catch the night breeze. That was when he saw a wink of light in the hay-loft over the livery across the street. He knew, even before he heard the gun report, what it was he had seen and, even though it was too late, he reflexively jerked away from the window, as the bullet crashed through the glass and slammed into the wall on the opposite side of the room.

There was another shot on the heels of the first shot, but by this time John Henry had moved away from the window and dropped down to the floor. He reached up to extinguish the lantern.

"What was that?" someone shouted from down on the street.

"Gunshots. Sounded like they came from the —"

That was as far as the disembodied voice got before yet a third shot crashed through the window. If John Henry thought the first two shots had cleaned out all the glass, he was mistaken, for there was another shattering, tinkling sound of bullets crashing through glass.

With his pistol in his hand, John Henry climbed out of the window, scrambled to the edge of the porch, and dropped down onto the street.

Because he was now in the darkened shadows between the hotel and the saloon, he knew that whoever was over in the livery couldn't see him. That also meant that he couldn't see the man who had been shooting at him, which made the disadvantage equal.

John Henry circled around behind the saloon, then ran up between the saloon and the restaurant which was next door.

"Who is shooting?"

"What's going on?"

"Has anybody been hit?"

"Get off the street! Everyone, get off the street!"

John Henry didn't recognize the first three callers but he recognized the last. It was the voice of the deputy city marshal. John Henry saw him standing just in front of the saloon trying to see what was going on. He also saw, in the dim light cast through the windows of the saloon, the shooter. The shooter was armed with a rifle and stepping into the opening of the loft of the livery, he raised the rifle to his shoulder and took aim at the deputy city marshal.

"Deputy, get down!" John Henry shouted as he raised his pistol to fire at the shooter.

The deputy, hearing both John Henry's shout and the report of the gun, dropped onto the ground. As it turned out, that precaution wasn't necessary. John Henry's pistol shot had been accurate, and the shooter in the livery loft dropped his rifle, grabbed his stomach, then pitched forward, falling hard on the ground below.

With his pistol still in hand, John Henry rushed across the street to check on the man he had shot. He was lying facedown and very still.

"Who is this?" the deputy asked, arriving shortly after John Henry.

Using his foot, John Henry turned the

body over.

"His name is Redbone," John Henry said. "Lucas Redbone."

"Lucas Redbone?" the deputy replied. "I've heard of him, but what is he doing here in Arkansas? I thought he hung around out in Indian Territory."

"Normally, he does. Or he did," John Henry said, correcting himself. "I expect he was here to kill me."

"Let me get this straight, now. He was here to kill you, but you wound up killing him."

"Yes."

The deputy laughed. "Marshal Sixkiller, remind me never to get you pissed off about anything."

Chapter Eighteen

"You may wonder why I invited you back," Parker said.

John Henry chuckled. "I didn't exactly consider it an invitation, Judge. I looked at it more like an order."

"Yeah, you might say that. But invitation or order, you have wondered about it, haven't you?"

"I confess that I have given it some thought," John Henry replied.

"Railroads."

"Railroads?"

"Yes, sir, railroads. The government is about to grant the authority for a railroad — one railroad — to pass through Indian Territory on the way to Texas."

"Yes, I think I have heard something about that."

Judge Parker took another swallow of his drink.

"Well, this is something you may not have

heard. The government says that the railroad that reaches the Indian Territory first will be the one that gets the rights to cross through Indian Territory. That means there is going to be a race between them.

"Now, whichever railroad wins, the race is going to make millions of dollars, and whichever railroad loses is going to be left sucking hind tit. And that kind of setup is a recipe for trouble. I want you to monitor the progress of the railroads."

"All right," John Henry agreed.

Colonel Robert S. Stevens, president of the KATY Railroad was meeting with his chief engineer, Otis Gunn, and his construction boss, John Scullin. On the table between them, maps had been rolled out and held flat by inkwells and paper weights. The maps showed what progress the railroad was making toward Indian Territory. More specifically, the maps were detailing the difficulties they were having and the problems they were facing.

The railroad would not survive unless it could go all the way through to Texas to tap into the lucrative cattle shipment business. But, in order to do that, it would have to cross through Indian Territory. And to win that right, the KATY railroad was in a race with the Border Tier Railroad.

The Border Tier was a formidable opponent, for it was owned by James Joy, who also owned the Chicago, Burlington and Quincy, as well as the Michigan Central. In addition, he had an interest in the New York Central, and he had secured control of the Hannibal and St. Joseph, merging it with the Burlington. Once he completed construction of the Kansas City, St. Joseph and Council Bluffs line, it gave him a through railroad from New York City, via Chicago, Council Bluffs, and Kansas City to the entire frontier.

James Joy had turned his attention to securing a railroad south from Kansas City through the Indian Territory and across Texas, all the way to the Gulf. At the moment, his Border Tier line was at about the same stage of construction as was the KATY. And that meant that the race was going to be bitterly fought.

Colonel Stevens of the KATY line was well aware of the difficulties facing his railroad as he listened to Gunn and Scullin point out the troubles they were encountering.

Scullin, an Irish immigrant, spoke with a heavy accent. "Colonel, sure 'n' m'boys is strung out all the way between here and the border they are, and the half of 'em loafin' and gettin' into mischief for the want of materials and supplies."

"What do you need?" Stevens asked.

"And where would you want me to be startin'? 'Tis ever'thing we are needin'. We need pilin's, masonry, iron, ties, rails, spikes."

"He's telling you the truth, Colonel," Gunn said. "Right now we're being held up at every river, stream, creek, and gully crossing for the lack of iron and timbers to build a bridge."

Colonel Stevens listened to the two men who were the most critical components of his getting the railroad to the Kansas border in time and, in so doing, ensuring the survival of the KATY. He nodded, and stroked his chin before he answered.

"Otis, John, I can't stress this enough. We have to win this race, do you understand? We have no alternative, for if we don't get the right to go through Indian Territory down into Texas, the KATY will not survive. That being the case, I don't want anything to hold us up. If the work trains aren't getting through, then hire teams and wagons. Take on as many men as you want, and hire them from anywhere you can. Buy whatever you need and if you can't buy it, then by

God, just take it. I'll settle accounts later. And get the material laid out ahead of your work crews. I don't want a bunch of men standing around leaning on their shovels and picks because there isn't material to work with.

"From now, until we reach the border of Indian Territory, money is absolutely no object. Spend whatever you need — just get the railroad there ahead of Joy. Do you understand that?"

"You say money is no object. Do we have enough money to do that?"

"I'll hock everything I have, and everything any of my family or friends have. If we succeed, we'll be paid back many times over. If we fail, we'll all be bankrupt, and I might be going to prison for fraud. Understand, this is an all or nothing effort."

"Colonel, if you can get me the material on time, I guarantee that I will get your railroad through. I'll drive the men night and day, rain or shine, drunk or sober."

Stevens smiled. "That's what I want to hear."

Tahlequah, Indian Territory
Marcus Eberwine was a heavy man with large jowls and a protruding lower lip. His skin was whiter than that of the average

white man, and he had eyes that were so light a blue that they were nearly without color. His hair was white, not the white of age, but the white of hair that was without color. Because of his pale and porcine appearance, in such contrast to the average resident of the Indian Territory, he stood out wherever he was.

But even without his distinctive differences, he was a man who would have been noticed because he was one of the wealthiest men in the entire Territory. He owned the Two Feathers Ranch, though as a white man he couldn't actually own it. He did have it on a fifty-year lease, however. But his main source of income was Eberwine Freight Line, which was the most profitable business in all of the Indian Territory. Eberwine had fifty wagons, and he employed one hundred and fifty men, nearly all of whom were Indians, to run his operation.

For most of the retail businesses in The Nations, Eberwine Freight was their supply lifeline, though that lifeline came at great expense. Eberwine charged as much to ship the freight as the freight cost, which meant that if a store owner at Fort Gibson ordered a bolt of cotton material for which he paid five dollars, he would have to pay an additional five dollars to Eberwine's freight line, just to have that bolt transported.

Eberwine also insisted that the merchants who did business with him sign contracts which included a clause that would allow for as much as a thirty percent "loss in shipment." This was supposedly due to such things as weather, accidents, and mishandling. In truth, it was merely a way for Eberwine to skim thirty percent off the top of each shipment.

This morning Eberwine was in his office looking at his ledger when Mr. Deckert, his secretary, came in.

"Mr. Eberwine, Willie Buck is here to see you. If you would like, I can get rid of him for you."

"Why would I want you to do that, Mr. Deckert?"

"Why? Mr. Eberwine, Willie Buck is little more than a criminal. He has been arrested many times."

"And for what? Trying to sell whiskey? That's not much of a crime now, is it? Anywhere else in the country, selling spirits, or running a saloon is an honorable and profitable pursuit. And the fact that Willie Buck has spent no time in jail shows that, even here, the law tends to turn a blind eye toward that minor violation. Besides, Willie Buck is well connected in the Cherokee nation. We couldn't even stay in business if we didn't have people like him in our camp. Show him in."

"Yes, sir."

Buck was tall for an Indian, muscular and athletic. Although he had formed the Indian Independence Council as a means to enable him to take advantage of the opportunities presented by the war, he had expanded his ambition. Now, he wanted to unite the different nations in the Indian Territory under his leadership, then withdraw all connections from the United States and form the independent nation of Tahlequah with himself as the leader.

"What can I do for you, Mr. Buck?"

"I think it's what we can do for each other," Buck replied.

"Oh? And what would that be?"

"Are you aware that the railroads are getting closer and closer to Indian Territory?"

"Yeah," Eberwine said. "I have heard something about it, but I haven't been paying that much attention to it."

"Well, you should be paying attention to it. Right now there are two railroads racing toward the Territory, and the first one to reach the border will be granted the right to take the tracks all the way across Indian Territory, and into Texas. And, they intend to

219

build a settlement every ten miles along the right of way. That would be a settlement of whites. If it reaches the point to where there are more whites in Indian Territory than there are Indians, this land will no longer belong to us."

"That won't be good for you, will it?" Eberwine asked.

"No, it won't. But how good will it be for you, if you have to compete with a railroad for your freighting business?"

"You have a point. Do you also have a solution?"

"Yes, I have a solution," Buck offered.

"Let's hear it."

"Suppose we made it difficult for them to build the line. Too difficult."

"How?"

"Well, if, say, their building materials would get burned, or if the track they laid one day would be torn up the next, that would make progress difficult, wouldn't it? What if the graders and track layers were too busy fighting off attacks to construct the railroad? Something like that might make them abandon the project."

"How are we going to do that, without having it come right back to us?"

"Easy," Buck said. "When we attack the KATY line, we'll let it be known that we represent the Border Tier Railroad. And when we attack the Border Tier, we'll be attacking for the KATY line. Pretty soon we'll have them fighting each other so much that nothing will be built. And the beauty of it is, by that time, we'll be staying out of it, watching them destroy each other."

Eberwine laughed. "Are you sure you are Indian? That plan has all the deviousness of a white man."

"Yes, well, I've been around enough white men to pick up their evil ways," Buck replied with a chuckle.

"All right, let's do it. We'll stir the pot, so to speak."

Percy Martin was wanted in Indiana, Ohio, and Illinois. So far he was not wanted in Missouri, Arkansas, or Kansas, and Eberwine was paying him to act as an enforcer among his employees, and as a collector for debts Eberwine considered overdue.

He was very careful to have Martin crowd the line toward illegality in his dealings with employees and debtors, but not cross it. As he explained it to Martin when he hired him, "From time to time I shall require certain services that only someone like you can perform. Should that time come, I would want you immediately available, and not in jail somewhere. Therefore, until such time as I need you, I want you to stay out of trouble."

When Eberwine began to contemplate Willie Buck's suggestion of instigating a war between the two competing railroads, Percy Martin was the first name that came to his mind.

"You sent for me, Mr. Eberwine?" Martin asked, stepping into Eberwine's office.

"Yes."

"Who's getting out of line? Who do you want me to straighten out?"

"It's not like that this time," Eberwine said. "This time I'm going to ask you to do something that is very much illegal. But you will be adequately compensated for it."

"What does that mean?"

"It means I will pay you well."

"How well?"

"Five hundred dollars."

"Damn!" Martin said, his eyes shining in excitement. "Five hundred dollars? Who do you want me to kill?"

"Nobody. At least, not yet, and not purposely, though some of the things I'm going to ask you to do might result in someone dying. Will that bother you?"

"For five hundred dollars? Hell no, it doesn't bother me a bit. That is, as long as I ain't the one doin' the dyin'."

"Good. I'm sure then that we can do business."

CHAPTER NINETEEN

"You're serious? You're goin' to give us twenty-five dollars apiece just to pull up this rail?" Evers asked.

"That's right."

"After we pull up the rail, then what?" Tinker asked.

"Then nothing. You get your twenty-five dollars and I don't care what you do with it."

"What if a train comes along after we pull up this rail?" Evers asked.

"What if it does?"

"Well, hell, a train can't run if there ain't a rail for it to run on, can it?"

"No, I don't think it can."

"So if a train comes along with this rail pulled up, it'll more'n likely wreck, won't it?"

"More'n likely," Martin agreed.

"Whooeee, damn!" Evers said. "That'll be a sight to see!"

"Not unless you get this rail pulled up."

"Come on, Tinker, let's get this pulled up. I'm goin' to enjoy watchin' this."

After the rail was removed, Martin, unnoticed by the other two men, left a folded piece of paper lying on the rail, held down by a rock.

"Let's go," Martin said, walking toward his horse.

"Go? Hell, you mean we ain't goin' to stay around and watch the wreck?"

"You want to go to prison?"

"Prison? No."

"Well, that's where we'll all be goin' if anyone finds out we did this. My advice is to get out of here now, while we still can."

"Damn. I wanted to watch."

"You can stay if you want to. But I've got another job that will pay twenty-five dollars if you want it. But if you don't, I can always find someone else to do it."

"No, no, I'll do it," Evers said.

The three men mounted their horses and rode away, but Evers stopped once, turned in his saddle, and looked back. "Damn, I'd like to see that train wreck, though."

"Not me," Tinker said. "I just want to get the hell out of here."

Engine number 275 of the Border Tier

Railroad was just south of Girard, Kansas, pulling six cars loaded with rails, ties, and spikes. The rails made for a heavy load so the train was traveling at little more than ten miles an hour, smoke pouring from the stack and steam gushing from the cylinders.

Austin Mueller was the engineer, and he was sitting on a small, triangular seat by the right window, with the stub of a pipe clamped between his teeth. Ray Cathcart was the fireman, and he was throwing chunks of wood into the boiler furnace.

"You know what I've always wanted to do?" Mueller asked, taking the pipe out. "I've always wanted to get out on the high iron with nothing more than the tender behind me, and open this thing up to as fast it can go. Why, I bet we could get her up to sixty, maybe seventy miles an hour! Jumpin' Jehoshaphat! Now, that would be a ride, wouldn't it, Ray?"

"A ride for you, maybe," Cathcart replied. "Now me, I'd be all asshole and elbows keeping the furnace fed."

Mueller laughed. "Maybe so, but it would sure be —" Mueller stopped in mid-sentence. "What the hell! Grab ahold on to somethin', Ray!" he shouted.

Mueller pulled on the brake and the train began sliding along the rail, steel screeching on steel heading for a place where one of the rails had been removed.

"What is it?" Cathcart called.

"Jump!" Mueller shouted.

The two men jumped off the train, and hit the ground rolling. Then they got up and moved away from the track. It was good they did, because as the engine hit the breach in the track, the great driver wheels dug into the dirt and that turned over the engine. The boiler burst with a huge explosion and a gush of steam.

Behind the engine the flatcars, laden with rails, kegs of spikes, cross ties, and railroad working tools, also went off the track and turned over, spilling the material over a wide area.

Mueller and Cathcart stood there, now out of harm's way, watching as the cars continued to twist and tumble, the air filled with the cacophony of steel crashing against steel.

"What the hell happened?" Cathcart asked. "What did you see?"

"One of the rails was missing," Mueller said.

"You mean it come loose?"

"I think it was more than that. I think somebody pulled it up of a pure purpose," Mueller said.

With the tumble of the cars and the falling and shifting of the cargo ended, it was now safe to go to the point on the track where the rail had been removed. Wisps of steam were still drifting up from the overturned engine.

"You're right, Austin," Cathcart said. "Lookie down there. There's the missing rail a' lyin' there just as pretty as you please. And you can bet that it didn't get there without someone carried it there."

"Who the hell would do somethin' like that? Why, if we had been haulin' passengers, a lot of 'em would'a got themselves kilt," Mueller said.

"And we damn near did," Cathcart replied.

The two men walked down the grade to look at the rail, and that's when Mueller saw it, a folded piece of paper on the rail, held in place by a rock that was so large that he almost didn't see the paper.

"What is that?" Cathcart asked.

"I don't know," Mueller said. "But I reckon we're about to find out."

Mueller opened the folded piece of paper and read the note that was attached:

We will do whatever it takes to be the first railroad into the Indian Territory.

"Son of a bitch. You know who done this, Ray?"

"Who?"

"The KATY Railroad, that's who. Them cheatin' bastards will do anything to get to the border first."

"I don't believe they'd wreck a train," Cathcart said.

"You, don't? Here, read this." Muller handed the note to Cathcart.

"I'll be damned," is all Cathcart said after he read it.

Ten miles south of Humboldt, Kansas, Otis Gunn had established a staging area for the material he was gathering for construction of the KATY line. Here were stacks of treated timbers to be used as cross ties, as well as kegs of spikes and fishplates.

Under cover of darkness, Martin, Evers, and Tinker sneaked into the supply yard. Using kerosene as an accelerant, they soaked the stacks of timbers and the kegs of spikes and fishplates. Then they splashed kerosene on the wooden building that held the tools needed for laying track. That done, they struck matches and set fires which, within a few minutes, became a roaring inferno. Also consumed in the fire were the timbers, already precut, that were to have been used

for bridging a deep gully. Before withdraw-
ing, Martin left a note attached to an
unburned tie.

Two blocks from the fire, Corey McElwain
stepped out of the Railroad Saloon. He
smelled smoke as soon as he stepped outside, and looking down toward the railroad
storage area, he saw orange flames lifting
into the sky. He knew, immediately, what he
was seeing.

"Fire!" he called. "The railroad supply
dump is on fire!"

A couple more people came out of the
saloon then, summoned by his shout, and
they began shouting as well. One of them
pulled his pistol and began shooting into
the air. By now, several others had heard
the commotion and they, too, came out to
see what was going on.

Someone ran down to the fire station and
began banging on the steel triangle, signal-
ing to all the volunteer firemen that they
were needed. Soon the whole town was
turned out and the pumper wagon was
drawn from the station and rushed down
the street toward the fire.

Almost as soon as the volunteer firemen
got there, though, they knew that there was
no hope of extinguishing the fire, or even

preventing the fire from spreading. It was a huge fire, covering at least half an acre of land, burning every building and every stick of timber in the equipment supply area.

"I've never seen a fire quite that large!" one of the fireman said.

"Get on it! Get it put out!" Otis Gunn shouted. "This is damn near all the material we've got!"

"We're doing what we can, Mr. Gunn," the fire chief said. He shook his head. "But with a fire this big, there just isn't much we can do."

The firefighters quickly emptied their pumper of water, but the fire was so large that the pumper had no effect whatever.

The only thing they could do was refill the pumper, then start directing the water toward the buildings that were nearest the burning supply compound. This they did in hopes that the fire wouldn't spread any farther. And in that effort, at least, they were successful, because the fire was contained.

By the next morning the fire was out, not due to anything done by any of the firefighting volunteers, but simply because the terrible fire had consumed all available fuel. Those who had fought the fire all through the night, and that included most of the town, were standing around, dazed, not only by exhaustion, but by the enormity of the event.

"Somebody needs to get word to Colonel Stevens," one of the railroad workers said.

"It's already been done," Otis Gunn said. "I sent a telegram to him more'n an hour ago, tellin' him about the fire."

"What's this goin' to do to us, Mr. Gunn? You think it'll stop the railroad from buildin'?" one of the track layers asked.

"If I know Colonel Stevens, it won't do much more than slow him down," Gunn said.

"Mr. Gunn?" the fire chief called. "Come over here, you might want to see this."

Gunn walked over toward the fire chief who showed him a note.

"I'll be damned. Some son of a bitch set this fire of a pure purpose," Gunn said.

As soon as he learned about the fire, Colonel Stevens, and his construction engineer, John Scullin, put together a special train to take them to the site. Otis Gunn met them, then walked over to the blackened area where the supply depot had been.

Most of the people of the town who had come to help fight the fire were still there, wandering around. New gawkers had come as well, and it was easy to tell the difference between those who had actually fought the fire, and those who were the merely curious because the firefighters had blackened faces, while the Johnny-come-latelies were clean skinned. The smell of burned wood permeated the whole town. Little wisps of smoke were still drifting up from the site as railroad workers walked through the destruction to see if anything could be salvaged.

The Humboldt fire chief came over to talk to them.

"I'm just real sorry about this, Colonel, but by the time we got here, the fire was too big for us to deal with," the chief said. "I'll tell you the truth, the fire was so big that, for a while there, I didn't know but what we might lose the entire town. We wet down the closest buildings to the fire, but that was all we could do."

"I can't imagine how this started," Stevens said. "Careless smoker? What?"

"I don't see how someone's pipe, or even a cigar, could cause a fire this large," the chief said. "No, sir, this fire was going in too many places at the same time for it to be an accident."

"Look here, Chief, are you telling me the fire was deliberately set?"

"Yes, sir, that is exactly what I'm telling you."

"Show him the note, Chief Hanlon," Gunn said.

"What note?" Stevens asked.

Chief Hanlon held out a folded piece of paper.

"Where did you get this?"

"It was tacked on to a cross tie."

"It couldn't have been," Stevens said. "It's not in the least charred."

"Yes, sir. Well, the cross tie it was tacked to was lying across the track well away from the fire. Like it had been put there on purpose, just so's this note wouldn't get burned."

Stevens unfolded the paper, and read the note.

We will do whatever it takes to be the first railroad into the Indian Territory.

He got a set, angry expression on his face. "I'll be damned," he said. "It was Joy."

"Joy?" Scullin asked.

"Probably not him, personally. But it was his men." Stevens showed the note to Scullin.

Scullin read it, then he clenched his teeth and his temple throbbed in anger. Finally, he spoke.

"Yes, sir, but don't you be worryin' none about this, Colonel," Scullin said. "Because what I plan to do is take me a bunch of Irish lads and we'll be for teachin' Mr. Joy and his outfit a thing or two. Yes, sir, you can count on that."

"Scullin, don't kill anyone," Stevens said. "The last thing we need now is to get bogged down in some murder trial."

"We won't be needin' to do any killin' to teach this lesson. But you can bet there will be a few boys wishin' they was dead by the time we get finished with them."

"Where are you going?"

"I'm told that end of track for the Border Tier is just north of Columbus. Like as not the gandy dancers will be comin' in town tonight. We'll just be there to meet 'em. After we get through with 'em, they won't be wantin' to lay track for a while, that's for sure."

"What about the men you take with you? Will they be up to working tomorrow?"

"Now is it kiddin' me you are, Colonel Stevens? Sure 'n' 'tis Irishmen I'll be takin' with me, and there's niver been an Irishman who couldn't fight until midnight and answer the call the next mornin'."

Stevens smiled. "Then, by all means, take your Irishmen and do battle for the KATY."

Chapter Twenty

It was a little after nine p.m. and business was booming in the Ace High Saloon. At least ten of the customers were from the Border Tier track-laying crew. They were drinking, and flirting with the bar girls, in general having a good time when seven men came into the saloon, then stood just inside the bating doors.

"And would there be any scum-sucking, low-life Border Tier men in here?" Scullin shouted.

"Well, now, what have we here?" one of the Border Tier men replied. "Is there a circus nearby? I think a bunch of monkeys have escaped."

With a guttural yell, Scullin and the six men with him charged into the middle of the floor, met by ten of the Border Tier men.

The KATY men were slightly outnumbered but, by a strange coincidence, all of them happened to be carrying a small club, cut from two-inch thick dowels. Some of the saloon patrons who were not part of the Border Tier pitched in as well, though they were so quickly dispatched that nobody else joined. Instead, those who were not railroad workers, as well as the bar girls, and even the piano player, backed up against the wall, out of the way, watching as the fight continued.

There were curses, shouts of anger and pain, and the crash of furniture.

The battle lasted for no more than three minutes as Scullin and his boys made quick work of the Border Tier men.

"Get out of here!" Scullin yelled, holding aloft his truncheon. "Get out of here before we break all your skulls!"

The few Border Tier men who could still walk carried or helped the others clear the saloon. When all were gone, Scullin gave a loud yell.

"Huzzah, boys! Now, let's drink up!"

The victorious KATY men rushed to the bar and the bartender was suddenly busy again. The bar girls, now with the Border Tier men gone, resumed their flirtations, but this time with Scullin and his men.

Two days later six KATY men — none of whom had taken part in the raid on the Ace

High saloon, were attacked as they were grading the right of way for the KATY. There were nine Border Tier men, and like the KATY men in the Ace High fight, all were equipped with truncheons which were just the right size to be easily handled, and to inflict painful injuries. When they left, three of the KATY men wound up with broken bones.

For the next few days the fights continued, as the KATY sent raiding parties out after the Border Tier workers, and the Border Tier responded in kind.

Willie Buck showed Marcus Eberwine a copy of the *Doster Defender* newspaper.

Fighting Threatens Railroad

There are two railroads vying for the goal of transiting Indian Territory, James Joy's Border Tier, and Colonel Robert Stevens's KATY Railroad. This contest has deteriorated into a physical battle between the two companies as, on several occasions, there have been clashes between great groups of men.

These battles have not only caused several injuries, to include broken bones and severe cuts and abrasions, but have also brought to a complete halt all construction. The West, indeed the entire nation, is waiting for the successful crossing of Indian Territory, which will bring Texas beef to the Eastern markets, but that seems unlikely unless the two companies declare a truce between them.

Eberwine read the article, then smiled. "Willie Buck, my boy!" he said, thumping the paper with the back of his hand. "I believe we may just have won the war."

"Were you in the war, Eberwine?" Buck asked.

"No, I, uh, managed to avoid that unpleasantness."

"Well, I was in the war."

"Oh? Were you a member of Colonel Sixkiller's regiment? It was the Second Cherokee Mounted Rifles, I believe."

"No, I want nothing to do with any Sixkiller."

"Oh, yes, of course. I heard about the episode of him arresting you, and destroying a wagonload of your liquor. I can see how that would make him your enemy."

"It didn't start there. Sixkiller and I have been enemies for many years. Anyway, the reason I asked if you had been to war was to make a point. It is far too early to say that we have won more than a battle."

■ ■ ■ ■

The railroads continued to war against each other until James Joy sent word to Robert Stevens that they should meet.

"Look here, Colonel, I don't like the looks of this," Scullin said. "I mean, what if he gets you off by yourself and — does something to you?"

"Mr. Scullin, James Joy is a fierce opponent who will take advantage of any situation, but I scarcely think he would do anything to harm me."

"Och, and 'tis not so sure I am of that," Scullin said. "You saw what he did to our materials storage depot. Why . . . if Mr. Gunn had been staying in the shack there, instead of at the hotel, he could have been killed in that fire."

"Do you expect him to murder me?" Stevens asked.

"No, I'm not for thinkin' that. But what if he has it in mind to snatch you, and hold you prisoner to keep the KATY from buildin' any farther?"

"I'll tell you what, Mr. Scullin. If it will make you feel any better, you can go with me as my bodyguard."

"Aye, lad, 'twould make me feel much

better."

Joy had suggested that they meet in Garnett, Kansas, which was not only a neutral site, but was accessible by railroad.

"I see you've brought your strong man with you," Joy said.

"Aye, and 'tis keepin' an eye open I will for any of your underhandedness," Scullin said.

"My underhandedness? And who was it that attacked my men in Columbus?"

"See here, Joy," Stevens said. "Can we not compete like honorable men?"

"There was nothing honorable about you wrecking my supply train, nor was there anything honorable about your thugs beating up my men," Joy replied.

"Wrecking your supply train? Why, I did no such thing. But if I had done it, it would be no less honorable than you setting fire to my supplies," Stevens replied.

"I did not set fire to your supplies," Joy said, "though I certainly had every right to do so, since you wrecked my supply train."

"I told you, I did not wreck your supply train."

"Oh? Then how do you explain this? It was left at the site of the wreck."

Joy showed Stevens the note.

We will do whatever it takes to be the first railroad into the Indian Territory.

Stevens looked at the note. "I'll be damned," he said.

"Uh-huh. It's hard to lie about it when the evidence is put before you, isn't it?" Joy asked.

Stevens reached into his own pocket and pulled out a note. "This note was left at the scene of the fire, when your men — or somebody — burned my supplies."

"Or somebody? What note?"

Stevens handed the note to Joy.

We will do whatever it takes to be the first railroad into the Indian Territory.

"That's — that's the same note," Joy said.

"And the same handwriting. Look how the letter *f* is formed. It is backwards on both notes."

"What is this?"

"Someone, and I don't know who it is, doesn't want either one of us to cross into Indian Territory," Stevens said.

"But why?"

Stevens shook his head. "I'm afraid I can't answer that, James. I have no idea who it is, or why he is doing it. But it is pretty obvious that he intended for us to do just as we have done, start warring with each other."

"What do you propose we do about this?" Joy asked.

"We could swear a gentleman's oath, here and now, that neither of us will use physical force against the other, nor will we make any attempt to destroy the other's property," Stevens suggested.

"I so swear," Joy said, extending his hand.

"Just so that we are clear about this, the oath we are taking declares that I will not use physical force against you, or your men, nor will I attempt to destroy any more of your equipment, or your track already laid. And you are making the same promise to me. Is that how you understand it?"

"It is."

The two men shook hands, and their agreement was made.

Over the next week, both the Border Tier and the KATY railroads continued to make progress, neither railroad impeded by the activity of the other. The renewed effort was noticed by newspapers all through Kansas, Arkansas, and Missouri.

The *Doster Defender,* which had earlier highlighted the difficulty, now printed a story filled with hope that the railroads would continue their competition, fairly.

Competing Railroads Make Agreement

James Joy and Robert Stevens, both known to be men of great honor and integrity, have shaken hands on an agreement to compete fairly. The prize of their competition, to be awarded to the first railroad to reach the border between Kansas and the Indian Territory, is to be a government-sanctioned right of passage through the Territory into Texas.

Of late, there has been some difficulty as fighting has broken out among the railroad workers, resulting in some injuries. There was also damage done to the real property of each of the railroads, though it has been determined by Joy and Stevens, that the damage was the result of a third party, perhaps trying to stir up trouble between them. The identity of the third party is not known, nor is there known the reason for such perfidy.

Eberwine had enjoyed the earlier article detailing the troubles between the two railroads, but this article troubled him. Not only had the railroads made peace with each other, they seemed to have figured out that the trouble between them was being caused by a third party.

It was in the open that there was a third party behind the trouble, but nobody knew who it was. Better yet, nobody knew the reason for the attacks on the railroad, for if someone had been able to ascertain the motive, they could surely trace it back to him.

It was time to take another step, and to that end, he called upon Percy Martin again.

"I've got another job for you," Eberwine said.

"You want me to wreck another train?"

"No. I just want you to make a nuisance raid against the town of Ladore."

"Ladore? Why?"

"Why should it matter to you, as long as it is worth another five hundred dollars?"

Martin smiled. "Five hundred dollars?"

"And anything you manage to take from the town. Do you think you can do that?"

"What do you mean, anything I manage to take from the town?"

"Ladore is at the end of track for the KATY railroad. There are a lot of workers there. This is the end of the week, and most of them have just been paid."

"You're saying I should rob the workers?"

"No, far be it from me to tell you how to take advantage of a small town with no law, and filled with people who have money in

their pockets. People who are railroad workers, I might add, and who are unarmed. I
would think that if there was enough trouble
stirred up in the town, that it might have
the effect of delaying the building. Do you
think you could do something like that?"

"Yeah," Martin said. "Yeah, I know I can
do something like that."

CHAPTER TWENTY-ONE

Two days later Percy Martin and six more heavily armed men rode into the town of Ladore, which was just across the border into Kansas. Ladore had sprung up at the end of track for the KATY Railroad and, like end-of-track towns all across the West, it was a place designed to take advantage of the most basic needs of the men who were building the railroad. There was a livery, grocery store, and apothecary, but the most lucrative businesses in Ladore were those that involved whiskey and prostitution.

Percy had been hired by Marcus Eberwine to do what he could to disrupt the building of the railroad. He was initially paid five hundred dollars, but had the bonus of being able to keep anything he managed to round up during the operation.

Neither Evers nor Tinker, nor any of the other men who were riding with him, knew anything about the money Martin had been given by Eberwine. Martin told them only that if they would come into Ladore, there would be an opportunity to "make a little money, and have some fun, besides."

"Hey, Martin," Evers asked, "how are we going to make any money here? Hell, there ain't even so much as a bank."

"That's goin' to make it even easier," Martin said.

"How?"

Martin pointed to a hastily constructed, ripsawed lumber building. The sign on the outside, roughly painted, read RAILROAD SALOON.

"Suppose we go in there and have a few drinks. We can discuss this inside."

"Sounds like it might be a good idea, if I had enough money for a drink," Tinker said.

"I'll buy the drinks for all of us. By the end of the day I figure everyone will have enough money to pay me back."

The others, agreeing to the proposition, swung down from their saddles and tied their horses off, then walked into the saloon.

"Get a table. I'll get us a bottle and some glasses," Martin said.

The men couldn't find one table big enough for all of them, so they pulled two together. Martin stepped up to the bar.

"Yes, sir?" the bartender said.

"Give me a bottle of whiskey and seven glasses."

"If there's seven of you, one bottle won't go very far," the bartender said.

"How much is your whiskey?"

"Three dollars a bottle."

"Three dollars? Look here, I ain't askin' for sippin' whiskey. All we want to do is get drunk."

"Well, you ain't goin' to do it for less'n three dollars. And as many of you as there are, you'll be needin' at least two bottles, and that'll be six dollars."

"All right, all right, if that's the best you can do. Bring it over to that table," he said, pointing to the other men.

The men drank for the rest of the day, going through four more bottles of whiskey. Then, as it started to get dark outside, Martin held up his hand. "All right, boys, it's time to start makin' a little money."

"How we goin' to do that?" Evers asked.

"Ever'one in this town is workin' for the railroad, and the railroad pays good wages," Martin replied.

"So?"

"I know that the railroad paid today, and if there ain't no bank for 'em to put their money in, whereat do you reckon that money is goin' to be?"

"Ha!" Tinker said. "They'll have the money on 'em."

"That they will," Martin said. "It's goin' to be like takin' candy from a baby. They's seven of us. We'll just sort of wander through the town and take whatever we want from anyone we might happen to run across."

"Yeah," Evers said. "Yeah, I like that."

The seven men left the saloon just as the evening crowd was beginning to come in. They weren't a block away before they came upon their first victim, a man who was walking up the road toward them.

"Hey!" Martin called out to him. "Where you goin'?"

"I'm goin' to the saloon, if it's any of your business," the man answered.

"You can't go to the saloon without you got money. And I'd say you didn't have one cent on you."

"Don't you worry about me. I got money."

Martin smiled. "You don't say." He nodded to the others and, too late, the man realized that he had made a mistake. The men were on him before he could cry out. He was knocked down and beaten senseless, then robbed.

"Damn!" Tinker said. "The son of a bitch didn't have but eight dollars on him."

"I'll take that," Martin said, holding his

hand out.

"Why should you get it?" Evers asked.

"I paid for all the whiskey, remember? Don't worry, we'll split up the next one."

"Yeah? Well, we damn sure better," Evers insisted.

"That wouldn't be a threat, would it, Mr. Evers?" Martin asked.

"Not a threat, just puttin' in my claim is all," Evers replied.

With their action shielded by darkness, the men wandered around the town, pouncing on the hapless railroad workers, beating them, then relieving them of any cash they might have on them. In this way, they managed to attack six more men, coming up with a grand total of one hundred and nine dollars, which they divided among themselves. As the division didn't come out even, Martin pocketed the extra money.

"Hey, what do you think that buildin' is down there?" one of the men asked, pointing to a rather large building about a quarter of a mile south of the rest of the town.

"Looks to me like it's a house," Tinker said.

"If it is, it's a pretty big house," Evers noted.

"Yeah, well, anyone livin' in a house that big has got to have money, don't you think?"

Evers asked.

Martin smiled. "Yeah, I think."

The men walked through the darkness until they reached the building.

"This don't look like no house to me," Tinker said.

"It ain't. Look at that sign," Martin said. "It's a boardinghouse."

"A boardinghouse? You mean a place where people pay money to stay?" Evers asked.

"Yeah, a boardinghouse where people pay money to stay," Martin said.

"I wonder if they have any of the money with them?"

"Where else would it be? Like I said, there ain't no bank here," Martin said. "Come on, let's pay them a little visit."

When the seven men went inside, they found themselves in a little entry area, separated from the rest of the floor by a counter. On the other side of the counter was what appeared to be the apartment where the owner and his family lived. There was an older man and two young women sitting at a table, eating, but when Martin and the others came in, the man got up and, wiping his lips with a napkin, came toward them.

"I'm sorry I wasn't at the counter," he

253

said. "My daughters and I were just having our supper. My name is Roach."

"You run the place do you, Mr. Roach?" Martin asked.

"I do, indeed. But if you are wantin' a bed, I'm afraid we are all full up. However, if you'd like, you can sleep out in the barn. The hay is clean, and it'll only cost you a nickel apiece. A dime each if you want a blanket."

"Yeah, we'll do that," Martin said. "With blankets."

"All right, the blankets are under here," the man said, leaning over to reach under the counter.

That was when Martin brought the butt of his pistol down hard on the man's head.

"Papa!" one of the young women at the table shouted.

"Get the women," Martin ordered as he knelt down and hit the unconscious man again.

"No! No!" one of the young women said. "Please, don't hit him again!"

"Shut 'em up, but don't kill 'em. We'll have some fun with 'em," Martin said.

The two girls, ages seventeen and nineteen, were gagged so they couldn't call out, then dragged from the house to the nearby woods. There, they were stripped down, and the men began taking their turns with them.

Evers was about to go to one of them when Martin reached out to grab him by the shoulder and pulled him away.

"It's my time," Martin said.

"The hell it is," Evers replied. "This here is first come, first served, and I was here first."

"I said it was my time," Martin said. He pushed Evers away and Evers responded with a right cross to Martin's jaw, knocking him down.

"Ha!" Evers said. "I reckon that'll teach you to mess with ole Harry Evers."

From his position flat on his back, Martin drew his pistol and fired at Evers. Evers went down and Martin regained his feet, then walked over to Evers's form. He looked down at him, then, with his foot, turned the body over. There was a black bullet hole in the middle of Evers's forehead.

"Son of a bitch!" Martin said. "Now that was quite a shot!" He looked at the others, who were looking at him in shock. "Like I said, this one is mine. Anyone got an argument with that?"

"What did you kill him for?" Tinker asked.

"The son of a bitch hit me," Martin replied. "I don't let anyone hit me and get away with it. Anyone got 'ny argument with that?"

No one did.

"Come on, honey, me 'n' you's goin' to have some fun," Martin said to the younger of the two girls.

When Percy Martin woke up at about two o'clock in the morning, the two girls were gone. The men were still here, but all five of them were passed out drunk. Martin went through their pockets to take what money they had, then he left.

Less than half an hour after Martin left, the two girls, Betsy and Carol, returned, leading at least ten armed men.

"That's them," Betsy said, pointing to the sleeping figures.

The self-appointed leader of the posse was a man named Jim Abell and he walked over to the closest sleeping man and kicked him hard, in the side. The man grunted.

"Get up!" Abell said. "Get up, you son of a bitch!"

"What is it? What do you want?" the man said.

"What is your name?" Abell asked. He was holding a shotgun leveled toward the man on the ground.

"Tinker. Gerald Tinker. Who are you?"

"I'm the man that's going to hang your sorry ass, along with all your friends. Get up, now! All of you!"

By now the others were awake and, gradually, they began to stand.

"You, too!" Abell called to one of the men who had made no effort to stand.

"Won't do you no good to yell at him," Tinker said. "That's Harry Evers. He ain't goin' to stand."

"Oh? And why won't he stand?"

"He ain't goin' to stand 'cause he's dead. Percy Martin killed him."

"Which one is Percy Martin?"

Tinker looked at the other four men. "He ain't here," Tinker said. "He's gone."

"Hey!" one of the other men said. "My money's all gone!"

"Mine, too," another said.

"Martin! That son of a bitch took all our money!"

Ladore had never incorporated itself as a city, so it had no city government, no mayor, and no marshal. But it had a population of over two hundred and fifty people, all of them connected with the railroad in one way or the other, so they declared themselves a town, then held court in the saloon,

257

which was the biggest building in town. They selected Jim Abell to act as the judge, and two of their members, both of whom had some college, were appointed as prosecutor and defense counsel. Next, they empaneled a jury.

"Before this trial even starts, let me tell you what argument I will not hear for the defense," Abell said. "I will not hear, as argument for the defense, that we have no right to try these men."

"But, Your Honor, without that, the defense has no case," Gilmore said.

"You are an intelligent man, Mr. Gilmore. Come up with a defense," Abell ordered.

Larry Nickel, the citizen selected as the prosecutor, presented a strong case which included the tearful testimony of the two Roach sisters, Betsy and Carol. Ed Roach, the girls' father and owner of the boarding-house, made just as powerful a presentation as he sat in the witness chair with his head in bandages from the pistol-whipping he had suffered at the hands of the five men who were being tried.

For the defense, Gilmore argued that the man who had actually done the pistol-whipping was Percy Martin, and that Martin had avoided capture. And when the girls said that they had kept their eyes closed during the assaults on them, Gilmore suggested that they could not positively connect the individual defendants with a specific rape. He was willing to concede, however, that Percy Martin, the man who escaped, and Harry Evers, the man Martin had killed, probably were guilty of rape.

"And, it would be easy to see how these poor young women, so brutalized and degraded, might be led into thinking that all the men took part in the rape, when only two were guilty — the two who are not present today."

Abell congratulated Gilmore for his "valiant effort," then charged the jury with finding a verdict.

The jury reached the verdict in less than five minutes, and Abell sentenced the five men to be hanged by the neck until dead.

"You got no right to do this!" Tinker shouted. "This ain't no real court!"

"It's as close to a court as you men are going to get," Abell said.

"Hey, Abell, where are we goin' to keep these men till we can get us a gallows built?" someone asked.

"We don't need a gallows," Abell said.

"How are we goin' to hang 'em, if we don't have a gallows?"

"The hackberry tree just south of town,"

Abell said. "It's got one long, strong limb that reaches out. All we have to do is trim away a few of the smaller branches from that limb, and we can use it. And what makes it so perfect is it is long enough to hang all five of 'em at the same time."

CHAPTER TWENTY-TWO

John Henry had been sent to Ladore by Marshal Sarber to look into the trouble between the railroads.

"In what was either a brilliant move, or something incredibly stupid, the federal government has said that only one railroad could enter The Nations, and that prize was to go to the first railroad to reach the border," Sarber had told him. "As I'm sure you can well imagine, that competition has caused all kinds of trouble."

"Between the railroads?"

"You guessed it. They are not only doing everything they can to be there first, they are doing whatever they can to see that their competition doesn't make it. That's where you come in."

"I understand. You want me to see that the competition between the railroads is fairly contested."

"That is exactly what I want," Marshal

Sarber had told him

And, with that charge, John Henry Six-killer left Fort Smith to look into the situation.

Even before John Henry reached the town of Ladore that afternoon, he saw the frenzied activity of buzzards ahead. There were too many of them for it to be something small. He might have thought they were gathering around a dead horse or cow, except for the way they were behaving. These buzzards were flying in circles, only rarely committing to a diving attack to whatever it was that had drawn them.

John Henry knew, even before he reached the town, that the buzzards were circling a human corpse. The fact that buzzards were frightened of men, even when they were dead, caused them to be somewhat hesitant. He knew also, though, that once they got over their initial fear, they would make fairly quick work of the corpse.

As he came farther into town he saw what had attracted the buzzards. Stopping, he sub-consciously ran his finger down the lightning bolt flash of the scar on his face, and studied the scene before him. It wasn't just one corpse that had attracted the buzzards, for there in front of him, suspended from a long, and solid branch of a hackberry tree, were five men. They were hanging by their necks, their heads crooked to one side in the way that was peculiar to a hanged man.

There had been nothing in Sarber's instructions that mentioned a lynching. Also, these corpses were still fresh. Neither buzzard attacks nor decomposition had yet sullied the corpses, so John Henry knew that this had to be something that had just happened.

As he rode by the dangling men, he saw that a sign had been pinned to one of them.

THESE FIVE MEN WERE
MURDERERS AND RAPISTS.

HANGING WAS <u>TOO</u> <u>GOOD</u>
FOR THEM.

Technically, Ladore was not a town, in that it had not been incorporated. And because it was not a town, it had neither law, nor a court, therefore it appeared to John Henry that the five men had been lynched. His first thought was that their deaths were somehow connected with the competition between the railroads to be first to reach the border of the Indian Territory.

But that would not explain the sign that referred to them as "murderers and rapists."

When someone saw John Henry paying attention to the five suspended corpses, he rode out to meet him. That was when he saw the badge on John Henry's chest.

"I see by the badge on your chest that you are the law. May I inquire as to what branch of law you represent?"

"I am John Henry Sixkiller, United States Marshal. And you are?"

"My name is Jim Abell, sir," Abell replied. "I must say, I thought what we did might attract the law, but I didn't expect anyone to come this quickly."

"Oh?"

"No, sir, I did not. Seeing as we only strung these men up this very morning."

"They do look fresh," John Henry admitted.

"How did you find out about it?"

"I saw them hanging here."

"No, I mean, how did you hear about them?" Abell took in the five hanging men with a motion of his hand.

"I didn't hear about them. I knew nothing about them until I saw them hanging here."

"This isn't what brought you here?"

"No."

"I see. Well, seeing as you are a U.S.

Marshal and all, I figured you were here because of this. Does this mean you aren't planning to look in to it?"

"You aren't going to try and say they were legally hanged, are you?"

"As legal you can get in Ladore, seeing as we have no law."

"Lynching is never legal."

"They weren't exactly lynched. We gave them a trial of sorts. It was a people's court, you might say."

"What did they do?"

"They commenced yesterday by beating up and robbing several of our townspeople. Seven of 'em, there were then. But that wasn't enough for them. No, sir. They topped it off last night by nearly pistol-whipping to death Ed Roach, one of our citizens. Then, with poor old Mr. Roach lyin' near to dead on the floor, they took his two girls with 'em out into the woods. What they did to those two poor, innocent girls isn't even fit to talk about."

"How did you catch them?" John Henry asked.

"Ha, that wasn't hard at all. They got drunk and passed out and the girls escaped. Soon as we found out about it, we just went out to the little patch of woods where the girls said it happened and, sure enough, there they were, drunk as skunks. All we had to do was pick them up."

"But you said you had a trial."

"We did have a trial, right back there in the saloon. Mr. Roach, even though his head is all wrapped up in bandages, came over to testify, and he identified them. His two girls did, too. And they also told us what all these men did to them. It was something terrible to hear, I tell you."

"Tell me more about the trial? Did you have a judge, jury? Did you have lawyers for the prosecution and defense?"

"Yes, sir, we did. And the two men we had be the defense and prosecuting attorneys both have college educations, too."

"You said there were seven of them, but there are only five here. Where are the other two?"

"There's only one more of 'em. One of them got himself killed, and we have his body down at the lumberyard where the coffins are being built. We'll be burying him alongside these. The one that killed him was a man by the name of Percy Martin. Martin is the one that got away."

"I see."

"Look here, Marshal, if you didn't come here to look into this — legal — hanging, what did you come here for?"

"The federal court has taken an interest in the competition between the two railroads," John Henry said.

"Oh. Well, then in that case, I expect you'll want to talk to either Colonel Stevens, or Mr. Gunn, or Mr. Scullin, but none of them are here. If you want to talk to them, you'll have to go up to Emporia. But if you'd like, I can get you on the next train that will be goin' back for supplies. That'll be about an hour from now, and it'll have you in Emporia by supper time.

"What about my horse?"

"You can board him here, if you want. Curly Lathom runs the livery, he'll take good care of him."

"All right, thanks, I may do that."

"The lynching?" Abell said.

"If you are telling the truth, Mr. Abell, the entire town was in on it."

"Yes, sir, like I said, we had a trial and everything."

"How many people live here in Ladore?"

"We've never taken an actual count, but we figure it has to be somewhere between two and three hundred people."

"I can't very well arrest two hundred people for lynching now, can I?" John Henry asked. "And the only difference between two hundred people here holding a trial, and two hundred people in an incorporated town holding the trial, would be some paperwork. Sometimes looking the other way, Mr. Abell, may be the wisest part of discretion."

"Yes, sir," Abell replied as a big relieved smile spread across his face. "I've always said that same thing."

"I would not recommend you hold any more trials before you get yourself incorporated."

"Yes, sir, I think that is a very good suggestion, and I can tell you that it is highly unlikely that such a thing would ever happen again."

"Where is the livery?"

"Right up ahead, on your right. You can't miss it," Abell promised.

John Henry rode down to the livery, made arrangements for his horse, then walked down to the railroad office, which was a railcar sitting at an end of track.

"Yes, sir, Marshal Sixkiller," a man said as he greeted him. "Mr. Abell said you would be taking our next work train back up to Emporia. If you'll just have a seat and make yourself comfortable here, I'll make all the arrangements."

"Thank you," John Henry said.

■ ■ ■ ■

As John Henry Sixkiller waited for his train at Ladore, ten miles to the west, Matt Dixon rode into Baxter Springs. Baxter Springs was at the end of track of the Border Tier Railroad. It was a "hell on wheels," with enough cafés, saloons, and bawdy houses to take care of the men who were building the railroad. Its population was growing almost daily as people flocked into the town to take advantage of the prosperity the railroad promised.

As Dixon rode in, he made a studied perusal of the town. It consisted of a combination of whipsawed lumber shacks with unpainted, still-green wood, and tents. Dixon rode up to the hitch rail in front of the End of Track saloon, dismounted, and patted his tan duster a few times, sending up puffs of gray-white dust, then walked inside. The saloon was busy, but Dixon found a quiet place by the end of the bar.

Dixon was a small, thin man with a hawk nose, dark, beady eyes, and pockmarked skin.

When the bartender moved over to him, Dixon ordered a beer.

At the opposite end of the bar from

Dixon, a dark-haired, dark-eyed man tossed his whiskey down, then ran his finger across the full mustache that curved around his mouth like the horns on a Texas steer. Dixon hadn't noticed him, but the mustachioed man had noticed Dixon. The man with the mustache was Angus Luber. Angus Luber was a bounty hunter, and because of that, he recognized Dixon as someone who had a bounty on his head.

"Dixon," Luber called.

Dixon didn't look up from his beer.

"Dixon!" Luber called again. "I'm talking to you, Mister."

There was a clear challenge in Luber's voice, and all other conversations ceased, and the drinkers at the bar backed away so that there was nothing but clear space between Dixon and Luber. Even the bartender left his position behind the bar.

"I think you've made a mistake," Dixon said.

"No, Dixon, you did. You made a mistake when you came in here."

Dixon looked up from his beer. "Did I now?"

"You sure as hell did. Your name is Dixon, isn't it? Matt Dixon?"

"You're mistaken, Mister. My name is John Smith."

"No, I don't think so," Luber said, confidently. "I've seen paper on you. You are a low-life bank-robbin', murderin' son of a bitch. And I'm callin' you out."

"Who are you, to call me out? I don't see any badge."

"You might say that I'm a man who takes advantage of opportunities when they are presented," Luber said. "For example, if I happen to see someone that the law wants — say, someone like you, who has a price on his head — well, that's just too good an opportunity to let pass."

"And just how do you intend to take advantage of that opportunity?" Dixon asked, lifting his mug for another drink.

"By takin' you down to the sheriff's office."

"And if I choose not to go with you?"

"Oh, you're goin' with me all right," Luber said.

"Well now, is that a fact?" Dixon asked. He wiped the foam from his lips with the back of his hand. "And how do you propose to get me there?"

"I propose to kill you," Luber said, easily. There was a collective gasp from those who were watching, intently, the real-life drama that was playing out before their very eyes.

Dixon set his beer mug down, then

stepped away from the bar. He flipped his duster back so that his gun was exposed. He was wearing it low, and kicked out, the way a man wears a gun when he knows how to use it.

"You've been doin' lots of talkin', Mister," Dixon said. "Seems to me like it's about time you showed us whether or not you can back up that talk."

Luber stepped away from the bar as well, and like Dixon, Luber was wearing his gun low, and kicked out. "Oh, I can back it up, all right."

"Is that so? And, just what might your name be, Mister?" Dixon asked.

"Luber. Angus Luber."

There was a collective gasp of surprise from the others who were in the saloon at the time, for all of them had heard of Angus Luber, the famous gunfighter. There were tales about Luber and his life on both sides of the law. The story was that the last judge he went before gave him a choice. He could either go to prison, or turn his prowess with a gun into a more productive pursuit, by apprehending wanted men. Luber chose the latter.

"So you are Angus Luber."

"I am. I see that you've heard of me."

"I've heard of you."

Among the outlaws, Angus Luber had the reputation of being someone that you didn't want to tangle with. But Matt Dixon had just the opposite reaction when he heard the name. He wanted to run into Angus Luber. He knew that if he became known as the man who shot Angus Luber, he would be able to sell his gun for a lot higher price.

"I can see that I'm not welcome here, so I reckon I'll just be goin' on," Dixon said. He had no intention of going on, but he thought if he could give the idea that he was afraid of Luber, then Luber might get a little cocky. And that would give Dixon a slight edge.

Edge, Dixon thought. That's what every gunfight came down to. Who had the edge — and how did he use that edge?

Luber smiled, a cold, evil smile. "No," he said. "You won't be goin' on, Dixon. You're either goin' to walk down to the sheriff's office with me, or I'm going to kill you here and now, and have your dead carcass carried down there. Which will it be?"

Now it was Dixon's time to smile, his smile just as cold and just as evil. "I reckon we're just goin' to have to dance, you and me."

Luber had been in several shoot-outs during his career as a bounty hunter, and he was fast. Without another word he made his move, pulling his pistol in the blink of an eye. But Dixon had anticipated Luber's move and had his own pistol out just a split-second faster, pulling the hammer back and firing in one fluid motion. In the close confines of the barroom, the gunshot sounded like a clap of thunder.

Luber's eyes grew wide with surprise at how fast Dixon had his gun up and firing. He tried hard to beat the bullet with his own draw, but he couldn't do it. Dixon's shot caught Luber in the chest and he fell back against the bar, then slid down to the floor. His gun arm was thrown to one side and the still unfired pistol was in his hand. He looked up at Dixon, who was still standing there holding the smoking pistol.

"How did you . . . ?" he tried to ask, but that was as far as he got before his head fell to one side.

There was a moment of stunned silence. Then one of the patrons nearest the bar walked over to examine Luber, who was still sitting on the floor, his body propped up by the bar. The customer called out to the others in the saloon.

"He's dead, folks. He's deader than a doornail."

"Bartender," Dixon said.

"Yes, sir, Mr. Dixon?"

"Set up drinks for the house."

"Yes, sir, Mr. Dixon," the bartender replied and, with a happy shout, everyone in the saloon rushed to the bar to give his order.

CHAPTER TWENTY-THREE

When John Henry stepped down from the train in Emporia, he was met by Colonel Stevens.

"Marshal Sixkiller, I am Colonel Stevens, president of the KATY Railroad. It is good to see you, sir, and welcome to Emporia."

"You were expecting me?" John Henry asked, surprised by the greeting.

"Mr. Abell sent a telegram informing me that you were coming. I've arranged a dinner for you, where you will meet Mr. Gunn and Mr. Scullin, my two top men. We may as well make your visit as pleasant as possible while we are discussing business."

"You won't get an argument from me," John Henry said.

John Henry accompanied Colonel Stevens to the restaurant where, in a corner in the back, a special table had been laid out. Here, John Henry met Otis Gunn and John Scullin, as well as two prominent Cherokees,

Colonel Boudinot, and General Stand Watie, both of whom had earned their military appellations when they had served in those positions in the Confederate army during the Civil War. John Henry knew both of them well, and they knew him.

"John Henry," Boudinot said as he took John Henry's hand. "I haven't seen you since you were appointed U.S. Marshal. Congratulations."

"Thank you, Colonel," John Henry replied. Then, he nodded toward Stand Watie, the other Cherokee. "General, my respects, sir."

"Captain Sixkiller," General Waite replied, and though as chief sheriff of the Cherokee John Henry was a captain in the Indian police, he knew that General Waite was referring to the rank John Henry had attained during the war.

"Gentlemen, I've invited Marshal Sixkiller to have dinner with us tonight so he could speak to us about the role of the U.S. Marshal in our race to get the railroad to the Indian Territory before Joy and his group get there."

"It's too late for that," Boudinot said.

"What?" Stevens replied with a gasp. "What are you talking about?"

"James Joy and his Border Tier Railroad

have reached Baxter Springs."

"The hell you say!" Stevens exploded. "This is the first that I've heard about it. When did it happen?"

"Just a few hours ago."

Stevens let out a sigh of frustration and disappointment. "Then it's over. All is lost."

Unexpectedly, Boudinot smiled.

"No, it isn't," he said.

"It isn't? What do you mean? How can this be anything but a disaster?"

"The Border Tier has reached Baxter Springs," Boudinot said. "Now, most people consider Baxter Springs to be right on the Territory line and, indeed, they even advertise themselves as such. But in fact, it isn't. It is actually a whole mile from the border.

"So far, Joy doesn't know this, and I'm told he has halted all work and they are going to sit there until after the party, next week, celebrating the victory."

"Next week? No, that's no good, that's too far away. Joy is sure to learn that he isn't actually at the line before then. And how long will it take him to go a mile?"

"How is he to learn? As an official representative of the Cherokee nation, I have already welcomed him into the Territory. And, I will be furnishing everything his workers might need for a wild party — food, drink. I've even arranged to have some women come down from Wichita.

"The Honorable I.S. Kalloch, famous politician and orator is going to speak. I expect, before the day is over, that you won't find a sober worker within twenty miles of the place."

"Still, he has only a mile to go. He can do that in a day. We still have thirty miles to go."

"We haven't told you the best part," Stand Watie added. "Even if he does cross the line, it won't matter."

"Why not?"

"He thinks he is opposite Cherokee land where the right of way has already been negotiated with the government. But he isn't. He is opposite Shawnee territory and even if he crosses from where he is, it will do him no good, because he has no right to be there. The Shawnee have not granted permission to enter their land, and they'll be turned around. Then, they will have to reroute for twenty-three miles back to Chetopa, in order to cross the border where it is legal," Stand Watie said.

"Ha!" Stevens said, hitting the palm of his hand with a clenched fist.

"We aren't out of the woods yet, Boss," Gunn said. "We are still thirty miles from

Chetopa, and that's farther than the Border Tier will have to go to make up for their mistake."

"I have a suggestion," Scullin said. "Let's hire as many of the Border Tier Railroad track workers as we can, just to deny them to Mr. Joy. Once he finds out his mistake he's going to have to go like hell to get there, but if we have hired away enough of his men, he won't have the labor source to do it."

"Gentleman, we are going to reach Chetopa three weeks from today or by damn I am going to know the reason why. General Stand Watie, Colonel Boudinot, you tell the folks in Chetopa that when our tracks cross into Cherokee nation, that I will throw a party for the entire town, and I'll give every man, woman, and child, a free railroad ride to Russell Creek and back."

After the railroad business was discussed, Stevens turned to John Henry, who during the discussion had been enjoying a rare, restaurant-prepared meal. He had just carved off a piece of beef and put it in his mouth when Stevens turned to him.

"I'm sorry, Marshal Sixkiller. I invited you to dinner, then ignored you to take care of business. Now, perhaps you can tell us what brings you to Emporia?"

John Henry held up his hand to signal that he would answer as soon as he chewed his food. Then, the meat swallowed, he spoke.

"I have been told that the competition between your railroad and the Border Tier Railroad has resulted in some destruction of property. Marshal Sarber is concerned that it might get out of hand and that some people might get hurt, or even killed. If that happens, it could spread out to endanger some innocent civilians."

"Marshal, I admit that when we first started this little race, there were a few incidents. But now both Joy and I are convinced that the first trouble, the most damaging trouble, was not done by the Border Tier or the KATY Line. I didn't do it, he says he didn't do it, and I believe him. We think it was some outsiders who wrecked the Border Tier work train, and burned our store of supplies."

"Why would an outsider do that?" John Henry asked.

"You've got me there, Marshal. I mean, if it was someone who wanted the Border Tier to beat us, why, they wouldn't have wrecked the Border Tier train now, would they? And the same thing in reverse. If it was someone who wanted the KATY to succeed, why would they burn our supplies? No, sir, it has to be someone outside. And, say, maybe this is where you can fit in. Maybe you can find out who it is that's doing this."

"That is my job, Colonel Stevens. I fully intend to find out who is at the bottom of this."

"I will make you this solemn promise. The KATY Railroad will fully cooperate with you in your investigation. And, we also stand ready to assist you in any way we can."

"Thank you, Colonel Stevens. I appreciate that."

John Henry spent the night in Emporia, then the next day took the Frisco Line to Paola, which would connect him with the Border Tier Line.

"Yes, sir, Mr. Joy is down at Baxter Springs," Robert Greenwell said. Greenwell was Joy's general manager. "The train from Kansas City will pass through here at nine o'clock tonight." Greenwell took a booklet from his desk drawer, pulled out a page, and wrote on it. "Here, give this to the conductor. It will grant you a free ride."

"Thanks," John Henry said.

There was a private car waiting at the depot to be attached to the train when it arrived. The car belonged to Charles Beam, who was one of the principal investors in the Border Tier Line. Beam wanted to see for himself that the railroad had reached the border of the Indian Territory.

"Sixkiller?" Beam said when he was introduced to John Henry. "That is a rather unusual name. It sounds almost Indian."

"That's understandable, Mr. Beam, seeing as my father was Indian."

"My word. You don't look Indian."

"By not looking Indian, do you mean I'm not wearing a warbonnet, and I don't have my face painted?"

"I . . ." Beam started, then he stopped and a sheepish smile spread across his face. "I guess you've got me there, friend. I'm sorry if I offended you."

"I'm not offended."

"Mr. Beam?" one of the railroad officials called. "Will you be wanting your car to remain in Baxter Springs for a while?"

Beam went over to speak with the railroad official while John Henry took a seat in the waiting room. After about fifteen minutes the train arrived. There was some delay as the train was connected to Beam's private car, then the conductor came into the waiting room.

"Board!" he called.

Fifteen miles south of Paola, Percy Martin

and three others were waiting.

"You sure this train is carryin' money?" a man named Peters asked.

"There's nearly two hundred railroad workers down in Baxter Springs," Martin said.

"So?"

"So, they have to be paid. More'n likely the payroll is on the train."

"More'n likely don't mean it is on the train," Peters said. "It just means that more'n likely it is."

"If you don't want to be a part of this, you are free to ride away now."

"Look here, Peters, I think Martin is right. And even if the train ain't carryin' a payroll, why it's goin' to have passengers on it, and you know they got money."

"I ain't ridin' away, I was just askin' is all."

"You got the wood ready to light?" Martin asked.

"Yeah, but why are we goin' to light it? If we leave it just the way it is, it'll wreck the train, then it'll be easy pickin's."

"Think so, do you? You ever walked through a rail car when it's lying on its side?" Martin asked.

"No, can't say as I have."

"You can't say you have, because it can't

be done. If we're goin' to be takin' money from the passengers, then we need cars we can walk through. Get it lit soon as we hear the train a-comin'. I want the engineer to see it in plenty of time to stop."

"All right. It's all ready to light."

"Better get it lit now," one of the other men said. "I hear it comin'."

CHAPTER TWENTY-FOUR

They had been underway for almost an hour when the train suddenly ground to a shuddering, screeching, banging halt. The sudden stop threw a sleeping boy from his seat and he began crying.

John Henry, who had been dozing in his seat, tried to look through the window, but because it was dark outside, and because the inside was illuminated with gimble-mounted coal-oil lanterns, the only thing he saw in the window was his own reflection.

"What is it?" someone asked.

"Why did we suddenly stop like this? There's no depot here!"

"If this is how James Joy is plannin' on runnin' his railroad once he gets it built all the way through to Texas, he certainly won't get my business," another complained.

John Henry was unable to see what was going on outside, but he had a gut instinct as to what was going on, so he pulled his pistol, then covered it with his hat.

Almost immediately a man stepped into the car from the front. He was wearing a white hood pulled down over his face, with only his eyes showing. The mask hid the man's identity, but John Henry knew that it would also restrict the robber's vision some-what.

"Everyone stay in their seats!" the man shouted as he brandished his pistol.

"Who do you think you are?" a passenger in the front seat demanded angrily. "You've got no right to come barging in here like this."

"This gives me all the right I need," the robber said, waving his gun around. "Now you just stay in your seat and be quiet, and you won't get hurt."

"The hell I will," the passenger said, and exhibiting more guts than sense, he stood up. When he did, the robber brought the butt of his pistol down, hard, on the top of the man's head and, with a groan, he fell back in the seat with his head bleeding. Several in the car shouted out in protest.

"Keep quiet!" the gunman demanded. "Everyone, just keep quiet and stay in your seats."

Another gunman came on, to join the first. "What happened?" he asked.

"Nothing I can't handle. Is everything under control out there?"

"Yeah," the second gunman answered. "Ever'one is doin' just what you told 'em. Semmes is coverin' the engineer, 'n Beardsley is goin' through one of the other cars."

"Peters, you dumb son of a bitch! You just told everyone on the train our names!"

"Sorry, Martin. I wasn't thinkin'."

"No, you'd need a brain for that, wouldn't you? Just start with the car behind us."

"All right," Peters said.

As the second gunman started down the aisle to go to the next car, he looked over and saw the badge on John Henry's shirt, and he gasped.

"Hey, Martin!" he called, bringing his gun around toward John Henry. "We got us a lawman on board!"

John Henry had intended to wait for a few minutes longer until he was able to get a better grasp of the situation, but his hand had been called. Peters was already pulling the hammer back on his pistol, so John Henry had to shoot, his bullet blasting a hole through his own hat. The gunman who had recognized him went down with a hole in his chest.

The gunman up front, the one called Martin, managed to get off a shot, but he was shooting fast and wild and his bullet buzzed harmlessly by John Henry's ear, plunging into the seat behind him. John Henry, his hat now discarded, brought his own pistol up and squeezed off a second shot. Martin was hit in the chest and he fell against the front wall of the car, then slid down until he was sitting on the floor. On the wall behind him a swath of blood traced his path downward. Martin clasped his hands over his wound, but blood began spilling through his fingers. Pulling his hand away, he looked at his bloody palm for a second, then his head fell to one side.

Two men had come into the car, and two men had died. During the gunfire, women screamed and men shouted. And now, as the car filled with the gun smoke of the three discharges, John Henry scooted out through the back door of the car, jumped from the steps down to the ground, then fell and rolled out into the darkness.

"Martin! Peters! What's goin' on in there?" someone called. "What's goin' on?"

By the train's ambient light, John Henry saw the train robber who was yelling at the others. This was the same one who had been covering the engineer, and now he was moving quickly toward the back of the train. As he ran through the little golden patches of light, it had the effect of a lantern blinking on and off so that first he was in shadow, then brightly illuminated . . . then shadow . . . then illuminated. John Henry aimed at him.

"Hold it right there! I've got you covered. I'm a United States Marshal! Put down your gun and throw up your hands."

Realizing he was standing in a patch of light, the robber moved out into the shadow to fire at John Henry. He was out of the light, but the muzzle flash of his pistol gave John Henry an ideal target and he returned fire. The robber's bullet whistled by harmlessly, but John Henry's bullet found its mark and the would-be robber called out, "Semmes, I'm hit!" Then the robber collapsed.

John Henry had accounted for three, and he knew there was at least one more, so he stepped up close to the side of the train, then began moving toward the rear of the train, trying to locate the one remaining man. He saw him then, just as he was stepping through the door and into the private car. John Henry snapped off a quick shot but missed, and he saw his bullet send up sparks as it struck part of the metal in the doorframe. He didn't get a second shot at him, because the outlaw made it inside.

John Henry hurried to the front end of the same passenger car he had been riding in, then backed up against the side of it so that the robber, who was now safely inside the private car, wouldn't have a clear shot at him. One of the passengers poked his head out to see what was going on.

"Get back inside!" John Henry shouted.

The passenger jerked his head back in, quickly.

John Henry peered cautiously around the corner, trying to see his adversary.

"Semmes," John Henry called, remembering the name. "You may as well come on out of there. All the others are dead. You're the only one left, and you don't have anywhere to go."

"Who the hell are you, anyway?" Semmes yelled.

"The name is Sixkiller," John Henry called back.

"Sixkiller? Yeah, I've heard of you. You're that Indian policeman, ain't you? What are you doin' here?"

"I'm a U.S. Marshal," John Henry said.

"What the hell? How'd you hear we was goin' to rob it?"

"A medicine man told me," John Henry said.

There was a beat of silence, then Semmes

called out again, "I'm comin' out. Don't shoot, Sixkiller! I'm comin' out!"

"Well, come on then," John Henry replied.

John Henry watched the back door of the private car. A second later it opened and Semmes appeared. But instead of coming out with his hands up as John Henry had expected him to do, he had Beam with him, and he was holding his pistol to Beam's head.

"You out here, Sixkiller?" Semmes called, searching the darkness. "You out here?"

"I'm here," John Henry answered. He stepped out so the outlaw could see him, and he raised his pistol to point it at Semmes. "Drop your gun and come on down here."

"Drop my gun? Are you crazy? Maybe you ain't noticed, but I got my gun pointed right straight at this man's head."

"Why?" John Henry asked.

"Why? 'Cause he's my ticket out of here, that's why. I figure he must be someone important, else he wouldn't be ridin' in a private car. And I don't reckon you'd like to see his brains blowed out now, would you?"

"To be honest about it, Semmes, I don't even know the man, so I really don't care one way or the other. The business between us has nothing to do with him. You may as well let him go."

"Ha! Let him go? The hell I will. Don't you understand, Marshal? I aim to shoot this man!"

"Put your gun down, and your hands up, Semmes. That's the only way you're going to get out of here alive."

"No, it ain't the only way I'm goin' to get out of here. It's like I told you. I got me an ace up the sleeve."

"And what would that ace be?" John Henry asked.

"What the hell do you mean, what is my ace? Damn it, man, are you blind? Can't you see that I got this man here?"

"Yes, I can see that you are holding your gun to that man's head. But my question is, what is that supposed to mean to me?"

"Just how dumb are you, anyway? What it means is, if you don't drop your gun, I am going to shoot him!" Semmes said, his voice becoming more agitated. "Are you listenin' to what I'm sayin', Marshal? If you don't drop your gun I'm going to shoot him. And I ain't bluffin'!"

"All right, do it."

"What?"

"I said do it. Shoot him now so you and I can get down to business."

"Are you crazy?" Semmes asked, shocked

by the answer he hadn't expected to hear.

"I'm an Indian. What does a white man mean to me? Go ahead, do it. Shoot him," John Henry said. "And once he's gone, it'll just be the two of us."

"You're bluffing."

"If you don't shoot him, I will," John Henry said. "Then I'll shoot you." John Henry moved the barrel of his gun slightly, so that he was now aiming at Beam. By now several of the passengers had detrained and they were standing out in the darkness, watching as this drama played out before them.

The engine was still, but not quiet, as it vented steam in a rhythmic series of loud gasps.

"You think the marshal is really going to shoot Mr. Beam?" someone asked.

"No, I don't think so," a voice answered.

"I don't know," another voice added. "I think he's serious."

"What's it going to be, Semmes? Are you going to shoot him? Or am I?" John Henry cocked his pistol, the sound of the hammer engaging the cylinder loud in the night.

"You son of a bitch! You're crazy! You know that? You're crazy!" Semmes shouted. In angry frustration, he pushed Beam away and aimed at John Henry. That provided

John Henry with the opening he needed, and he aimed and squeezed the trigger. The gun boomed and bucked in his hand, knocking Semmes back against the door of the car before he collapsed in a heap onto the vestibule floor.

"Are you all right, Mr. Beam?" John Henry asked. He was still holding his pistol out in front of him and smoke curled up from the end of the barrel.

"Yes, I'm fine, thank, you," Beam replied. He was silent for a moment. "Would you really have shot me, Marshal?"

"What do you think?"

"For a minute or two there, I thought maybe you would shoot me."

"Good."

"Good?"

"If you thought I was going to shoot you, then Semmes was thinking the same thing."

By now the conductor had left the train and he was joined by a few of the braver passengers. Even the engineer and fireman were on the ground and they began milling around, looking at the two bodies that were outside the train.

"There's two dead inside and two dead out here. Any more left that you know of?" the conductor asked the engineer.

"No," the engineer replied. "There was

just the four of 'em that stopped me."

"Why'd you stop?"

"Didn't have no choice," the engineer replied. "They put a barricade across the tracks." The engineer looked at a few of the stronger-looking passengers. "Any of you men want to bear a hand till we get the tracks cleared?"

At least three men joined the fireman and the engineer as they walked up front to clear the barricade from the track.

"You had no right to do that, you know," the conductor said to John Henry.

"Are you telling me I had no right to prevent a train robbery?"

"No. I mean you had no right to put Mr. Beam's life in jeopardy like that. He is an important man."

"Mr. Adams, is it?" Beam said to the conductor.

"Yes, sir. I'm sorry, Mr. Beam, and I want to personally apologize on behalf of the railroad for this man's action."

"Let me ask you something," Beam said. "Suppose this man, Semmes, had taken me with him as a hostage. How long do you think he would have let me live?"

"Why, I don't know," the conductor said.

"Well, I'll tell you how long he would have let me live. Just until we were out of sight of the train. Then he would have shot me dead, just as sure as a gun is iron."

"I guess, maybe that is so," the conductor said.

"So instead of chastising Marshal Six-killer, you should be thanking him for preventing the train from being robbed, and I do thank him for saving my life. It took courage for him to do that."

"Oh," the conductor said. "I guess I didn't consider that. Marshal, I take back what I said. And I reckon I owe you an apology."

"And I owe you my life," Beam said. "I wonder if you would do me the honor of accepting my invitation to finish this trip as my guest in my private car."

John Henry thought that, as a public servant, he should probably decline. But he had never ridden in a private car before, and it was highly unlikely he would ever get the opportunity to ride in one again. He smiled at the invitation.

"I'd be glad to," he said.

CHAPTER TWENTY-FIVE

As the train wheels clacked rhythmically beneath him, John Henry noticed that Mr. Beam's car rocked much more gently than the rough-riding car he had been in.

The car had a bar and Beam poured a drink and handed it to John Henry.

Over the course of his life, John Henry had drunk just about every type of alcohol available. He had drunk beer that was so green he could still taste the yeast, and whiskey that was aged with rusty nails and flavored with tobacco juice. Once he had even drunk champagne, but never had he tasted anything like the "sipping whiskey" he was drinking now.

"Do you like it?" Beam asked.

"I do, indeed," John Henry replied. His answer wasn't adequate to express how much he really did like it, but he never was a man for words.

"My grandfather, David Beam, started

our whiskey business," Beam said. "This is Jim Beam, named after my father, and a product of our finest line."

"How did you get from the whiskey business into the railroad business?"

"Well, I'm not in either, actually. My father and my brother are running the distillery, and I am but an investor in the railroad. I have an equal investment in the KATY Line, by the way."

John Henry chuckled. "Well, there's nothing like covering your bet."

"My sentiments exactly."

It was nearly midnight by the time the train reached Baxter Springs, but you couldn't tell it by the amount of activity. The railroad workers and the town were still celebrating the fact that they had reached the border ahead of the KATY.

John Henry stepped down from the private car and looked around at the ongoing celebration. On the platform all around him, there was a discordant chorus of squeals, laughter, shouts, and animated conversation among all the people

When John Henry looked toward the baggage car of the train, he saw that the four bodies had been taken down and laid out, side-by-side at the far end of the platform.

Already, the curious were beginning to gather around to look down at the four dead men. A man with a badge came toward him.

"I'm Sheriff Denman."

"Sheriff," John Henry acknowledged, with a nod.

"I'm told you did this."

"I did."

"Who are you?"

"My name is John Henry Sixkiller. I'm a —"

"I know what you are, Mr. Sixkiller. I've heard your name spoken a few times. You are a member of the Indian Police, and that's a pretty responsible position, but you had no business takin' these men on, whether they were tryin' to rob the train or not." Sheriff Denman pointed to the badge on John Henry's shirt. "That badge you're a' wearin' don't mean nothin' outside of the Territory."

"Maybe you had better take a closer look at the badge," John Henry suggested.

"What do you mean?" Sheriff Denman looked at the badge again, moving closer so he could see it more clearly in the glow of the gaslights that were illuminating the depot platform. "Wait a minute. U.S. Marshal? Are you telling me you are a United States Marshal?"

"Yes."

"What's an Indian doing as —" Denman started, then he interrupted his sentence. "Never mind. Just forget that I said anything. Of course, you bein' a U.S. Marshal, why, that changes ever'thing."

"I thought you might see it that way. By the way, is there a hotel in town?"

"No hotel," the sheriff answered. "You might get a room down at the End of Track Saloon if the whores aren't usin' all of 'em. But what with ever'one celebratin' like they're doin', well, more'n likely the whores are goin' to be busy all night long."

John Henry walked down the street from the depot toward the town. The End of Track Saloon was the most substantial-looking building in a row of ramshackle shacks and tents. There was a drunk passed out on the steps in front of the place and John Henry had to step over him in order to go inside.

Because all the chimneys of all the lanterns were soot covered, what light there was inside was dingy and filtered through drifting smoke. The place smelled of whiskey, stale beer, and sour tobacco. There was a long bar on the left, with dirty towels hanging on hooks about every five feet along the front. A large mirror was behind the bar but, like everything else about the saloon, it was so dirty that John Henry could scarcely see any images in it and what he could see was distorted by imperfections in the glass.

"Yes, sir," someone was saying. "By the time this railroad goes through Injun Territory, then on through Texas, why this here town will be the biggest town in Kansas."

"Biggest town in Kansas? Hell, it'll more'n likely be one of the biggest cities west of the Mississippi. There will be St. Louis, Denver, San Francisco, and Baxter Springs. Mark my words."

Out on the floor of the saloon there were eight tables, with nearly all of them occupied. A half dozen or so bar girls were flitting about, pushing drinks and promising more, for the right price. A few card games were in progress, but most of the patrons were just drinking and talking. There were two subjects of conversation, one being the railroad reaching the border and the other, the gunfight that had taken place in this same saloon earlier in the day. But by now they had also heard of what had taken place on the train and, already, there was speculation as to which of the two victors was the best.

"In my mind there ain't no doubt," one of the men at one of the tables was saying.

"The marshal took on four men. Four, mind you, and he kilt all four. You can't compare that with Matt Dixon killin' just one man."

"The hell you can't," another man contended. "That marshal done his killin' in the dark. Dixon called Luber out and stood up to him, face to face. And did you see Dixon's draw? Faster'n greased lightnin' it was. Why it was that quick I never seen nothin' more'n a jump of his shoulder and the gun was in his hand. In his hand and blazin', it was, and Luber was grabbin' his chest and fallin' down, already deader'n a doornail without gettin' off even one shot."

"Still, four to one," one of the others said, and the argument continued.

"Whoowee! Wouldn't you love to see them two go ag'in one another?"

"Which one do you think would get kilt?"

"Sixkiller, for sure."

"I don't think so. I think Sixkiller is the one who would do the killin'."

The men who were carrying on the conversation were unaware that the subject of their conversation was right there in the room with them.

When John Henry stepped up to the bar, the bartender was pouring the residue from abandoned whiskey glasses back into a bottle. He pulled a soggy cigar butt from one glass, laid the butt aside, then poured the whiskey back into the bottle without qualms. John Henry held up his finger.

"Yeah?" the bartender responded.

"I'd like a room."

"There ain't no rooms."

"I was told that you had rooms for the whores to use."

"That's right. We do have rooms, but they are for the women."

"Do they use the rooms alone?"

"What?"

"When someone buys a whore's time, does the whore go into the room alone?"

"No, of course not."

"Then I want a room with a whore."

"Why didn' you say so in the first place? Which one do you want?"

"I don't care."

"You've got to have a choice."

"Pick one."

"You're kidding me."

"No, you choose one."

The bartender looked over at a woman who was standing alone at the end of the bar. She was clearly older than any of the other women, and there was a drained look about her. She was alone and she was nursing a beer.

"Suzie," the bartender called. "This here man wants you."

"Really?" Suzie smiled at John Henry, but the tiredness didn't leave her eyes.

"You have a room?" John Henry asked.

"Yes, of course I have a room."

"How much if I spend the whole night with you?"

"The whole night? You want to spend an entire night with me?"

"Yes."

"Well, it'll be midnight in another few minutes, so it'll only be half price then, if you want to wait."

John Henry pulled out a silver dollar and handed it to her. "Why wait?"

"Mister, are you serious? You're willin' to pay full price now, instead of waiting no more than five minutes?"

"Yes."

Suzie led John Henry up the stairs, then down the hall to her room. It was very small, only slightly larger than the bed.

"I'll, uh, get us a towel," Suzie offered.

"We won't need one."

"What do you mean?"

"I'm tired, Suzie. To be honest with you, I came up here for the bed. All I want to do is sleep. I hope you don't mind."

"Mind? Mister, I could kiss you. You don't

know how wonderful it would be for me to just sleep all night." She smiled, showing two missing teeth. "And get paid for it besides."

There was a photograph of a young girl on the chest, and Suzie saw John Henry looking at it.

"That's my little girl," Suzie said. "She lives with my sister back in Kansas City. She doesn't know I'm her mother, and I don't ever want her to know."

"She's very pretty," John Henry said.

"Yes, and very sweet." The smile left Suzie's face. "She must never learn who her mother is, or what I do for a living."

"You obviously love her," John Henry said.

"Yes, I do. Very much."

"Any child who has a mother's love is lucky," John Henry said. Sitting on the edge of the bed, he started to remove his boots.

"Wait," Suzie said. "At least let me take your boots off for you." Suzie turned around, straddled one of John Henry's legs, then pulled off the boot. She did the same thing with his other boot.

"Thanks," John Henry said.

John Henry awakened the next morning to the aroma of freshly brewed coffee. When he opened his eyes, he saw Suzie putting a coffeepot, two cups, and a plate of biscuits on the chest.

"Coffee and biscuits," Suzie said. "Not much of a breakfast, I admit. But I thought it might hold you till you can get a proper breakfast in you."

"Suzie, it is a wonderful breakfast," John Henry said. "Even more so, because I will be able to share it with you."

Suzie's smile was almost a blush, and, for just a moment, the tiredness in her eyes went away.

Suddenly from outside there was a series of loud pops, followed by the high peal of a woman's laughter.

John Henry moved over to the window and pulled the curtain to one side as he looked down on the street. The street was full of men and women who seemed to be celebrating.

"What's going on down there?" John Henry asked.

"I imagine they are still celebrating that the railroad reached the border," Suzie said. "They don't know yet that they haven't really reached it."

John Henry looked at Suzie in surprise. That was exactly what he had heard when he met with Colonel Stevens, Stand Watie, and others of the KATY Railroad. He didn't know that anyone here realized that, though.

Fifteen minutes later, John Henry was down on the side of the street, watching the celebration. When the sheriff saw John Henry, he smiled and came over to him.

"What's the celebration about?" He wanted to hear if Suzie had been correct in her assessment of the cause of the celebration.

"Two things," the sheriff said. "We are celebrating that the railroad has reached Indian Territory. And, of course, you are also the cause of our celebration."

"How am I the cause of your celebration?"

"I take it you haven't gone down to look at the display on the porch of the general store," the sheriff said.

"No."

"Go take a look, Mr. Sixkiller. I think you will be proud."

Finishing his biscuit, Sam walked down toward the general store. There were several people — men, women, and children — standing around the front porch looking at whatever it was the sheriff said was displayed there. When John Henry got closer, he drew in a sharp breath of surprise.

There, in four wooden coffins standing up against the wall, were the bodies of the men who had tried to hold up the train the night before. All four outlaws were shirtless so the bullet holes that killed them could be clearly seen, "Hey, everyone! Here's the feller that kilt these outlaws!" someone shouted, noticing John Henry looking at the bodies.

"It's Marshal Sixkiller!" someone shouted.

"Three cheers for the marshal!" someone else called. "Hip, hip . . ."

"Hooray!"

"Hip, hip . . ."

"Hooray!"

"Hip, hip . . ."

"Hooray!"

John Henry held up his hand to silence them, then walked up for a closer look at a hand-lettered sign propped up at the foot of the coffins:

**HERE ARE THE BODIES OF FOUR
BANDITS KILLED BY UNITED STATES
MARSHAL JOHN HENRY SIXKILLER**

**THESE OUTLAWS WERE KILLED
WHEN THEY TRIED TO ROB A
BORDER TIER TRAIN**

The sign and the celebration made John Henry uncomfortable. He didn't enjoy killing, but it wasn't something he backed away from. In any life-or-death confrontation, he knew he must be prepared to kill without hesitation, if need be. But it had never been anything that he took pride in.

CHAPTER TWENTY-SIX

Tahlequah

Marcus Eberwine cracked a raw egg, then dropped it into his beer. He swirled it around a couple of times, then drank it down.

"How can you do that?" Willie Buck asked.

"It's good for you," Eberwine answered.

"Deckert said you wanted to see me."

"Yes." Eberwine belched. "It seems that John Henry Sixkiller, our own intrepid Indian policeman, chief sheriff, and now United States Marshal has been personally assigned to keep a watch on the progress of the railroads as they approach Indian Territory."

"Yes, that's what I've heard."

"I propose that we take advantage of that," Eberwine said.

"Pardon me, but you don't what you are talking about. I can't imagine anyone in the whole of the Indian Territory less likely to be taken advantage of than John Henry Sixkiller," Willie Buck said.

"Oh, we won't take be taking advantage of him; we will be taking advantage of the situation. This is the way we'll do it." Eberwine showed Willie Buck a letter.

From the office of William Ross, President of the Cherokee

To: Marcus Eberwine

Mr. Eberwine, it has been approved by the president and Council of the Eastern Cherokee, in session assembled, to accept your generous offer to act as liaison between the Eastern Cherokee and the KATY Railroad, and between the Eastern Cherokee and the Border Tier Railroad, the two companies currently engaged in the effort to be first into Indian Territory.

This liaison is to be provided without prejudice with regard to the separate railroads until such time as one of the railroads shall succeed in crossing into Indian Territory. At that time, you will represent the president and the council of the Cherokee.

William Ross
Chief and President
Eastern Cherokee

"What does that mean?" Buck asked.

"That means that John Henry Sixkiller will be working for me, be he United States Marshal or not. And as soon as the winning railroad enters the territory, he will be required to report to me, for further instructions."

"Eberwine, you won't be able to tell him to stop the construction, or even to slow it down," Buck said.

"No, nor is that my intention. We will be monitoring the progress through him, which will give us an inside position on how best to combat it."

"How will that work?"

"Just leave that to me," Eberwine said. "Oh, and from here on, I think it would not be good for us to be seen together. After all, you are chairman of the Indian Independence Council and you will be fighting against the construction until the United States grants the independence of the new nation of Sequoyah. And because of my involvement with the railroad, I will be able to tell you where your attacks will be most

313

effective."

Buck smiled. "Yes," he said. "Yes, that is a very good idea. It's like I always say, Eberwine. You are a very smart man."

Eberwine poured a beer for Buck, then refreshed his own. He held his glass out in a toast. "I like to think so," he said.

"How soon do I start?"

"As soon as I learn which railroad will be our most likely target," Eberwine said.

As Eberwine and Willie Buck were discussing the tactics they would use to stop the railroad, Colonel Stevens was in Emporia, holding a conference with his chief officers.

"I want a work train made up right away. Put my private car on it, right behind the engine and tender. Load the train with as much building material as you can get on it, and let's move everything to end of track."

"All right, Boss," Gunn said.

"We are going to be the first railroad into Indian Territory, come hell or high water. The success or failure of this operation will be determined in the next two weeks. Millions of dollars are at stake. Millions."

"I'll get the train loaded right away," Gunn promised.

■ ■ ■ ■

Despite Gunn's promise of "right away," it took twenty-four hours to load the train with rails, cross ties, bridge timbers, spikes, and fishplates. When the train was loaded, and Stevens's private car, which was named the Prairie Queen, was attached, they got underway.

The length of the train, and the heavy load it was carrying, meant that it could barely manage a speed of ten miles per hour. Because of that, it took nine hours to get from Emporia to Humboldt. There, the train was pulled off to a siding where it spent the night. The next day, the train passed through Cherryvale, and thirty miles beyond to the end of track.

It was raining when the train reached the end of track, and not just a gentle rain. The rain was coming down in torrents, with streams of water rushing alongside the track.

"Colonel, when you said come hell or high water, you weren't kidding," Gunn said. "Here's the high water for you. It's raining hard enough to drown frogs."

"That may be so, Otis, but we aren't frogs," Stevens said. "Let's get out and see what's going on."

Donning slickers and a poncho, Colonel Stevens and Otis Gunn stepped down from the Prairie Queen to have a look at where things stood.

"There's nobody working," Stevens said, obviously upset by the fact. "Where the hell is everybody?"

"I imagine they are staying out of the rain," Gunn said.

"Why? They aren't made of sugar. They aren't going to melt."

Walking a hundred feet or so beyond the end of track, Stevens saw that a very large bridge was resting on timbers standing in a creek. The bridge was not yet secured, even though it was raining hard, and the creek was rising.

"Look at that!" Stevens said, pointing toward the bridge. "Damn it! That bridge isn't secured and the water is running faster than bloody hell! It's going to push the bridge off the pilings!"

Even as he was talking, some of the top tier of the timbers worked loose, then started floating rapidly downstream.

"We've got to stop that! If we lose that bridge, it'll cost us several days!"

John Scullin, upon seeing the train arrive, now came up to greet Stevens.

"Colonel, we weren't expecting you here today."

"Obviously not," Stevens said, showing his displeasure. He pointed to the bridge. "We are about to lose that bridge, and not one man is out here working. Not one!"

"Colonel, you can't expect the men to work in conditions like this."

"I can expect them, and I do expect them. Where are they? And please don't tell me they've gone back to Humboldt."

"No, sir, they're here. Every one of them," Scullin said. He pointed to four rather substantial tents. "They're all inside the tents, out of the rain."

Stevens started toward the tents, splashing through the mud puddles, some of which were knee deep. As Scullin had said, all of the workmen had taken shelter from the rain, and they were in tents, playing cards, talking, and napping. No one was working.

"What are you men doing in here?" Stevens shouted. "Why aren't you working?"

"Colonel, it's rainin' too hard," one of the men said. "You can't work in rain like this."

"Who says you can't? You have to!" Stevens pointed to the bridge. "Don't you understand that if you don't get this bridge secured it can wash away? If we lose that bridge, it'll take nearly a week to get it put back again."

"That's a possibility," one of the men said. "But, Colonel, what can we do about it? Especially in weather like this."

"I have hired the best engineer and the best construction foremen in the business. And they are here with you. I'm sure that, under their direction, you can find some way to secure that bridge. I am so sure of it, that I will give a twenty-dollar bonus to anyone who will work until this bridge is secured."

"Twenty dollars?" one of the men called back.

"Yes, twenty dollars, and you won't have to wait until the next payday to get your money. I'll give it to you as soon as the bridge is secured."

"I don't know about the rest of these folks, Colonel, but you got me," one of the men said as he began putting on his poncho.

"Me, too. Twenty dollars is a lot of money."

"Hell, Lee Roy, you'll just spend it on whiskey and women," another called.

"Well, can you think of anything better to spend it on?" Lee Roy replied, to the laughter of the others.

Within five minutes, twenty-five men had agreed to the offer, and they came out of the tents, grabbed their tools, and headed for the bridge. If they were harboring any hope for the rain to ease up, it was a false hope, for the rain increased in intensity.

The men began working in almost impossible conditions. They would get a timber in place, but before they could secure it, it would wash away in a swirling pool, sometimes taking one or more of the men with it. One of the workers was knocked out when a heavy timber hit him in the head, and he started floating away, belly down, face underwater. It was Scullin who saved him from drowning, racing after him, picking him up from the water, and to the cheers of the others, throwing him across his shoulder to bring him back to safety.

Another man got a broken arm, and several others received painful bruises and cuts, but the men did not stop working. They toiled in a constant downpour, working by lanterns once it grew dark, even though the rain was falling so hard that it was difficult to keep the lanterns lit, even with the storm shutters. Finally, at midnight, both Scullin and Gunn inspected the bridge and declared that it was secure and sound. It was a tired crew that turned in that night but, by seven o'clock the next morning, the crew was at work again. Thankfully, the rain had stopped, though the way that had been prepared for the tracks was under water, and much of the grading had washed away.

Compared to the Herculean effort of the night before, though, laying the tracks up to, and across the bridge, seemed almost child's play. By four o'clock in the afternoon, the tracks crossed the bridge, and were laid for a thousand feet beyond. It was now time to test the bridge.

"We'll run the train across as soon as we unload it," Gunn said.

"Why are you going to unload it?" Scullin asked.

"Why, to lighten the load, of course."

Scullin shook his head. "We're goin' to need the material to go on from here, aren't we?"

"Yes, of course."

"Then I see no reason to lighten the load. We're goin' to need the material, and we need to know if the bridge is going to hold up. If it will hold up for this load, it will hold up for anything."

"I don't know," Gunn said. "That seems like quite a risk to me. If the bridge collapses under the load, we'll have a wrecked train and scattered material that might take two weeks or longer to clean up."

"I think the bridge will hold up."

"John, how confident are you that the bridge will hold up?" Stevens asked. "The reason I ask is, Otis is right. If the bridge collapses under the load, I am ruined. It won't make any difference if it is two days or two weeks, the KATY won't recover."

"Colonel, I'll tell you how confident I am. I'll ride up on the boiler," Scullin said. "If the bridge gives way, and the engine crashes, that boiler is going to explode and I'll be a cooked goose."

"You are that sure of it, are you?"

"Yes, sir, I am."

Stevens chuckled. "Well, you don't have to ride on the boiler. Let's just cross our fingers and send it across."

Scullin smiled broadly. "Yes, sir!"

Anxiously, all the workers gathered around to watch the train start across the bridge.

"I think they ought to offload it first," one of the men said.

"Why, don't you have confidence in your work?"

"Well, yeah, except, maybe you didn't notice but we wasn't exactly workin' under the best of conditions last night. In fact, I don't think there's ever been any worse conditions. Who knows how good of a job we done? Besides which, I ain't never seen a train as heavy loaded as this here train is."

"I say it'll make it across, no problem."

"You willin' to ride on the engine as it crosses, are you?"

"I'm willin' to lay money that it makes it across. Are you?"

"Yeah, I'll put some money on it. I bet five dollars the bridge falls in."

"You're on."

"Wait a minute, I want some of that action," someone else called.

"Yeah, me, too," another said.

Over the next few moments, several hundred dollars were bet on whether or not the train would be able to cross the bridge without the bridge collapsing under its weight.

The fireman climbed into the engine and built the fire. It took about half an hour to get the steam up, and Stevens, Scullin, Gunn, and everyone there stood around the engine as it came alive, listening to the water gurgling in the boiler. The fireman stuck his head out of the window of the locomotive and called down to the engineer.

"Steam's up, Doodle. If we're going to drive this train across the bridge, now is the time to do it."

"Here goes, boys," Doodle said as he

started toward the locomotive cabin.

"Doodle, wait," Scullin said to the engineer. "If you don't feel comfortable taking it across, you can stay here. Gordon, you can climb down from the cab, too. I know how to drive the thing. I'll take it across."

"Thank you, Mr. Scullin, but I'm the engineer," Doodle said. "I reckon this is my job. I don't need you though, Gordon," Doodle said to his fireman. "You got enough steam up to get across."

"I ain't climbin' down," Gordon said. "Like you said, this is my job."

"Wait a minute before you start across, Doodle," Stevens called up to him. "I'll be in my car. I'm going across, too."

"You got room for me in that car?" Scullin asked.

"I sure do," Stevens replied with a smile.

"I'm going, too," Gunn said, and the three men climbed up into the Prairie Queen.

"Hell, I ain't goin' to be left behind!" one of the workers said, and he climbed up onto one of the loaded flatcars. At least a dozen others joined him.

Doodle had gained the cabin by now, and he leaned out of the window and looked back along the train until all the boarding activity was completed and the train was clear. He blew the whistle, then opened the throttle, and with loud puffs of gushing steam, the connecting rod turned the driver wheels and, slowly, the train started toward the bridge. The workmen gathered around the bridge on both sides of the creek, watching as the train approached.

"She's on it!" someone shouted, though the shout wasn't necessary — everyone could see that the engine had eased out onto the bridge. It rolled across and anxious eyes studied the bridges and the timbers for any unwanted activity.

The bridge held solid as the train rolled across. Once the last car had cleared the bridge, Doodle began blowing the whistle, and the workers sent up a mighty cheer. Everyone cheered, even those who had lost money on the bets, but those who won the bets cheered the loudest.

In Stevens's private car, he poured three glasses of whiskey, then held his glass up, joined by the others. They drank a toast, then Stevens pulled out his pocket watch and checked the time.

"We crossed the last major obstacle at four — oh — three p.m.," he said. "Gentleman, I have never felt more confident than now that we will be the first railroad across the border."

Chapter Twenty-Seven

John Henry was sent back down into Indian Territory to meet with Marcus Eberwine. According to Marshal Sarber, who had given John Henry his assignment, Eberwine had been appointed by the Cherokee Council to be the chief liaison between the Indians and whichever railroad won the race to come into Indian Territory.

If it had been up to John Henry, Eberwine would not have received the appointment. John Henry knew who Eberwine was. He was a businessman who employed a lot of Indians, and because of that, he had a lot of people depending on him for their living. But John Henry was absolutely certain that Eberwine took advantage of his position of power within the Cherokee nation by charging such exorbitant prices on goods that he brought in by his freight wagons.

Shortly after John Henry entered Indian Territory he saw a disturbing sign. The sign had been erected alongside the right of way that would be granted for whichever railroad first crossed the border into the Indian Territory.

WARNING TO
THE WHITE MAN'S
RAILROAD
WE DON'T WANT YOU!
STAY OUT OF OUR LAND!

INDIAN INDEPENDENCE COUNCIL

John Henry paused long enough to read the warning, then he looked around to see if anyone was monitoring the sign. He knew that, during the war, Willie Buck had created something called the Indian Independence Council, which he claimed was fighting for the total independence of the Indian Territory from both the Union and the Confederacy. After the war, Willie Buck had made a big thing about surrendering to the Union Army, and was paroled, along with all the other Rebel commanders.

But that was during the war. He was unaware of any activity by the Indian Independence Council since the war had ended. He was sure that Willie Buck had something to do with it, but he decided that he would check with Captain LeFlores. If there was anyone in the whole Territory who would know about it, John Henry was convinced it would be LeFlores.

It had been a couple of months since John Henry was last in Tahlequah, and he exchanged greetings with several people that he recognized, including a few who had fought with him during the late war.

"John Henry, you are making us proud!" Charley Silverthorn called to him.

"Hello, Charley," John Henry called back. "How is your boy?"

"Growing tall and strong. Soon, he will be taller and stronger than I am."

"I'll bet he is already better looking," John Henry said, and both men laughed.

John Henry rode up to a building that served as the Cherokee government offices. Here was the office of President William Ross. Here, too, was where the two houses of the Cherokee Government assembled when they held session. Captain LeFlores, who was chief of the Indian Police, had his office here as well, and it was to LeFlores that John Henry reported.

"Hello, John Henry. Or should I say Marshal Sixkiller?" a smiling LeFlores said by way of greeting.

"Captain," John Henry replied, touching

the brim of his hat.

"What brings you to Tahlequah? Not that I'm not pleased to see you, you understand."

"You mean you don't know?"

LeFlores looked puzzled. "No. Why? Should I know?"

"Maybe not. I just thought you might know. I've been summoned back to meet with Marcus Eberwine."

"Marcus Eberwine? What do you mean, summoned back to meet with him? What are you to meet with him about?"

"I'm told that he has been appointed as liaison between the Cherokee and the railroad."

"Damn, I haven't heard that. I was hoping you were here to arrest the son of a bitch on some charge. To which railroad will he be the liaison?"

"At the moment, it is nonspecific. I expect he will be liaison to whichever railroad is first into the Territory, and as yet, we don't know which that will be. But my guess is that it will be the KATY."

"Who appointed Eberwine? The railroads?" LeFlores asked.

John Henry shook his head. "No. It is my understanding that he was appointed by President Ross."

"William Ross," LeFlores said, slurring

the name. "He wouldn't make a pimple on his father's ass. How in heaven's name he became our chief, I'll never know."

"It was the council," John Henry said.

"Yes."

"Captain LeFlores, what do you know of the Indian Independence Council?"

"The Indian Independence Council? You mean that outfit that Willie Buck started during the war? What about it?"

"Is it active again? I mean, have you heard anything about it?"

"No, I haven't heard anything. Why do you ask?"

"When I first came into the Territory I saw a sign that said the Indians do not want the railroad, and it warned the railroads to stay out. The sign was posted by the Indian Independence Council."

"Nonsense. Why wouldn't they want the railroad here? It will benefit the entire Territory."

"Yes, I would think so as well. But apparently Willie Buck is against it. That is, assuming he is affiliated with the Indian Independence Council."

"Well, I tell you the truth, I wouldn't put it past the son of a bitch. He is certainly ornery enough. Though, why he would be against the railroad, I have no idea. I'm glad you told me about it, though. It sounds as if it might be a group that could cause us trouble. I'll get the police to keep a lookout for it to see if we can actually find out who they are, and what they have planned."

"Thanks, I appreciate that," John Henry said.

LeFlores looked at John Henry, chuckled, and shook his head.

"What is it?" John Henry asked.

"You've come a long way from the young man who wanted nothing more than to avenge your father's murder. You became the best policeman on the entire force, then you were chief sheriff, and now you are a United States Marshal. And, you have compiled quite an impressive record along the way."

"I had a good teacher," John Henry said. He smiled broadly, then pointed. "You."

"You give me too much credit, John Henry."

"I like to give credit where credit is due."

"I appreciate that. And, do me a favor, will you? Watch yourself dealing with Eberwine. I know he is a big man in the Territory, he employs a lot of people, and he has a lot of money. But I've never trusted him, and if he is involved in the railroad business, I just don't believe he is up to any good."

"Thanks for the warning. I'll keep my eyes open."

Leaving the office of his friend, John Henry rode down to the far end of town where he saw a neatly painted white building with green trim. A large sign was posted on top of the building declaring it to be the office of the Eberwine Freight Company. Behind the building was the freight yard, a great, enclosed lot that was at least five acres. Half of the lot was corral for scores of mules, the other half had more than a dozen freight wagons, some ready to go, a few up on stands with one or more wheels removed as they were undergoing maintenance. From the corral a mule started braying, and another picked it up.

As John Henry was dismounting, Marcus Eberwine came out onto the front porch to greet him.

"Marshal, it was good of you to accept the invitation to come," Eberwine said.

"It was a bit more than an invitation. I'm just following orders."

"Perhaps so, but I am glad you are here. And, I see no need to make our visit all business, though of course we will discuss business. But first, we may as well enjoy the meeting. I thought you might be here in time for lunch, so I've had my cook prepare a meal for us. Come in, we'll visit and discuss this railroad situation."

John Henry had never had a direct run-in with Eberwine, though he could remember the distress of his father when one of his friends had lost his store to Eberwine.

"How did you get into such debt with him, Michael?" James had asked.

"He charges so much for the goods that he brings in that I can't make a profit," Michael had responded. "I can't raise the prices, my customers are my friends. I have dealt with them for years. But my debt to Eberwine grew so deep that he went to court and took the store from me."

John Henry recalled that conversation, and felt that doing business with Eberwine today was, in a way, a betrayal of Michael Santone. He would have preferred not to socialize with Eberwine, but he didn't know any easy way to avoid the lunch.

If John Henry had expected something like a ham sandwich, or perhaps some cold chicken, he was very much mistaken. Inside the office building he saw a table, covered with a crisp, white table cloth, set with gold candelabra, shining silverware, classic china, and delicate crystal stemware. The lunch, served by a white-coated server, consisted of tinned oysters, freshly caught trout, baked sweet potatoes, wine, and canned peaches in heavy cream.

John Henry picked at his meal, while Eberwine consumed his with great gusto, so enjoying his eating that he didn't even notice that John Henry barely touched his food. After the meal was over and the white-jacketed server cleared away the table, Eberwine suggested that they move to another part of the room where two overstuffed oxblood leather chairs faced each other, separated by a small, round table. There were papers on the table, at least one of which, John Henry noticed, was a map.

Another servant, this time a very attractive young woman, approached the two men carrying a small, wooden box. When she reached them she opened the box, displaying its contents — at least two dozen aromatic cigars.

"These are from Cuba, you must try them," Eberwine said. He took one out and handed it to the woman. She used a silver cutter to snip the tips, then she licked the side, handed the cigar to Eberwine, and held a match under it. Eberwine puffed until the end glowed red and his head was enwreathed by smoke.

She took a second cigar out and snipped the tips, but before she licked the side, John Henry shook his head and reached for it. She lit his cigar as well.

"I think it is absolutely uncivilized to discuss business in any way other than in the convivial atmosphere of good cigar smoke," Eberwine said.

"It is a good cigar," John Henry said, wanting Eberwine to lead the conversation.

Eberwine removed the cigar and studied the end of it for moment before he spoke again.

"Tell me, Marshal, you have been a part of this railroad operation for some time now — which one do you think will be first to reach the border?"

John Henry had his own belief about which one he thought would be first, and he had shared that idea with Captain Le-Flores, but he had no intention of sharing it with Eberwine. At least, not until he had some feel of what Eberwine's role was in this operation. "I don't know the answer to that," he said. "Both of them are building as quickly as they can and, at the moment, I would say that they are about even."

"But surely you have an idea of who is in

the lead. Or at least, who you think might win. I don't wish to breach any agreement of confidentiality you may have with them, but I think it would make my job easier."

"What, exactly, is your job, Mr. Eberwine?"

"Why, I thought you knew." Eberwine stuck the cigar back in his mouth, then spoke around it. "I am to be the liaison between the railroad and the Cherokee people. But I don't know exactly what that will entail until I know which railroad I will have to deal with."

"Have to deal with? You say that as if you aren't welcoming a railroad into Indian Territory."

"On the contrary, sir. Who would not welcome the railroad, and the prosperity it is sure to bring to all of us?"

"Evidently, there are some who don't want the railroad."

"You would be talking about the Indian Independence Council?'

Eberwine's mention of the Indian Independence Council surprised John Henry.

"You mean you know about them?"

"Yes, of course I have heard of them. They have certainly let it be known that they are displeased with the idea of a railroad coming into the Indian Territory."

"It's strange that you would know that, when Captain LeFlores did not."

"Are you telling me that the captain of the Indian Police is unaware of the opposition of the Indian Independence Council to the railroad? My, that doesn't give one much confidence in our police, does it? I mean, you know about it, and you aren't even one of us."

"One of us?"

"Well, I meant that figuratively, of course. Of course, you are Cherokee, even though you are no longer a full-time resident of the Territory, being as you are a United States Marshal. And I'm not Cherokee, though my heart is certainly with the Cherokee nation. But tell me, how is it that you know about their opposition to the railroad, and Le-Flores does not?"

"I wouldn't have known about it if I hadn't seen a sign that they posted. I know the Indian Independence Council was something that Willie Buck put together in order to justify his looting during the war. I didn't know he was still involved with it."

"Do you think it's Willie Buck?"

"Who else would it be?" John Henry asked.

"Yes. Who else indeed? But you are right about their opposition to the railroad. I got a letter of demand from them as soon as it was announced in the *Cherokee Advocate* that I was to be the railroad liaison. I do know, though, that it is composed of a group of Indians, and not just Cherokee, who want the Indian Territory to be independent from the United States. As I understand it, they want to establish a separate nation, a nation to be called Sequoyah, I believe."

"Do you still have that letter?"

"Yes, would you like to see it?"

"I would, if you don't mind."

Eberwine rose from his chair and walked over to his desk. Pulling open one of the drawers, he removed the letter, then brought it back to John Henry.

"My first thought upon getting it was to tear it up and throw it away. As you will see when you read it, it is quite belligerent. But, upon second thought, I decided to keep it, just in case they decided to act upon one of their threats and someone in authority might want to see it."

John Henry nodded, then took the letter and began to read:

Dear Mr. Eberwine:

We, the members of the Indian Independence Council, have read with interest the news of your appointment as Railroad Liaison.

The railroad must not, and will not, be built. Be warned, we will not stand by and allow any further incursion by the white man into our lands until such time as we have gained full and complete independence from the collection of states that call themselves the United States of America.

In your capacity as liaison, we caution you to order the railroads currently under construction to halt at the border. Any attempt made by the railroad to cross into Indian Territory will be resisted, by violence if necessary.

Once our independence is gained, we will build a railroad system through our new nation and, at that time, enter into agreements with American railroads that will allow trade and commerce.

Any attempt to build a railroad before our independence is gained, and agreements made, will end in disaster.

Sincerely,
Indian Independence Council
Willie Buck, President

John Henry looked up after he finished

reading the letter. "I'm surprised he signed it."

"Oh, I think he fashions himself a patriot. I'm sure he is quite sincere in wanting the Territory to secede."

"We tried to secede once before, and it brought us nothing but trouble," John Henry said.

"Yes, you are talking about the Civil War, when the Five Civilized Nations opted to secede from the Union and join the Confederacy. That wasn't a very smart move, I will admit. But this isn't anything like that. What the Indian Independence Council wants, as I understand it, is complete independence, not to be affiliated with any other country, but to be a nation itself."

"That wouldn't be a very wise thing to do. In the first place, we would be completely landlocked by states and territories of the United States. What sort of independence would that be? Besides, even if these people are serious about secession again, and make a declaration of independence, wouldn't it make sense to support the railroad, rather than oppose it? A railroad would give us a connection to the outside world."

"Yes, but I think their point is that the white man would own the railroad. I believe they want us to own the railroad."

"Us?"

"Again, I am speaking figuratively. I meant, of course, that they want the Indians to own the railroad."

Chapter Twenty-Eight

Eberwine walked John Henry to the door. "I'm sure, Marshal, that with you on the job we will have no difficulty in bringing the railroad to the Indian Territory."

"I appreciate your confidence in me, Mr. Eberwine."

"How can I not be confident? You have made quite a name for yourself as a U.S. Marshal, and before that, as an Indian policeman."

"As I said, I appreciate your confidence," John Henry said.

After John Henry Sixkiller left his office, Eberwine walked over to stand in front of the window and watch as the marshal mounted his horse and rode away. Not until then did he call out.

"You can come out now, Mr. Dixon. He's gone," Eberwine said.

Matt Dixon had been hiding in a back room of Eberwine's office, peeping through a crack at the U.S. Marshal who was meeting with Eberwine. As soon as the marshal left, Dixon came out of the back room and, without being invited, walked over to the desk to take a handful of Eberwine's cigars.

In a world without guns, Dixon, because he was small, and almost anemic looking, would scarcely be noticed. But this was a world with guns, and Dixon had the two attributes that served him well in his chosen profession as a hired gun. He was fast and accurate, but many gunfighters were fast and accurate. Dixon possessed that additional character trait that made him a man to be feared by even the fastest and most skilled. Dixon could kill without compunction. Dixon could take a man's life with no more thought than he would give to stepping on a bug.

Eberwine had sent for Dixon, and was going to hire him. But even Eberwine felt uneasy in his presence. He winced, as Dixon put at least five of the expensive cigars in a pocket. He lit one, causing Eberwine to wince again as he scratched a match across Eberwine's desk.

"Is that the man you want me to kill?" Dixon asked as he held the match to the end of his cigar.

"Well, I wouldn't exactly put it that way,"

Eberwine said.

Dixon squinted at him through the tobacco smoke. "No? How would you put it?"

"I want him — out of the way — so he won't interfere with my plans."

"If he is dead, he is out of the way."

"Yes," Eberwine said. "I suppose if you put it that way. But I'm not going to tell you how to do it. I just want him, uh, out of the way."

"It's going to cost you fifteen hundred dollars," Dixon said.

"Fifteen hundred? Are you serious?"

"I'm very serious. I know that you can afford it, Eberwine."

"I only paid Percy Martin five hundred dollars."

"Uh-huh. And how did that work out for you? Martin's dead, isn't he?"

"Yes," Eberwine agreed.

"You get what you pay for. I'm going to cost you fifteen hundred dollars. Seven hundred fifty now, and another seven hundred fifty when Sixkiller is — out of the way."

"All right," Eberwine said. "All right, I'll give you what you ask. I just want the job done.

After successfully crossing the creek,

Stevens's group, perhaps inspired by the success of completing the building under the harshest possible conditions, worked prodigiously. For the first few days after crossing the creek, the railroad progressed at a rate of three miles per day, including when they set a record of four miles and one hundred feet of track laid in one day.

Their progress did not go unnoticed, and when word got back to Octave Chanute, he rode over to have a look himself. Stunned and upset by what he saw, he hurried back to Fort Scott to report to James Joy.

Unlike Robert Stevens, Joy had chosen to stay away from end of track, especially after he learned that Baxter Springs was not only outside Indian Territory, but was opposite Shawnee land, not Cherokee land.

"I'm tellin' you, Mr. Joy, they are going to beat us there," Chanute said. "They are laying track like you've never seen. They are in Chetopa."

"In Chetopa? How far is that from the border?"

"Three miles. The way they have been laying track, they'll make it in one day."

"How far are we from Cherokee land?"

"Eight miles, three days, two at the absolute best," Chanute said.

"Damn, to get this close and be beaten by that upstart Stevens? No," Joy said. He slammed the side of his fist down on his desk. "No, by God I will not be beaten by him!"

"Mr. Joy, if we worked twenty-four hours a day, and doubled our work force, I don't believe we could beat the KATY into the Indian Territory."

"Then if we can't work any faster, we will slow them down," Joy suggested.

"What do you have in mind?"

"I want you to arrange a visit," Joy said. "Offer a twenty-dollar bonus to anyone who is willing to go over to the KATY operation and find some way to slow them down."

"How do you propose to do that?"

"Use your head, Octave!" Joy yelled. "If, say, some of their track was removed, it would slow them down, don't you think?"

"What about the truce you made with Colonel Stevens?"

"Did Boudinot welcome us into the Cherokee Nation, or did he not?" Joy asked.

"Yes, sir, he did."

"And were we in the Cherokee Nation?"

"No, sir, we were not."

"And has he, or has he not, allied himself with Robert Stevens and the KATY Railroad?"

"He has."

Joy smiled and nodded. "Would you not consider that, by that duplicitous action, the truce was broken?"

Chanute laughed out loud. "Yes, sir, indeed the truce was broken."

"By KATY."

"Yes, sir, by KATY."

"Therefore if several of our men pay a visit to the KATY people in Chetopa and slow down the operation, it cannot be said that we broke the truce. It can only be said that we were responding to their dishonest welcoming of us to the Cherokee Nation. How many men can you gather?"

"For twenty dollars apiece I can gather over a hundred men," Chanute said.

"Then, by all means, do so. I will have the money ready when the men return."

Scullin pulled out a handkerchief and wiped the sweat off his brow as he watched the men working with purpose and rhythm. So pleased were they with the fact that the goal was in sight . . . with its one-hundred-dollar bonus per man for winning the race, that the men were singing as they worked.

Hail to the day and deed
Hail to the iron steed

Hail to the iron rail
Hail to the KATY, hail
Border Tier can go to hell.

Scullin laughed at the song the men had composed, but the laughter died in his throat when he saw several wagons and horses approaching.

"Colonel Stevens," Scullin said, pointing toward the approaching men.

"What is it?" Stevens asked.

"I don't know, but I don't like the looks of it," Scullin said. Then he recognized the track boss of the Border Tier. "Son of a bitch! It's O'Brien and his men."

"What do you think they want?"

"I don't think they want to congratulate us."

"But, no, Joy and I have a truce."

"Not anymore you don't. Men! Gather 'round!" Scullin shouted. "Gather 'round, men! We're about to do battle with the heathen bastards of the Border Tier!"

The wagons and horses continued to approach. Then they stopped and men started pouring out of the wagons, screaming and yelling in fury as they ran toward the KATY men, now gathered around Scullin.

"At 'em, boys, at 'em!" Scullin shouted, and though Stevens retreated to the rear,

Scullin advanced to the front, becoming the first of the KATY men to land a blow.

Both the KATY and Border Tier men had hammers and pickaxes that could have been used as weapons, but those were thrown aside and, with ancient Irish war cries, the two sides went against each other with fists flying.

The Battle of Chetopa was on, and the citizens of Chetopa, aroused by the screams of rage and battle, poured out of their homes to witness the fight.

In order to show impartiality, John Henry Sixkiller was halfway between Chetopa and the current end of track for the Border Tier Railroad. The distance between the two points was ten miles, which meant that John Henry was five miles away from Chetopa when he saw Sheriff Gurney coming toward him at a gallop.

Realizing that it must be something important to bring Sheriff Gurney out here so fast, John Henry started galloping toward him so that he was able to close the distance quickly.

"What is it, Sheriff?" John Henry called when he pulled up on Iron Heart.

"Marshal, you have to come quick!" Sheriff Gurney said. "There's a hell of a fight going on back in town between Joy's men and Stevens's men. There's more'n two hundred engaged if there is a man."

"Is it a shooting fight?" John Henry asked, anxiously.

"No, thank God. At least, there wasn't no shooting when I left. As far as I could tell, they're just goin' after each other with nothin' but their bare hands, but there's so many of 'em, I don't see how we're goin' to avoid some real serious injuries."

"How much do you have left in your horse?" John Henry asked.

"I don't know, he's purt' nigh give out, gallopin' all the way out here like I done. I'll follow you back, but I won't be able to keep up with you."

"That's all right, get there when you can," John Henry said, urging Iron Heart into a gallop.

John Henry could hear the shouts, screams, and curses before he got there, even over the thundering sound of hoofbeats as Iron Heart galloped, without letup, for the entire five miles. When he got to town, he saw a great crowd of what looked to be over a thousand people. At first he thought they were all fighting, but as he got closer he saw that most were just gathered around, watching the melee of flying fists.

Pulling his pistol, he fired it into the air as he rode Iron Heart right into the middle of the brawlers. The intrusion of the horse knocked several of the men down and had the effect of separating the others. He fired a few more times until, finally, the fighting stopped and everyone looked toward him.

"You men back away from each other, farther!" John Henry ordered.

When they didn't move quickly enough, he fired into the ground, first just in front of the feet of the Border Tier men, and then in front of the KATY men. That drove them farther apart and the men of the KATY and the men of the Border Tier stood across from each other, bloodied and bruised but, for the moment, quiet.

"Mr. Scullin!" John Henry called.

"Aye, Marshal," Scullin replied, his nose bloody, his knuckles split, and his face bearing the smile of a man who loves a fight.

"What is going on here?"

" 'Tis a fight, Marshal, and a glorious one it be," Scullin said.

"I can see that. How did it start?"

"These black-hearted Border Tier men attacked my men while we were at work."

"Who is in charge of the Border Tier men?" John Henry asked.

"That would be me," a man said, stepping forward. Like Scullin, he was bloodied and bruised.

"Paddy O'Brien," Scullin called out to him. "Sure 'n' there's never been the day when a man from Donegal County could beat a man from Cork, and that's the truth of it."

"I'm the better man than you, John Scullin, an' you'll be forgettin' that soon, I don't think."

"Mr. O'Brien, what are you and your men doing here?" John Henry asked.

"Why, Marshal, t'wasn't nothin' but a friendly fracas that brought us here. A few blows among friends, you might say."

"Take your men back where they belong."

O'Brien turned to his men and nodded and, nursing broken noses and fingers, they started toward their horses and wagons.

"Paddy, m'boyo," Scullin called out. "As soon as we cross the border into The Nations, come see me. We'll share a pint, and speak o' Ireland like the friends we once were."

CHAPTER TWENTY-NINE

With Joy's men gone, work could continue unhampered on the KATY Line. And because the KATY was within a few days of reaching the border, John Henry decided that his best bet would be to stay with the KATY until the border was crossed. He telegraphed his intention to Marcus Eberwine.

CROSSING INTO INDIAN TERRITORY IMMINENT BY KATY RAILROAD WILL REMAIN WITH KATY UNTIL CROSSING. JH SIXKILLER

"Wait, Mr. Deckert," Eberwine said after he read the telegram Deckert had given him. "I have a telegram I need to send. I want you to take it to the telegraph office."

"Yes, sir," Deckert said, standing by as Eberwine wrote out his telegram.

■ ■ ■ ■

Matt Dixon was in the End of Track Saloon in Baxter Springs, drinking whiskey and playing solitaire. He was playing solitaire because everyone was too frightened to play poker with him. Finding no play for a red six of hearts, he looked through the down cards until he found a black seven, then turned it up so he had a play. It was cheating, yes, but he reasoned that, since he was cheating himself, what difference did it make?

A boy of about fifteen came into the saloon.

"What are you doing in here, Mickey?" the bartender asked.

"I have a telegram for Mr. Dixon," the boy replied.

"That's him back there in the corner, playing solitaire," the bartender said, pointing.

"That's him? He ain't very big, is he? From all I've heard of him, I thought he would be a big man."

"How big do you have to be to kill someone?" the bartender asked as he went back to wiping his glasses.

Mickey stared at him for a long moment before he got up the courage to walk back

353

to his table.

"What do you want, boy?" Dixon asked, as Mickey approached, then stopped but said nothing.

"Are you Mr. Dixon?"

Dixon looked up from the cards he had spread out on the table. "I said, what do you want?"

"I, uh, have a telegram for you."

Dixon held out his hand, and Mickey handed it to him. He continued to stand there.

"Is that all?" Dixon asked.

"Yes, sir, only, the way I get paid is when folks give me a tip after I've handed them the telegram."

"It is, is it?"

"Yes, sir."

"Well, here's a tip, boy. Don't come pussyfooting around me no more. I don't like it."

Realizing then that no money would be forth-coming, Mickey walked away from the table.

"Mickey," the bartender said as Mickey walked by.

"Yes, sir?"

"Here," the bartender said, giving him a nickel.

"Thanks, Mr. Green," Mickey said, a

smile brightening his face.

"Did you give that boy some money?" Dixon asked after Mickey had left.

"Yes, sir. The boy don't have a daddy, and his mama is sickly. The boy gettin' paid for deliverin' telegrams is the only way they have of making a livin'."

"If you're dumb enough to want to give him money, it's none of my concern," Dixon said. "But you ain't doin' it for me."

"No, sir, this wasn't no reflection on you," the bartender said. "I was just, uh, tryin' to help the boy and his mama out, is all."

"A woman can always make money whorin'. What does his mama look like?"

"She couldn't do that, Mr. Dixon. Like I said, she's just real sickly."

"Ha! What the hell does she have to do but lie there when a man is with her?" Dixon asked, then he laughed at his own joke.

Not until then did Dixon open the telegram.

SIXKILLER IN CHETOPA. SECOND PAYMENT PLUS BONUS WHEN JOB IS DONE.

John Henry was in the Railroad Saloon having his lunch and a beer when Matt Dixon came in. John Henry had never met

Dixon, and didn't know who he was until the little man came over to his table.

"Are you Marshal John Henry Sixkiller?" Dixon asked.

"Yes," John Henry replied. The question had been more challenging than inquisitive, and John Henry dropped both his hands in his lap.

"Yes, I'm Marshal Sixkiller," John Henry replied. "Is there something I can do for you, Mister . . . ?" He let the sentence hang, inviting the little man to supply his name.

"My name is Dixon. Matt Dixon. And what you can do for me is die."

"If it's all the same to you, Mr. Dixon, I'd prefer not to die," John Henry replied. His voice was calm.

"It's not all the same to me. They tell me you are good with a gun, Marshal. Is that true?"

"There have been those who have tried to kill me, but so far I've managed to stay alive."

"Have you ever heard of me?" Dixon asked.

"Oh, yes, I've heard of you."

"What have you heard?"

"I've heard that you enjoy killing."

Dixon smiled. "That's right. And I especially like killing big strong sons of bitches like you. I'll just bet you wish you could mop this floor up with my ass, don't you?"

"Yes, that is a pleasant thought," John Henry replied.

"I know what people like you are like."

"Really? And what are people like me like?"

"You see someone small like me, and you think I'm of no consequence. You think you can just brush me off like a fly. But this" — Dixon patted the handle of his pistol — "makes me as good as the biggest and strongest man that ever lived."

"No, it doesn't make you as good," John Henry said. "It may give you a little backbone, but it doesn't make you as good."

"I'm tired of talkin', Sixkiller," Dixon said. "I've heard that you are fast with a gun. For an Injun," he added with a smile. "How about it, Mr. Sixkiller? Me and you. You want to try it now? Go for your gun." Dixon moved his hand down to hover just over his own gun.

The conversation had started easily enough, but it quickly progressed to a dangerous level, and now a challenge had been issued. From a nearby table a woman's laughter halted in mid-trill and the piano player pulled his hands away from the keyboard so that the last three notes of his melody hung raggedly, discordantly, in the air. All conversation ceased and everyone in the crowded saloon turned to see if the event they had all been speculating on was about to take place. Most of the onlookers were experiencing some trepidation as they watched the drama being played out before them. But there were some who were watching with morbid curiosity, anxious to see where this was going. Was there going to be a gunfight? If so, who would win?

"Well, Mr. Dixon, let's think about this. I mean even if you beat me, what satisfaction will you get? It wouldn't be a fair draw now, would it?" John Henry asked, replying to the man's challenge. "I mean I'm sitting down, and you're standing up. I would be at a disadvantage trying to draw."

Dixon's smile broadened. "Yeah, well, that's the way of it. It's the luck of the draw, you might say." He laughed. " 'Luck of the draw.' That's funny, ain't it? I mean, seein' as we are about to draw against each other. Now, Sixkiller. Let's do it now. I don't plan to wait around all day while you're getting' up your courage."

"Oh, you don't have to wait," John Henry said. "You see when I saw you come over to my table, I thought you might have something like this in mind. So I've already pulled my gun. I'm holding a gun under this table right now and it's pointed straight at your belly."

Dixon blinked a couple of times, then he laughed nervously. "Who are you trying to kid, Sixkiller?" he asked. "You didn't pull your gun. It's still in your holster. I can see it!"

John Henry looked down at the pistol in his holster. "Well, so it is," he said easily. "I guess I would really be in trouble now, wouldn't I? I mean if that was the gun I was talking about. But I'm not talking about that gun," John Henry explained. "No, sir, the gun I'm talking about is the one I keep up my sleeve. I learned some time ago to do that. It's a derringer, two barrels, forty-one caliber. I can shoot right through this table and put a hole in your stomach big enough to stick my fist in."

"You're bluffing. You don't have a holdout gun under there. I know you don't."

"Well, now," John Henry said. "I guess you are just too smart for me, Dixon. You've figured it out, haven't you? It could be that I don't have a gun under the table, couldn't it? Or, maybe I do. I guess you are just going to have to go ahead and draw to find out."

"Don't think I'm going to let you stand

up and draw," Dixon said. "You're the one so dumb that you didn't stand up when you saw me come in."

"You've got a point there. I guess I'm just going to have to sit here and let you draw on me."

"Do you think I won't draw on you?"

"Oh, on the contrary, Mr. Dixon. I'm counting on you to draw. I mean, what if you didn't draw? Why, when I blow a hole in your belly, some might call it outright murder. On the other hand, if you would go ahead and draw now, and if everyone in here sees you draw, why I'll have all the witnesses I need to prove that I killed you in self-defense."

"You're — you're bluffing," Dixon said.

John Henry noticed a little line of perspiration beads breaking out on Dixon's upper lip. His pupils had grown larger, and his nostrils were flaring.

"I might be bluffing. I probably am, bluffing," John Henry said, his voice as calm as if he were in conversation with a casual friend. "Go ahead, Mr. Dixon. Draw. Let's see whether I'm bluffing or not. You could be right."

Dixon stood his ground for a moment longer, trying to decide whether or not he would call John Henry's bluff. His eyes narrowed, a muscle in his cheek twitched, and he began sweating more profusely.

"I tell you what. Suppose I count to three, and you draw on three," John Henry said. "No, that won't work, will it? I might decide to shoot on the count of two. Then where would you be?"

"I don't think you have a gun under that table," Dixon said.

"Like I said, you are probably right. So what do you say, Mr. Dixon? Do you want to call my bluff?"

"Wait a minute, I see what you are doing now," Dixon said.

"Oh? What am I doing?"

"You're trying to draw me into a trap."

John Henry laughed. "Draw you into a trap. You're just real clever, Dixon, the way you manage to work that word *draw* into a sentence."

Dixon was growing visibly more nervous.

"Draw, damn you. Can't you see that all these folks are wanting to see the show?" John Henry demanded.

"No," Dixon replied, holding his hand up in front of him, palm out. "No, I ain't goin' to draw. One thing I learned a long time ago is not to get into a gunfight until you know all the angles. I don't know all the angles here."

"That's true, you really don't know, do you? Of course, you said that you don't believe I have a gun here. And maybe I don't. That would be one thing going for you, I believe."

"Yeah, and it might be going against me," Dixon said. "Because the truth is, I don't really know one way or the other. And I'm not about to get into any fight unless I know there are no surprises."

"Yes," John Henry agreed. "That's always been my policy. I don't enter any confrontation unless I know exactly where I stand. I mean, I wouldn't invite you to draw, unless I was holding a pistol in my hand. That is, of course, if I'm actually holding a pistol in my hand. What about it, Mr. Dixon? Shall we open the ball?"

"Shit!" Dixon shouted. Now he put his hands out in front of him. "All right, all right, I ain't goin' to go for my gun now," he said. He pointed at Sixkiller. "But you and me has got us a score to settle, Mister."

"Dixon?" John Henry called out as the diminutive gunman started to leave. Dixon turned toward John Henry.

"I don't figure you would be coming after me unless someone paid you to do it. Who paid you?"

"You're pretty smart, ain't you?" Dixon

asked ominously.

"I try to be."

"What if I told you we were working for the same man?"

"I'm working for the U.S. Government," John Henry replied.

"Are you now? You know, don't you, that I'm going to have to kill you?"

"I know you are going to try," John Henry replied. "But you have to know, also, that I'm going to try, just as hard, not to get killed."

"I'll be seeing you around," Dixon said. "Soon," he added ominously.

"I'm sure I will be." John Henry watched as Dixon left through the swinging bat-wing doors. Then he brought his hands up from under the table. They were completely empty.

"What the hell?" one of the saloon patrons gasped. "Did you see that? The marshal just run a bluff on Matthew Dixon!"

"I never thought I'd live to see anythin' like that," another commented.

Without comment or gesture, John Henry got up from the table and walked over to the bar. He handed the bartender his empty mug.

"I'll have another."

"Yes, sir, Marshal!" the bartender said.

"And this one is on the house! Yes, sir, it's worth it to see what I just seen."

As the bartender turned toward the beer barrel to refill the mug, John Henry pulled his pistol and faced the door.

"Draw now, you son of a bitch!" Dixon shouted, darting back inside the door. His gun was in his hand and he fired a shot at the table where John Henry had been sitting.

"I'm over here, Dixon," John Henry said calmly, standing at the bar.

Dixon swung his pistol around for a second shot, but before he could pull the trigger, John Henry fired. The impact of the bullet knocked Dixon back out through the bat-wing doors.

John Henry held the smoking pistol in his right hand and continued to look toward the door as, nervously, the bartender put the beer mug down on the bar beside him. John Henry didn't even look around, but reached back with his left hand to get the beer. He took a long swallow as he continued to stare at the door.

If Dixon had any friends, none of them came in after him.

Chapter Thirty

The next morning John Henry visited Colonel Stevens in his private car. The car was blocking Maple Street in Chetopa, and everyone in the town was standing in the street, staring through the window at John Henry and Colonel Stevens as they were talking.

"I heard about the run-in you had with Matthew Dixon last night," Colonel Stevens said. "Hell, ever'body has heard about it. It's the only thing anyone wants to talk about."

"I guess those sort of things do create a lot of talk," John Henry said.

"Why do you think he came after you like that?"

"That's a good question. He said something interesting though. He said that he and I were working for the same man."

"Working for the same man? What does that mean?"

"I don't know," John Henry said. "I have been puzzling over it."

"We'll be crossing the Territory line at noon tomorrow," Stevens said. "The Border Tier is still some six miles away, which means we have won. I don't expect any last-minute skullduggery, but I would be obliged if you would spend the rest of your time here with us, until we cross into The Nations."

"That sounds like a reasonable request," John Henry said. "I'll stay with you."

"Colonel Stevens!" Gunn said, calling into the car from the door.

"Yes, Otis, come in, come in."

Otis Gunn was smiling, broadly, and holding up a piece of paper, waving it back and forth.

"This just came by telegram. I thought you might want to read it."

"You are smiling," Stevens said. "May I take from that that it is good news?"

"Yes, sir, you can," Gunn said.

"Then you read it to us."

"All right," Gunn answered. Clearing his throat, he began to read. " 'On the 6th, instant, the KATY will be completed to the south boundary of the state of Kansas. I have passed over this railroad, making a careful and critical examination of its construction and equipment, and hereby certify that said Missouri, Kansas, and Texas Railway Company have constructed a first-class railroad, beginning at its junction with the Kansas Pacific Railway at Junction City, from thence in a south-easterly course to the headwaters of the Neosho River, and thence across the valley of said river to the town of Chetopa.' "

"That's a very good endorsement," Stevens said.

"It was good enough to get the job done," Gunn said.

"What do you mean?"

Gunn broke out into a big smile.

"We also got a telegram from Secretary of the Interior Cox." Gunn cleared his throat, than began to read. " 'I find that at the Kansas and Neosho Road, the Border Tier is not authorized at present, under said legislation, to enter the Indian Territory and build the line, and that to complete its right at this time to do so, it would have been necessary for said road to have been completely constructed to a point in the Neosho Valley at or near the crossing of the boundary line by the Neosho, and where it could enter the Cherokee country without crossing the reservation of any other Indian tribe. This, the said company has not done.' "

With his smile even broader, Gunn looked up from the telegram toward Stevens. "You know what this means, Bob?"

John Henry looked toward Colonel Stevens, and saw his eyes glistening. He looked away quickly, so as not to embarrass him.

"Yes, Mr. Gunn, I know what it means," Stevens answered in a voice that cracked. "It means we have won."

From the *Southern Kansas Advance:*

KATY Wins Railroad Race Will Be Allowed to Enter Indian Territory

At ten o'clock on Monday morning the KATY Railway reached the south line of Kansas. The construction train was ordered up to the foot of Maple Street by Colonel Stevens, and through the enthusiastic efforts of the band, hundreds of our citizens were soon on their way to the depot to be in for a free ride.

The end of the track is two miles and one hundred rods south of Chetopa. Arrived there, we found the Irish brigade which had hammered and shoveled its way from Junction City, one hundred and eighty miles, to the Indian Territory in less than nine months, resting their picks and hammers at last on Cherokee soil, on the grassy slopes looking down to Russell Creek.

To Colonel Stevens fell the task, and the honor, of driving the last spike on the Kansas side of the line. Three or four false blows greatly amused the Irish track brigade, but the task was completed, the spike driven, and the race to the border was won.

In a brief speech, Colonel Stevens reminded the crowd that "we shall not stop here. Our course lies onward to the Red River. Nor shall we pause there, but continue to the Rio Grande. Beyond this even, we are casting our eyes through the chaparral and over the steppes of Mexico, till our engine stands panting in the palaces of Montezuma and the halls of the Aztecs."

The first railroad spike driven on Indian soil was driven by Colonel Elias C. Boudinot, a Cherokee Indian, and an attorney.

"My own people," said Boudinot, "along with the Creeks, Choctaws, Chickasaws, and Seminoles, the Five Civilized Tribes, have always been pre-eminent to the wild Indians of the plains by virtue of what we have learned by contact with the white man. I stand in no fear or dread of the railroad. It will make my people richer and happier. I feel that my people are bound closer together and to the government by these iron bands."

Chapter Thirty-One

One week after the border crossing ceremonies, the KATY was five miles into the Indian Territory when a surveying party was set upon by three men. The surveying party was unarmed, and they stood by helplessly as the three armed men destroyed their instruments and destroyed their charts and maps.

"Why are you doing this?" Willard Fairman asked. Fairman was the chief surveyor.

"This is Indian Territory. This is our land, this does not belong to the white man, and we don't want your railroad here," one of the armed men said.

"But we have permission from the Cherokee Council. Colonel Boudinot himself welcomed us when we crossed the border."

"The Council does not speak for us," the Indian said. "Show this paper to Colonel Stevens."

Fairman and his surveying team returned

to end of track where Steven's private car, the Prairie Queen, had been converted into his office. Stevens and Scullin were in a discussion when Fairman and his entire team stepped in.

"Willard?" Scullin asked, surprised to see not only his chief surveyor, but the entire surveying team. "What are you doing here? Why aren't you out surveying?"

"You can't survey without tools, and we've got no surveying tools."

"What do you mean? What happened to them?"

"They were destroyed."

"Destroyed? How?"

"By Indians."

"What?"

"Read this," Fairman said, handing the note to Stevens. Stevens read the note, then passed it over for John Scullin to read.

The railroad company KATY is trespassing on Indian land. You are not welcome here. Leave our land at once, or suffer the consequences.

Indian Independence Council

"What is this Indian Independence Council? I've never heard of it before," Stevens said. "Who are they?"

CHAPTER THIRTY-THREE

"It wasn't anything," Willie Buck said, answering Eberwine's query about the cause of the shooting. "Just some of the men shooting at ghosts, that's all."

"You're sure?"

"I'm sure."

Willie Buck was good at his job. He had also known John Henry since both were boys, and he knew that John Henry Sixkiller was a person who did what he set out to do. That meant that no matter where he was now, he was going to turn up here, at the main house. This is where Sasha Quiet Stream was, and she was John Henry's goal.

He found himself wishing that John Henry would show up here. He had spent a lifetime being outdone by Sixkiller. It would give him a lot of satisfaction to be the one to kill him tonight. And then, after John Henry was killed, Willie Buck had his own plans for the girl, plans that he hadn't shared with anyone else.

"What are you doing hanging around here? Why aren't you out looking for him?"

"You really want me to leave you here, by yourself, to face him alone?" Willie Buck asked.

"No, no, I guess not."

"We've got men combing the entire range," Willie Buck answered. "Maybe someone will get lucky. But the real place to look for him is right here."

"Right here? What do you mean?"

"I mean he's goin' to come here to get the girl," Willie Buck said. "And when he does, we'll get him."

"Surely he won't try it now that we're on to him, will he?" Eberwine asked. "I mean he'd be a fool to try it right under our noses."

"Eberwine, I have known John Henry Sixkiller since we were children together." Willie Buck put his finger to his temple. "I know how he thinks. Leave this to me. I promise you, he will come here, and we will kill him tonight."

"All right," Eberwine said after a thoughtful pause. "We'll try it your way."

"That's more like it," Willie Buck said. "Now, you men, get rifles!" he ordered the others. "Get into your positions! Sixkiller is going to be comin' around sooner or later."

"What about the others?" one of the cowboys asked. "The ones that are still ridin' around out there."

"What about them?" Willie Buck asked.

"We got eight men out there. Shouldn't we send someone out there to bring them in?"

"What the hell for?" Willie Buck asked. "They'll just get in the way."

"But what if they find John Henry?" one of the men asked. "Will we still get our bonuses? I mean, even though we aren't lookin' for him?"

"When we kill him, the one hundred dollars is for everyone," Willie Buck said. "That would include the men who are back here."

"Yeah, but there's a thousand dollars for the one that gets him," one of the cowboys complained. "I don't see anyone who stays here collectin' on that money."

"Then go join the others if you want to," Willie Buck said easily.

"Really? It's all right with you if I go out to look for him?"

"Sure," Willie Buck said. "And since John Henry is wandering around somewhere out there between us and them, who knows? You might get lucky and run across him yourself. You can take him, can't you? If you can, you won't even have to split the thousand dollars."

"Yeah, that's right, isn't it?" the cowboy said with a broad grin. "Maybe I'll just . . . hey, wait a minute!" he said, suddenly realizing the implications of it. "There's no way I'm going to go up against Sixkiller by myself. What good is a thousand dollars if I'm dead? I'm not going out there."

"Does that mean you're staying here?"

"You're damn right it does."

"Then you'll do what I tell you."

"Sure, Willie Buck, whatever you say," the cowboy acquiesced meekly.

Willie Buck scattered the men out, putting them in defensive positions all around the house. Once that was done, they waited.

And they waited.

Though John Henry was surprised at the number of defenders there were here at the ranch, he wasn't surprised by the preparations they had made for him. From where he was, John Henry used his binoculars to make a careful survey of the defensive positions Willie Buck had constructed. That knowledge would come in handy when he made his move.

He located seven men at various positions on the ground around the house. The seven men had overlapping fields of fire, and that meant that there was no way to make a direct approach to the house without coming under fire from more than one of the defenders. In addition to the men on the ground, there was a man in the hayloft of the barn. John Henry had to congratulate Willie Buck on constructing his defense. A good-sized army couldn't get through.

But John Henry wasn't an army. He was one man, sneaking through the cracks.

John Henry had also seen Eberwine. He had been out on the porch for a few minutes talking to Willie Buck, then he went back into the house. John Henry hadn't been all that surprised to see that Eberwine was with Willie Buck. He knew now what Matt Dixon meant when he said that they were both working for the same man.

John Henry swept his binoculars across the front, looking in through each window. One of the downstairs windows had a gap in the middle of the drapes, as if someone had been looking through them. All the other drapes hung as straight as if they were sewn shut.

John Henry lowered the binoculars.

"Hang on, Sasha," John Henry said quietly. "I'm coming for you."

As the sun dipped lower in the west, John

Henry decided to try to improve his position. There was another protected spot off to his left, a little ridgeline that protruded like a finger pointing toward the house. The end of the finger was a hundred yards closer than he was now, and from there, John Henry would be able to see more clearly what was going on. But if he was going to do it, he was going to have to do it now, before it got too dark to see. To reach it, however, he would have to cross an open area about fifty yards wide.

John Henry moved back down off the rock and walked over to his horse. "Iron Heart, I'm going to be asking a lot of you," John Henry said. "But I know you can do it."

Gripping his pistol, John Henry put his foot in the stirrup and lifted himself up. But he didn't get in the saddle. Instead, he remained bent over, hidden behind his horse. Once he had his balance and a good hold, he urged his horse across the open area. Iron Heart broke out into the clearing at a full gallop.

"Whose horse is that?" someone shouted.

"I don't know. Maybe one of the men who went after him. He must have been killed."

"Why did his horse come back here?"

"Where else would he go?"

"I don't know. But it spooks me."

"Wait a minute! It's Sixkiller! The son of a bitch is hangin' on to the other side!" someone shouted.

Knowing now that he had been spotted, John Henry raised up and fired across the top of his horse.

Those who were closest began shooting, and even after John Henry had made it all the way across and was completely out of their line of fire, they kept up their shooting until, finally, Willie Buck shouted at them to stop.

"Cease fire! Stop your shooting! You're just wasting ammunition!" Willie Buck was shouting.

The firing fell silent.

"Where'd he go?"

"Was he hit?"

"Does anyone see him?"

"Everyone just keep your mouth shut and your eyes open!" Willie Buck ordered.

John Henry was in a good, secure position now. He was close enough to observe everything. Close enough even to overhear the men when they shouted at each other. Realistically, he knew this was as close as he was going to be able to get until it got dark. But with the sun already a bloodred disk low on the western horizon, he knew that darkness wasn't too far away.

Before it was too dark to see, John Henry made a careful examination of the house. Once he saw Eberwine peering anxiously through the downstairs window. He would like to have seen Sasha, just to reassure himself that she was in the house and that she was still alive, but he just had to have faith that she was.

"Hey, Willie Buck!" someone called. "Can you see him from where you are?"

"No," Willie Buck said.

"John Henry!"

John Henry recognized Sasha's voice. "I'm coming for you, Sasha!" he called back.

"Yeah, John Henry, you do that!" Willie Buck said. "We're waiting for you. Oh, and after we kill you? I'm going to have some fun with your woman."

John Henry didn't answer Willie Buck, nor did he say a word from that moment on. He would wait until one o'clock in the morning. If he was lucky, he might catch some of them napping.

John Henry didn't have to wait that long. It was no more than an hour after dark when he got an unexpected break. The men who had spent the day searching for him were just coming back now. They were tired, hungry, and frustrated over not yet having

Fairman looked at the other two members of his surveying team, but he didn't answer right away.

"What is it, Fairman? What are you not telling me?"

"Uh, when we first started surveying inside the Territory, we came across a sign they had put up."

"What did the sign say?"

"I don't remember the words exactly, but it was something like, 'Warning, we don't want the white man's railroad.' And the bottom line said that it was the Indian Independence Council."

"Where is the sign now?"

"We tore it up."

"You didn't think that would be something that might interest the colonel?" Scullin asked.

"Tell the truth, Mr. Scullin, I didn't want to trouble anyone with it," Fairman said. "I knew we had permission from the Indians and from our government, so I figured it didn't make any difference what the sign said. I'm sorry if I made a mistake."

Stevens stroked his chin for a moment, then he shook his head. "You didn't make a mistake. Even if you had told me about the sign, I probably would have had you do exactly what you did do."

"What should we do now?"

"There's no question about it," Scullin said. "We have to continue the survey. See Forney, our equipment manager. Tell him I said to give you a complete new set of surveying tools."

"Yes, sir," Fairman said, though his answer was hesitant, and he made no effort to leave the car.

"Well, go ahead," Scullin said. "Go back out there and pick up where you left off."

"There might be a problem with that."

"What problem?" Stevens asked. "We do have spare equipment, don't we?"

"Yes, sir, that's not it. Colonel, they didn't do anything this time but tear up our equipment, but they were armed. If we go out there again, I'm not so sure they will be satisfied with just destroying some equipment."

"That's no problem," Scullin said. "I'll send some armed men out with you."

"No, wait," Stevens said, holding up his hand. "That's not such a good idea."

"Colonel, you don't mean they should go out unarmed again, do you?" Scullin asked.

"No. For now, I'd say we don't go out at all."

"What are we going to do, Colonel? We can't lay track if we don't have our route surveyed."

"I'll send for the army," Stevens said.

"You'll send for the army? How long is that going to take? I mean, that's likely to cause quite a delay, isn't it?" Scullin asked.

Stevens smiled. "What difference does that make? We won the race, didn't we? We've already been certified as the only railroad with the authority to build into Indian Territory. Time is no longer as important to us as it once was."

"The railroad has stopped construction," Willie Buck said to Marcus Eberwine.

"Have they left the territory?"

"No, they're still there. But they aren't building."

"How do you know they aren't building?"

"We attacked their surveyors."

"Did you kill any of them?"

"No, but we stopped the construction."

"Are you prepared to kill anyone?"

"If need be," Willie Buck answered.

Eberwine nodded, but said nothing.

Emporia, Kansas

When Octave Chanute went into James Joy's office, he was drumming his fingers on his desk and staring out through the window.

"You look pretty pensive," Chanute said.

"Pensive? You call it pensive?"

"What would you call it?"

Joy thought for a moment. "Yeah, you can call it pensive, I guess. Otherwise, I would have to admit that I'm defeated."

"Not necessarily so," Chanute said.

"What do you mean, not necessarily so? Stevens is building in Indian Territory, I'm not. What else would that be but defeat?"

"Well, if Stevens really was building in Indian Territory, I suppose you could call it defeat."

The expression on Joy's face turned from one of depression to curiosity. "What do you mean, if he *really was* building? Are you saying he isn't building?"

"Take a look at the *Cherokee Advocate,*" Chanute said, handing the paper across the desk to Joy.

"What am I looking for?"

"It's right there on the front page. I don't think you'll have any difficulty finding it."

Joy took the paper from Chanute, opened it to scan the front page, then he smiled.

"I'll be damned," he said.

"Read the story."

Railroad Construction Stopped

Construction of the railroad into Indian Territory has been halted due to a raid by a group of renegade Indians who call themselves the Indian Independence Council. It is not known who the members of the Indian Independence Council are, but by their action they are denying the good people of Indian Territory the many benefits that would be derived by having a railroad that could both provide rapid transportation, and freight service. The railroad will allow us to ship our cattle and agricultural goods to the rest of the nation, as well as bring goods in at a price much less than the cost of wagon freight.

Every Cherokee, indeed, every citizen of the Indian Territory, regardless of tribe, should hold these renegades in scorn. We pride ourselves on our civilization, yet this kind of action makes us no different from the wild aborigines of the plains.

I call upon all good citizens of The Nations to report anyone known to be a member of the illegal Indian Independence Council to the proper authorities.

"What is Stevens going to do about this?" Joy asked when he finished reading the paper.

"I've heard that he is going to call the army in."

"Ha! That will never happen! The last thing our government wants is a war with any of the Civilized Tribes. Octave, my boy, this isn't over yet. I'm going to submit an appeal."

"Who are you going to appeal to?"

"Why, to the person who made the determination in the first place. He made the decision; he certainly has the power to change his mind if given sufficient reason. And I am going to give him reason."

To Secretary of the Interior
The Honorable J.D. Cox

Sir, I ask that the award of the right to build a railroad through the Indian Territory, awarded to the KATY Line be revoked, or at least suspended until such time as my appeal can be acted upon.

My appeal is based upon the following reasons:

1. There is no satisfactory evidence placed before your department that the character of the KATY is that of a good and completed road.

2. The KATY has failed to establish a satisfactory relationship with the Indians through which the proposed road will

pass. Without cooperation of the Indians, no railroad can, nor should it be built.

3. The Border Tier Railroad promises to make such compromises with the Indians as to guarantee their full cooperation and unrestrained right of passage.

James Joy
President, Border Tier Railroad

Fort Riley, Kansas
Colonel Albert J. Smith, commandant of the 7th Cavalry at Fort Riley, put his fingers together forming a steeple as he sat back in his chair to listen to Robert Stevens.

"We have permission of the United States Government, and we have the permission of the Cherokee governing council," Stevens said. "It must be obvious that the ones who are attacking us represent only a few."

"Who are the Indian Independence Council?" Colonel Smith asked. "I don't think I've ever heard of them."

"As I understand it, they were an irregular band of Indians who fought during the Civil War."

"Really? For whose side?"

"From what I've been told, it was their own side. They want to establish the Indian Territory as an independent nation, and evidently they look at the railroad as a threat to that endeavor," Stevens said.

"Still, Colonel Stevens, what you are asking is for me to have a military presence inside the Indian Territory. Why, that would be the same thing as launching an invasion. I don't think the Indians would appreciate that."

"Colonel, without some protection, we won't be able to build the railroad, and that's a fact."

"I'm sure you will come up with some solution, Colonel Stevens," Smith said, standing to indicate that the meeting was over. "But sending the military in, isn't it."

"What did the army say?" Gunn asked when Stevens returned to Chetopa.

"They won't send in any troops."

"So, what do we do now?"

"I'll send for Marshal Sixkiller. He is both a United States Marshal and an Indian. Who better to handle this for us?"

CHAPTER THIRTY-TWO

Mr. James Joy
President, Border Tier Railroad

Mr. Joy:

The award to KATY Railroad was made in accordance with the information delivered to this office by James M. Harvey, Governor of the State of Kansas, to wit:

That the Union Pacific Railway, Southern Branch, renamed the KATY reached the northern boundary of the Indian Territory, in the valley of the Neosho River, on the west side and about one mile therefrom, at 12 noon on the 6th day of June, 1870, and that at that time there was no other railroad nearer than sixteen miles of that point.

1. That on the 9th day of June, 1870, Governor Harvey, the officer specified by Act of Congress to pronounce upon

the completion of this railroad, certified over his official seal and signature, that the same was a first-class completed railroad to the northern boundary of the Indian Territory.

To that end, Mr. Joy, your appeal for reconsideration is denied, and no further appeal or correspondence with regard to the railroad to be built in Indian Territory will be considered.

Your Obedient Servant,
J. D. Cox
Secretary of the Interior

"What do we do now?

"Nothing," Joy said, dejectedly. "For us, it is over."

John Henry was with the advance surveying party, eating a biscuit and a piece of bacon as he watched the men at work.

"Marshal!" Fairman called to him. "It looks like we have company coming!"

Fairman pointed to the west where three men were riding hard toward the group of workers. All three had pistols in their hands, and all three were shooting. One of the surveyors was hit, and he went down.

John Henry jacked a shell into the Winchester he was carrying, raised it to his shoulder and fired. One of the three riders was unseated. When he fired a second time, a second rider was unseated, and the third rider turned and rode away.

"You stopped 'em!" Fairman shouted. "You stopped 'em!"

John Henry went quickly to the wounded surveyor, and saw that he had been hit in the leg. He treated him and, because the man said he was able to ride, John Henry rode back with him to end of track, where he was put on a train to be taken back to Emporia, which had the nearest doctor.

Tahlequah

"We've got to get rid of John Henry Six-killer," Willie Buck said. "We aren't going to get anything done until he's gone."

"He's not an easy man to get rid of," Eberwine said, thinking of the incident with Matt Dixon.

"We just haven't been going about it the right way," Buck said.

"You say that as if you have an idea."

"I do have an idea."

"Well, let's hear it. I'm always open to new ideas. It's for sure that nothing we have tried so far has worked."

"We just haven't used the right bait," Buck said.

"And you have the right bait?"

"Not yet. But I can get it."

"Good. Then get it."

"It's going to cost you."

"What do you mean it's going to cost me? I thought we had a mutual interest in keeping the railroad out."

"Our interest is going to be more mutual when you make me a full partner in your freight wagon business."

"Why should I do that?"

"Because you have no choice. You either make me a partner and keep half of your business, or stand by and watch the railroad come in and lose all your business."

Eberwine drummed his fingers on his desk as he stared, angrily, at Willie Buck. "You have just taken our relationship into a new dimension," he said.

"Yes, I have. So, what will it be? Do I get rid of Sixkiller for you?"

"All right, you have backed me into a corner," Eberwine said. "If you get rid of Sixkiller, then half the business is yours. If you fail, you get nothing."

"If I fail, there won't be anything to divide anyway," Buck replied.

"What do you have in mind?"

"Sasha Quiet Stream."

"Who is that?"

"A better question would be 'What is that?' Sasha Quiet Stream is bait for the trap."

John Henry was having breakfast with Stevens and Gunn when one of the track workers knocked on the door of the Prairie Queen.

"Yes?" Stevens called out.

"Colonel Stevens, some Injun just gave me this note and told me to give it to Marshal Sixkiller."

"All right, bring it in," Steven said.

The track worker came in, handed the note to John Henry, then turned and started to leave.

"Wait," John Henry called.

The man stopped as John Henry read the note.

"What is it, Marshal?" Stevens asked.

John Henry's face reflected anger, as he showed the note to Stevens.

Once, many years ago you rescued Sasha Quiet Stream from me. Now I have her again. Are you still the hero? If you want to see her alive again, come to the Two Feathers Ranch. Willie Buck

"Who is Sasha Quiet Stream?"

"She is an innocent young woman."

"Does she mean something to you?"

"Yes," John Henry said without further elaboration. He got up from the breakfast table.

"What are you going to do?"

"I'm going to get her."

"Marshal, you are an intelligent man. I'm sure you know that this is exactly what they want you to do. They are using her as bait to try and draw you into a trap."

"Yes," John Henry said. Again, it was a one word response, without elaboration.

Eberwine had Willie Buck bring Sasha to the Two Feathers Ranch, which Eberwine owned. Willie Buck had brought six men with him, and Eberwine had ten men working at his ranch. That was sixteen men, eighteen if you counted Willie Buck and Eberwine. That certainly should be enough to handle one man. And, as an additional inducement, Eberwine had offered one hundred dollars per man, to be paid when they brought Sixkiller's body to him, with an additional one thousand to be paid to the man who actually killed him. At the moment, Eberwine was in the house with Sasha, who was tied to a chair.

"Why are you doing this?" Sasha asked. "I

thought you were a friend to the Indians."

"Oh, I have a lot of Indian friends," Eberwine said. "It's just that Marshal Sixkiller isn't one of them."

Leaving her behind, Eberwine stepped out onto the front porch of his ranch house. Willie Buck was standing on the porch. Dennis Redbone was there as well. Dennis was Lucas Redbone's brother and he was aching for revenge against John Henry.

"I want all the men well out of sight. Keep one in the loft in the barn as a lookout," Eberwine said.

"Why? He can't get here without coming through the pass. Why don't we just go down there and shoot him when he comes through?" Willie Buck suggested.

"We're going to do that. I've got four men down to the pass, you can send out another four. Tell them to shoot him on sight. We'll keep eight men back here, just in case he gets through the men we send for him."

"How is he going to get through?" Dennis Redbone asked. "We're not waiting for a troop of horse soldiers. John Henry is just one man."

"Your brother thought that, too, didn't he?" Eberwine asked. "Where did it get him?"

"All right, all right, we'll do it your way. I

just want him dead, whatever it takes."

"Well, then we are all reading off the same page, aren't we?" Eberwine replied.

John Henry saw four men coming toward him. He was sitting calmly on top of a large round rock, watching, as four riders approached a narrow draw. The draw was so confined that they would not be able to get through without squeezing into a single file. It was a place that no one with any tactical sense would go. But these were not men with a sense of tactics.

John Henry stood up so he could clearly be seen against the skyline. He stood there until he knew he had been seen.

"Look! There he is!" The voice of one of the four men floated up to him.

"He's up there!"

"Let's get him!"

The riders galloped through the draw, bent on capturing or killing John Henry.

A couple of the men in front thought John Henry made an easy target, so they pulled their pistols and began shooting up toward him as they rode. John Henry could see the flash of the gunshots, then the little puffs of dust as the bullets hit around him. The spent bullets whined as they ricocheted through the little draw, but none of the missiles came close enough to cause him to duck.

John Henry had rolled himself a cigarette and now he leaned over, and using the burning tip, lit two fuses. A little line of sparks started at each fuse, then ran sputtering along the length of fuse for several feet alongside the draw. The first explosion went off about fifty yards in front of the lead rider, a heavy, stomach-shaking thump that filled the draw with smoke and dust, then brought a ton of rocks crashing down to close the draw that the riders couldn't get through.

The second explosion, somewhat less powerful, was located behind the riders. It also brought rocks crashing down into the draw behind the riders, and that effectively closed the passage off, trapping the riders inside. It was going to take them quite a while to dig their way out of this.

John Henry scrambled down off the rock. He had left his horse on the other side, and now he mounted and rode on, leaving behind the four trapped men.

John Henry rode no more than a quarter of a mile before he saw another four riders. Attracted by the sound of the explosions, they were hurrying over to see what it was.

"There he is!" someone shouted excitedly,

pointing toward John Henry.

"Get him!" another yelled.

All four riders started after John Henry at a full gallop.

John Henry turned Iron Heart into a nearby thicket. The tree limbs slapped painfully against his face and arms, but they closed behind him, too, so that he was hidden from view. John Henry slowed his horse just enough to hop off, then he slapped him on the haunch, sending him on. After that he squatted down behind a juniper and waited.

In less than ten seconds, his pursuers came by. As the last rider came by, John Henry reached up and grabbed him, then jerked him off his horse. The man gave a short, startled cry as he was going down, but the cry was cut off when he broke his neck in the fall.

The rider just in front of that rider heard the cry and he looked around in time to see what was happening.

"Hey! He's back here!" he called. This rider had been riding with his pistol in his hand, so he was able to get off a shot at almost the same moment he yelled.

The bullet grazed the fleshy part of John Henry's arm, causing a deep, painful crease. John Henry fired back, knocking the rider off his horse.

The other two riders suddenly realized that in the space of a few seconds, John Henry had cut the odds down to two to one. Those odds weren't to their liking, so they turned and galloped away.

John Henry called Iron Heart to him, mounted, and continued on toward the main house.

Eberwine had gone back into his house and now he stood there, looking through the window of his study. In addition to the pistol in his holster, there was another on the desk behind him, loaded and easy to get to. He couldn't imagine Sixkiller getting through everyone else to get to him, but he wasn't going to take any chances.

Eberwine closed the drapes, then looked around at his prisoner.

"What was all the shooting?" Sasha asked.

"Oh, I expect it's your hero come to rescue you," Eberwine said. "What a fool he is. He has fallen right into the trap, just as Willie Buck said he would."

"You may be the one who is in the trap," Sasha suggested.

Eberwine chuckled. "Oh, you think so, do you? One can almost admire the man for engendering such childish faith in others."

There were several more shots fired from outside, not too far from the house. Startled, Eberwine hurried over to peek through the drapes.

"Sounds like he's getting closer," Sasha said.

"I'd better go check on things," Eberwine said, starting toward the door.

"Mr. Eberwine?" Sasha called.

"Yes?" Eberwine looked back toward her.

"I think you may die this night."

won the one-hundred-dollar bonus they were promised. They rode boldly and irately right up to the ranch. Unfortunately for them, they made no effort to identify themselves.

The men had completely forgotten about those who were out on the range and were totally surprised to see a large body of men ride up on them.

"What the hell? Marshal Sixkiller brought a posse with him!"

A rifle shot rang out from one of the defenders, and it was returned by the approaching horsemen, who thought they were being fired at by John Henry. Their return shot was answered by another and by another still, until soon, the entire valley rang with the crash and clatter of rifle and pistol fire.

The night was lit up by muzzle flashes. Bullets whined and whistled, and men fell, mortally wounded.

John Henry realized at once that he could take advantage of the opportunity that was just presenting itself. As the guns banged and crashed around him, he sneaked out of his hiding position. He mounted, then rode north for a couple of hundred yards, out of the line of fire. He had no intention of getting shot accidentally when none of them had been able to shoot him by design during the entire day.

During the fighting the barn had caught fire and the man who had been shooting from the loft of the barn had to abandon it. Now the burning barn cast an eerie wavering orange glow over the entire scene, illumination enough to provide shadows as targets, but not bright enough to allow anyone to be identified and thus end the confusion.

By the ambient light of the burning barn, John Henry was able to pick his way through to the house. Going around back, he found the back door unlocked, and he let himself in. Moving quietly through the house, he looked into the parlor and saw Eberwine. Eberwine was sitting inside the fireplace seeking protection from the bullets, some of which were coming into the house. His knees were drawn up in front of him, and his arms were wrapped around his legs. His head was down on his knees so he couldn't see anything. His pistol was lying on the floor beside him.

He could see it all, because the room was dimly lit by the wavering orange light of the burning barn.

Sasha saw John Henry and her face lit up with excitement, but John Henry put his finger across his lips, urging her to be quiet. She nodded, showing that she understood.

John Henry walked over to the chair and cut the ropes that were binding Sasha. At that moment the shooting outside stopped.

"What the hell? We've been shooting at each other!"

When the shooting stopped, Eberwine opened his eyes, and seeing John Henry and Sasha, called out, "Willie Buck! In here, quick!"

The front door opened and Willie Buck came in. Seeing John Henry, he raised his pistol to fire. John Henry did two things at once. He pushed Sasha out of the way, and he shot Willie Buck. As Willie Buck went down, he pulled the trigger, but because he was twisting around as he was going down, the bullet from his gun hit Eberwine in the forehead. Eberwine went down as well.

"What's goin' on in here?" another man said, coming into the house.

"Drop it," John Henry said.

A quick perusal showed the man that both Eberwine and Willie Buck were down. He dropped his pistol and put his hands up. It was one of Eberwine's cowboys.

"How many are left out there?" John Henry asked.

"I don't think there's no more than four

of us," the cowboy said.

"I understand from some of the conversation I've overheard today that you were to get a hundred dollars each, if you killed me."

"Yeah, that's what Eberwine said."

"Who do you think is going to pay you that money now?"

"Nobody, I reckon."

"You go out there and tell the others that."

When the cowboy went out the front door, John Henry led Sasha through the back door. He didn't think any of the ones left would still be trying to kill him, but he didn't want to take any chances.

They reached Tahlequah just as the sun was rising.

When they arrived at the house of Sasha's parents, John Henry dismounted, then reached up to help Sasha down. He winced in pain, and it wasn't until then that Sasha noticed he had been wounded.

"Oh! You've been shot!"

"Not really," John Henry said. "It is just a crease."

"Please, come in. I'll clean it for you."

"All right," John Henry said.

John Henry followed Sasha into the house where her relieved parents welcomed her back home and thanked John Henry profusely for bringing her back safely.

Sasha drew some water from the pump, and warmed it. Then, using warm water and lye soap, she cleaned the wound. Afterward, she bandaged it.

"My shirt doesn't look like much," John Henry said.

"I've got a shirt for you," Sasha said with a broad smile.

"I don't think any of your father's shirts will fit me."

"It's your shirt."

"My shirt?"

"You let me wear it, remember?"

John Henry thought back to the time he had put his shirt over Sasha's wet body.

"Yes," he said with a big smile. "I remember."

Six months later
From the *Cherokee Advocate:*

Railroad Completed
Across Indian Territory

On the evening of Friday, February 3, a crew of KATY track layers, without fanfare or celebration, rhythmically, but wordlessly, drove the last spike in the last rail to complete the iron road. From this day and forever hence, the link is complete. The

Indian Territory is tied irrevocably with a slim silver ribbon to the great capital of Washington, the industrial East, the cattle-rich plains of Texas, and the minerals and wealth of California and the Pacific Shore. No longer isolated, the Indian Territory is now an integral part of the great, sometimes cruel, and always hard world.